A SLEEPING
MEMORY

A SLEEPING MEMORY

E. PHILLIPS OPPENHEIM

WILDSIDE PRESS

A SLEEPING MEMORY

Published by Wildside Press LLC.
www.wildsidebooks.com

A SLEEPING MEMORY

A SLEEPING MEMORY

CHAPTER I

THE fringe of a city fog was hanging about the
Edgware Road. The sky—such of it as could be seen
—was heavy with gray clouds, the pavements were
wet and sloppy with recent rains. The broad thor-
oughfare was almost deserted. The few foot passengers hurried along with upturned collars and drip-
ping umbrellas. It was a bad afternoon for the
shops. Before one of the largest two girls were
standing together.

It was the London headquarters of a wholesale
mantle and jacket maker, whose name loomed large
from the hoardings of half the great towns in England. Behind the plate-glass windows covering the
immaculate shapes of many wooden dummies were a
goodly collection of ready-made garments, whose
peculiar qualities, bravely set out in thick black letters, upon long strips of cardboard, might well have
exhausted the whole stock of feminine adjectives. A
tweed cape with a hood and a cunningly displayed
plaid lining advertised itself as the "Ranelagh Golf
Cape," a more gorgeous garment in the background
appealed to possible purchasers as the "Countess"
mantle, and gave modest reassurance as to the
quality of its trimming and its Parisian extraction.

The customers of the establishment were obviously of sporting tastes, and addicted to the diversions of the well-to-do. There were yachting jackets and shooting capes, driving cloaks, and—in a little window all to themselves—opera wraps! Everything was marvellously cheap. There were notes of exclamation following the prices. There were rows of electric lights to enhance the brilliancy of jet trimmings and steel buttons. Truly the place should have been a feminine Paradise.

Yet of all this magnificence there were but two spectators—two girls huddled together under one umbrella. The younger, large-eyed, anæmic, untidy, looked and spoke of what she saw with eager and strenuous toleration—a toleration which at times was merged into enthusiasm. Her companion, who was taller, and who held herself with a distinction which was oddly at variance with her shabby clothes, never attempted to conceal her contempt for this tinselly array of self-styled Paris models and cheap reproductions from the inner world of fashion. And indeed she seemed scarcely the sort of person for ready-made garments.

The younger girl's interest was apparently impersonal. She was essaying the part of a feminine Mephistopheles.

"I say, Eleanor, I think that one's quite stunning," she declared, pointing suddenly at one of the most atrocious of the models. "It's smart, ain't it? There was a lady came to the shop yesterday wearing one just like it. I declare you couldn't tell 'em apart. She was a lady too—really. She came in a carriage, and she had a little dog, and a real gold muff-chain, with funny little stones set in it—not one of them imitation things. It's cheap, too, only twenty-seven and elevenpence. Come in and try it on. I'll ask for it if you like!"

The girl glanced at the jacket and shivered. She made an effort to move away from the shop, but her companion's arm restrained her.

"Why, you haven't even looked at it!" she protested. "What a one you are to come shopping! Look at those steel ornaments. I call it most ladylike!"

"It is absolutely hideous, Ada," the other declared. "I would not put the thing on. Come away. There is nothing here. I am weary of looking at all this ugliness. Let us go and have some tea somewhere —and sit down!"

But Ada declined to move. She ignored her companion's weary gesture, and continued her expostulations. Her high-pitched Cockney voice sounded strangely after the other girl's soft speech and correct enunciation.

"Now, Eleanor, you must be reasonable," she declared vigorously. "It's all rubbish to be turning your nose up at everything just because it ain't exactly what you've been used to. A jacket you must have, and you cannot expect to go to Redfern with something under thirty shillings."

"I can make this do—a little longer."

"You can't! It's threadbare, and you'll catch your death of cold. This place is as good as any. If you don't like what's in the window, let's go in and see if they've got anything else. I know the young gentleman who's head-salesman here, and he won't mind a bit of trouble—especially when he sees you. I think I can get a bit off the price too. Come along!"

Her companion shook herself free from the arm

which was urging her inside. A sudden light flashed in her eyes, her lips quivered. Notwithstanding her worn clothes, her ill-shapen hat, and the hideous white glare in which they stood, one saw immediately that she was beautiful. The slight sullenness which in repose marred her features was gone. The faint flush which crept through the unnatural pallor of her cheeks restored her coloring, one realized the elusive blue shade of her eyes, the many coils of soft brown hair arranged with a grace which contrasted strangely with the worn hat and veil. She grew younger, too, with that little burst of feeling, the soft delicacy of her skin, the lingering girlishness of her figure asserted themselves. But she was very angry.

"You are blind, Ada!" she exclaimed passionately. "You see nothing! You understand nothing."

"Mercy me! I don't know so much about that!" Ada retorted, half indignant.

"Oh, don't be foolish! You're better off. Thank God for it—and come along."

"I understand that you'll catch your death o' cold in this wind with little more than a rag around you," Ada declared vigorously. "I've twice as much on as you, and I'm almost perished. I'd sooner have the fog than this. It's enough to kill you!"

The other girl shrugged her shoulders slightly.

"What if it does! Is life such a beautiful gift then to you and to me—to the thousands who are like us?"

"I'd sooner live than die, anyway," Ada declared bluntly. "Bearmain's is a bit rough, perhaps, but there's plenty of fun to be had if you set the right way about it."

The other girl smiled faintly.

"I am afraid," she said, "that I shall never find the right way. I should be glad to die to-day, to-morrow, this moment! Come, if my threadbare rags will take me to another world that disposes once and for all of the jacket question, I'll hug them and welcome."

Ada abandoned the subject with a little gesture of impatience. She attended church once every Sunday, and it sounded irreverent to her.

"Let's go and have some tea, then," she suggested. "You're tired now, and no wonder. Perhaps you'll feel more heart afterwards."

The girl whom she had called Eleanor laughed shortly, but did not move. She, who a few minutes ago had tried to drag her companion from the spot, seemed to find now some evil fascination in those long rows of resplendent garments.

"Look at them, Ada," she exclaimed bitterly. "They are for you and for me, and for the thousands like us. They are ugly, they are cheap, they are pretentious. That is what life is for us. And we can't escape. We are shut in on every side. It is horrible."

Her lips quivered—there was a break in her voice. Ada looked into her face with vague, wistful sympathy. She was sorry, but she did not understand. She looked once more at the jackets in the window.

"I can't see that the things are so dreadful—for the price," she said. "You haven't been used to ready-made clothes, I know, but after all I don't see where the difference comes in. I always look at it like this—if you can't afford the one thing you must have the other. That's reasonable, isn't it now?"

There was a moment's silence. Then both girls became suddenly aware that a man was standing upon the pavement only a few feet away, gazing through the shop windows with an absorption which was obviously simulated. He was in a position to overhear their conversation—he had already, in all probability, overheard some part of it. Without a glance in his direction the two girls turned away. The man, after a moment's hesitation, followed them.

The older girl drew a long breath of relief.

"Do you know, Ada," she said, "I think if I had stood much longer before that window I should have cried. Is there anything more depressing than ugliness?"

Ada sighed.

"I don't see that you're much nearer getting your jacket," she said, "and that's what we started out so early for."

Her companion laughed softly.

"Never mind," she said. "You needn't worry any more about that. I have quite made up my mind. I am going to buy some cloth and make it myself."

"There can't be much cut about it," Ada remarked doubtfully. "A jacket's just one of those things I don't see how one can make oneself. So much depends upon the style."

Again her companion laughed, and the man behind seemed to find it pleasant to hear, for he quickened his pace and drew a little nearer to them.

"You must wait and see it before you criticise, Ada," she said. "You shall help me to choose the material to-morrow."

Ada's face brightened.

"You'll get it at Bearmain's!" she exclaimed. "Well, Henry shall see that the price is all right I'll speak to him myself."

The girl nodded. She dismissed the subject of the jacket with manifest relief.

"Now for some tea," she said. "No, not at an A.B.C. to-day. I am so weary of those thick cups and saucers, and the endless chatter. I am going to take you somewhere else."

"You mustn't be extravagant," Ada protested timidly. "I think an A.B.C. is really very nice, and it's a good bit better than Bearmain's, anyhow. You're always for spending all your money directly you get it."

Her companion smiled. The accusation was by no means unfamiliar to her.

"Do you know," she said, "what I have often been tempted to do? To sell all my few remaining belongings, scrape together every penny I have, and for one long day—to live!"

Ada looked up at her perplexed.

"Isn't that what we're doing all the time?" she asked timidly.

The elder girl laughed tolerantly, but with a note of contempt underlying her mirth.

"You foolish child! What do we know of life, you and I, who spend ten hours of every day behind a counter, the servants of every impertinent, woman who wants a yard of calico. From the moment we wake to the moment when the bell rings and we are packed off like sheep to bed, we are slaves. We have to do it to eat and drink!—but it is not life, it is not even freedom. You don't understand. Always be thankful that you do not!"

"Tell me what you would do in that one day?"

The girl was suddenly thoughtful. Her eyes gleamed as though even the thought gave her pleasure.

"I will tell you," she said. "I would go into Bond Street and I would buy clothes—just for one day —everything. I would know the feel of cambric and lace, and I would buy perfumes and flowers. Then just a simple walking dress and a pretty hat—and oh! fancy for one day being able to wear gloves and boots like those other women wear. Then I would go to one of those old-fashioned hotels somewhere near Berkeley Square, have a maid prepare a bath for me, and change all my clothes slowly, and burn everything which reminded me of the Edgware Road! I would go out to lunch then to one of the best restaurants—Prince's, I think—and I would buy myself a great bunch of fragrant Neapolitan violets, and imagine that some one had sent them to me. And I would order the sort of dishes that make eating artistic, and I would drink wine, soft, white wine, with the flavor of Moselle grapes, and afterwards—"

"Yes, afterwards?" Ada interrupted breathlessly.

The girl's face was sad once more. In her eyes was the old hunger, her voice became almost a whisper.

"Afterwards would be beautiful too. I would take the train to a tiny little village in Surrey which few people know about—it is quite out of the world. When you leave the station you step into a narrow country lane with tall hedges full of birds, and you never meet any one except sometimes an old farm laborer. Then you climb and climb and climb, and at last you come to a very steep hill. The lane becomes a footpath, and at the top there is a little gate leading into a deep grove of pine trees—oh, you don't know what the odor of pines is like, Ada, when the sun is hot upon them. Then I should lie down— pine cones are softer than any mattress—and I think that the rest of that moment would be worth all these months of slavery. There are wild roses in the hedges with great pink blossoms, and the perfume is so faint and yet so perfect—and honeysuckle. You have been in the country sometimes. You know what the scent of honeysuckle is like. And the birds—it is wonderful to hear them sing; there is music, too, in the air when the west wind sweeps through the pine trees!"

"And—afterwards?" Ada asked again, in a low, fearful tone.

The girl looked downwards into her companion's rapt face, and smiled gravely.

"Afterwards I should lie quite still watching the white clouds pass across the sky—watching and listening! I think that all my weariness and bad temper would pass away from me then because the old life was finished."

"Finished?"

"Yes! After a day like that I could never come back again. If ever I should escape, Ada, if it were only for twenty-four hours, I should never come back again. One gets used even to slavery. I suppose it is that which keeps me at Bearmain's."

"But you must live! You do not mean—"

"That is what I do mean!"

"You would pray first?" the younger girl asked, in an awed whisper.

"I should speak to God—out there. Here I cannot even believe that there is a God. I should ask Him to look at the two worlds which He has made, and I would ask Him how, after a single day in the one, it were possible for such a creature as He made me to go back to the other. I would ask Him to show me where was the justice of those two worlds side by side, Heaven and Hell, yet even here in

London so far apart that you and I may beat our hearts in vain before the bars. That's the cruel part, Ada. The other world is always there. You can see into it. It isn't unworthiness that keeps you out. It is chance!"

They stopped short before the, door of a tiny restaurant. From inside came the glow of rose-shaded lamps, and a commissionaire looked somewhat critically at the two girls. They hesitated for a moment, acutely conscious of his disapproving glance, his burly figure filled the doorway. Suddenly the man who had been following them stood by their side. He addressed the elder girl, and his manner and tone were quietly deferential.

"The bars of the other world," he said, "are perhaps not so immovable as they seem to you just now. I must ask your forgiveness for having accidentally overheard a portion of your conversation."

The girl eyed him coldly, but without embarrassment.

"I do not think," she said, "that I have the pleasure of knowing you. Perhaps it is my friend with whom you are acquainted."

He appeared in nowise disconcerted at her steady gaze of inquiry, at the shoulder already half turned against him.

"I know," he said, "that I am a transgressor. I am a stranger both to yourself and to your friend. Yet I am going to ask you to do me the honor of having tea with me. I am almost old enough to be your father, and I shall take the liberty of introducing myself as soon as I can get at my card-case. I beg that you will accept my invitation."

Ada was already on the point of moving away. She had no doubt whatever as to what her com-

panion's answer would be. They had been accosted
before by boulevarders, young and old, and the departure of even the hardiest had been an abject
thing to witness. But this was a day of singular
happenings. The few scathing words which should
surely have been spoken remained unsaid. Ada
looked up, amazed at the silence. The man and
the girl were gazing steadfastly at one another.
Something was passing between them beyond
her comprehension, something which troubled her
vaguely as savoring of a world of greater things
than any which she had account of. She was a shop-
girl, pure and simple, one of her class in spirit as
well as fact, with all the limitations of a stereo-
typed conventionality, a puny imagination, and
a point of view which left her feet planted upon a
molehill. Yet even she recognized that this was an
incident, differing in some vague manner from any
other which had ever befallen them. The man was
no more a boulevarder than Eleanor was flighty.
She waited breathlessly for what might happen.

"You are very kind," Eleanor said quietly; "we
were just thinking of having some tea."

The commissionaire, to whom their meeting had
presented no unusual features, stepped on one side
promptly now, and touched his hat to their escort.
The door was swung open before them. Ada resigned herself to an amazed but cheerful compliance.
They entered the tea-rooms together!

2

CHAPTER II

INSIDE the little place seemed to the two girls unexpectedly bright and cosy. In the centre of the
round table to which their escort led them was a
great bunch of scarlet flowers, and the perfume of
hyacinths was like a breath of Springtime. The tea
appointments were dainty, the attendants deft and
smiling. From an inner room came the soft music of
violins. The rose-shaded lights were kind to the
girls' clothes, and even Ada, who showed some signs
of an embarrassment which was shared in no degree
by her companion, looked about her with mingled
pleasure and curiosity.

"I'm glad we thought of coming here, Eleanor,"
she whispered. "Isn't the music lovely, and what
dear little cakes."

Eleanor, who had loosened her jacket and was
leaning back in her cushioned seat, gave a little
sigh of satisfaction.

"It is so deliciously warm," she said, "and after
that terrible A.B.C. it is like Paradise! May I
have chocolate, please, instead of tea."

He had returned from finding a place for his hat,
and taking a chair opposite to them gave an order
to the smartly dressed waitress. He smiled across
at them pleasantly.

"And now!" he said, "for the conventionalities. I
have a card-case somewhere, I know."

He unbuttoned his coat and began a search for it.

Meanwhile the two girls surveyed him with covert but widely different curiosity. If indeed he was old enough to be the father of either of them, he bore his years remarkably well. He might possibly have been thirty-five, it was hard to believe him a day older. He was clean-shaven, with hard, well-cut features, smooth dark hair, and wonderfully clear gray eyes. He was dressed quietly, but fashionably, and with an attention to detail which the elder girl recognized at once and appreciated. He did not look in the least the sort of man to care about adventures or the consorting with those who were his social inferiors. He produced a card from a tiny silver card-case and handed it to Eleanor.

"You will find my name there," he said. "I live in Hans Crescent. Now you must tell me, please, how I may call you—and your friend."

"My name is Eleanor Surtoes," she said, "and my friend's Ada Smart. We are employed at a drapery establishment in the Edgware Road."

He bowed gravely. It was impossible to tell from his face whether he felt any surprise. Ada, who felt that such candor was wholly unnecessary, kicked her friend under the table without effect.

"The conventionalities," he remarked pleasantly, "are satisfied. It only remains for me to thank you for your confidence, and to assure you that it will not be misplaced."

"It is the first time," Ada interposed, "that either Miss Surtoes or myself have ever done such a thing as this—isn't it, Eleanor?"

She nodded.

"I do not understand," she remarked, "why you spoke to us—any more than I can understand our coming in here with you."

"I spoke to you," he said, "because I overheard some part of your conversation, and I was most anxious to make your acquaintance."

Eleanor flushed slightly.

"Your hearing," she said dryly, "must be remarkably acute."

"I am not going to offer any more apologies," he assured her. "I felt sure that you would acquit me of impertinence. I don't know why, but I was quite confident."

"You are evidently," she murmured, "not afflicted with nervousness."

"In my younger days," he answered, "I was brought up in a profession which does not recognize nerves."

"And now?"

"I was meant to be a physician, but I have never practised."

She nodded.

"Well," she said, "you overheard some of our conversation. Why did that interest you personally?"

He helped himself to some more sugar, and stirred his tea thoughtfully.

"I will tell you presently," he said. "Let me assure you at least that I am not a vulgarly curious person, a libertine, or a philanthropist."

Eleanor sipped her chocolate and leaned back in her chair with an air of lazy content. The pleasant warmth of the place and the sound of his cultivated voice engaged now in sustaining a perfectly effortless conversation with Ada were very soothing to her after the cold, wet streets, and her companion's good-natured but irritating chatter. Ada, though such adventures were far less foreign to her, was by no means wholly at her ease. She was conscious of being surrounded by better-dressed people of a different station in life, who glanced now and then curiously at the two girls. More than once their escort was saluted by friends, whose greetings he returned with easy indifference. Eleanor, watching him more closely than he was aware of, could not detect the slightest signs of disquietude on his part even when two ladies paused for a moment to speak to him, and scarcely troubled to conceal their amazement when they realized that the two girls were his guests. He met Eleanor's scrutinizing gaze with an answering flash of comprehension.

"My friends," he remarked, "have a right to look a little surprised to see me here with you. I do not frequent such places, and I believe because I do not as a rule find much to interest me in the society of your sex that I am considered to be a hardened misogynist. It is one of the penalties of bachelordom."

"You can easily escape from it!" she reminded him.

He shook his head.

"Marriage," he said, "is one of those experiments which, properly considered, is no experiment at all. The finality of the thing is so overwhelming."

She was suddenly thoughtful.

"I am a very persistent person, I am afraid," she said, looking up at him, "but I should like to know your real reason for speaking to us. It is a puzzle to me! I know quite well that you are not one of those who amuse themselves with such adventures, or we should not be here. At the same time, I do not think you were wholly disinterested. You haven't in the least a sympathetic appearance. You had a definite reason, I am sure. What was it?"

The man was Sphinx-like. There was nothing to be read from his face.

"You are quite right," he said. "I have never spoken to a woman before without a formal introduction, and only then when I have been compelled to. I am going to be ungallant enough to admit that your sex does not as a rule particularly attract me. I have other and very strong interests in my life."

She nodded.

"I imagined so. Hence my curiosity. Forgive me if I remind you that we must go in a few minutes, and you have not yet gratified it."

"That is very reasonable," he said. "I will satisfy it if I can to some extent. I think I told you that I started life as a physician. I still devote a good deal of time to one branch of the profession, although my studies are purely private."

"I am glad you do something," she said, smiling. "Idleness is a woman's natural state, but for a man it is demoralizing."

He nodded.

"Quite right! Well, it has always seemed to me, although few people will admit it, that my profession is one which brings any one engaged in it into a very close and actual sympathy with one's fellow-creatures generally. When I say sympathy do not misunderstand me. I make no false claims to being a sympathetic person. I should say perhaps understanding."

Ada sat listening with wide-open eyes. Her private opinion was that their escort was a little mad. Eleanor was puzzled but interested.

"Well!"

"I heard you speak, and I knew that your words

came from your heart. There was the ring of absolute truth about them. I do not know by what
accident you occupy your present position, or what
your chances may be of escaping from it. I take it
for granted that your own estimate of it is a faithful one. If so, you are in a hopeless state. Your
life must be intolerable !"

"My life," she murmured, "is worse than intolerable."

He assented cheerfully.

"I was privileged," he continued, "owing to my
exceptional hearing, to become still further your
involuntary confidant. You spoke of a certain
visionary day, of a long, sweet draught from the
cup of life, and afterwards—oblivion, what men call
death."

His eyes held hers—they were bright with a certain
steely radiance. She felt her heart beating fast, the
music in the room beyond seemed to her to come
from a far distance.

"I gathered, of course," he continued, "that you
were a pagan, pure and simple. You do not possess
what these silly women call soul. You are anxious,
fiercely anxious to make the best of the only life
which we can possibly know anything about. I
heard you speak, and the human note was strong
in all that you said. It occurred to me at once that
you were the woman for whom I had been seeking."

"You are very mysterious," she said slowly. "I
do not remember now all that I said, but I am quite
sure that there was not a single word which I did
not mean."

"You spoke," he declared, "as one in extremity.
You spoke as a woman who had none of the ordinary fear of death. You spoke as one who would

dare great things to pass from the evil place in which fate has set you into the world beautiful."

"I am afraid of death," she said, her eyes bright, her voice tremulous with a sudden passion, "only because I do not want to die before I have lived."

He nodded.

"There are many like that," he said, "but without the courage to own it. May I be quite frank with you? It may save you from embarrassment later on. I followed—not you—but the unit of humanity who felt as you felt. Personally I have interests in my life so absorbing that your sex for many years have been little else save shadows to me. That may sound ungallant, but it will help you to understand."

She smiled.

"It may," she admitted. "At present I am all at sea."

"I am going to be a little more explicit at any rate," he assured her. "I believe that in you I have found a person whose life is wholly distasteful to them, who would welcome oblivion, and who has no absolute fear of death."

"I fear death," she answered firmly, "less than I fear to-morrow and the whole future of to-morrows! Sometimes I see worse things than death before me!"

"You have no friends?" he asked.

"None!"

"No hope of deliverance?"

"None!"

"I do not wish," he said, "to seem impertinent or inquisitive. Yet it is apparent that you are not of the class which claims you now. You may have had family troubles which will right themselves."

"I have no family," she answered. "My father and mother are both dead. I am alone in the world, and there is no living person to whom I may look for help."

He glanced towards Ada, whose impatience was manifest.

"Your companion," he remarked, "looks at me as though I were a madman. I am afraid that she is in a hurry."

"She can wait," Eleanor answered curtly. "Go on!"

"Let me put an extreme case to you, then," he said, lowering his voice a little. "Supposing that you were suddenly removed from your present life, would there be any one who would have the right to search for you?"

"Not a soul!" she answered.

He nodded thoughtfully. A certain satisfaction was apparent in his pale, set face. Ada eyed him with deep distrust. To her the whole episode was capable of but one explanation. The man was plotting to get Eleanor into his power, and she was just in the mood to be an easy victim. She could scarcely keep her indignation from breaking out.

"Eleanor," she said, "it is time we were going. We are very much obliged to you, sir, for the tea, but when Eleanor says that she has no friends she says what isn't true, and she knows it. If harm came to her I'd never rest till I'd found out all about it."

He smiled at her good-naturedly.

"I am afraid," he said, "that you have misunderstood me a little. I was simply putting a supposititious case, which is not in the least likely to happen."

He rose to his feet, and accepted his hat from an attendant.

"Listen," he said. "If you are what you seem to be, and if you have the courage which I believe you to possess, I think that before long I can give you a chance of escape from your present slavery. I want you to reflect once more carefully upon the questions which I have asked you and the answers which you have made."

"They need no further reflection," she said. "All that I have told you I mean. Tell me what you mean by a chance of escape?"

His eyes rested for a moment upon Ada, who stood near watching him suspiciously.

"It is not a matter to be decided upon lightly," he said. "I have your address, and I will write to you before long."

He held out his hand.

"I must thank you very much," he said, "for your society—and for your confidence. Good afternoon!"

He parted from them upon the pavement with a pleasant but conventional farewell, and they watched him call a hansom and drive off. Then they looked together at his card which Eleanor had brought out all crushed up in her hand. She straightened it out, and they moved underneath a lamp-post.

> "Sir Powers Fiske,
>   131 Hans Crescent."

"I don't care if he's a hundred times a Sir," Ada exclaimed. "I don't like him. I wish we'd never seen him."

Eleanor said nothing. But she put the card carefully in her pocket.

CHAPTER III

OUTSIDE, the two girls passed into a street wet with rain, ill-lit, and almost deserted by foot passengers. A cold, damp wind blew in their faces, the change from the perfumed warmth of the brightly-lit tea-rooms made them shiver as they turned southwards. Ada passed her arm through her companion's, and together they struggled along.

"I wish you would hold the umbrella over yourself," Eleanor said, as they rounded a tempestuous corner. "Your skirt must be wet through."

"I'm all right," Ada declared. "My clothes are thicker than yours. Are you going to let me ask you something, Eleanor?"

"Why not?"

"What made you do it? You're always so particular—snap a fellow's head off almost if he speaks to you. Yet you followed him in there as though you had known him all your life!—and he was a bad 'un! Ugh!"

Eleanor laughed softly and mirthlessly.

"Why do you say that? I thought he was rather interesting."

Ada looked upwards in scornful wonder.

"You ain't so simple as all that, Eleanor, I know. Bother his fine talk, I say. I've met his sort before —all the gentlefolk who take the trouble to talk to any of us are the same. A lot of soft-sounding palaver, and as much real wickedness behind it as you'll find in a day's march. Not for me, thank you! Nor for you, Eleanor, eh?"

Again that upward anxious glance. Ada knew that this girl whom chance had made her companion was in a dangerous mood, and she knew, too, that between her and the man who had just left them had existed some sort of subtle sympathy wholly outside her powers of definition which irritated and alarmed her, but which she was powerless to ignore.

"I am not sure that you judge him rightly," Eleanor answered, "but after all it scarcely matters, does it? I do not suppose that we are either of us likely to see him again."

Ada was visibly relieved.

"I hope to goodness we shan't," she answered heartily. "I ain't nervous as a rule, but he scared me with his strange talk and the way he looked at you. I can't abide people who talk in riddles. Why couldn't he out with what he wanted like a man. I don't think you'd have had much more to say to him then!"

Eleanor looked doubtful.

"I believe now that he was honest," she said. "I can't help it. Yet he was certainly very mysterious. He frightened me, too, a little. Why was he so anxious to know whether I was afraid to die? What did he mean, I wonder?"

"Mean!" Ada gave vent to a contemptuous exclamation. "Mean! Oh, his meaning was plain enough. I've met his sort before, only not quite so barefaced. If ever you were to go near him, Eleanor, you'd find out fast enough. All that fine talk of his was simply rot. There's only one thing such as him could do for you, and only one price to be paid. It's sickening, but it's true."

"I daresay you are right," Eleanor said wearily.

"All the same, I can't help feeling that I should like to know more about him. Don't look so horrified, child! Remember that after all I have seen more of the world than you have. I, too, know something of the sort of men of whom you are thinking. I can't class him amongst them. It's quite impossible."

"He's there, all the same, wherever you put him," Ada declared. "I should like to know what else he spoke to us for, and talked to you as though you were the first woman he had seen in the world. He wasn't a boy, you know, looking out for a spree. He heard you talking as though you'd like to chuck yourself away for an old song, and he followed us deliberately."

"We are not going to talk about him any more," Eleanor said firmly. "Perhaps I was foolish, but there is no harm done, and it was a pleasure to hear a gentleman's voice again. Is that six o'clock? Where were you to meet Mr. Johnson?"

"I told them that we should be at the theatre at half-past," Ada answered.

Eleanor stopped short in the middle of the pavement.

"Them! Who?"

There was a moment's awkward silence. Ada had intended to keep that plural to herself until the meeting was actually over. She tightened her grasp upon her companion's arm.

"You mustn't be cross, Eleanor," she begged. "It's a friend of Henry's who's going with us. He's not at Bearmain's. In fact, he's not in our sort of business at all. Henry says he's awful good company, and you know how particular he is."

"I would rather go back, Ada," Eleanor said

doubtfully. "I didn't mind you and Mr. Johnson, because of course you would have plenty to talk about, but I am not in the humor for company."

"Oh, he'll do the talking all right," Ada urged. "He's that sort! You see, as Henry said, three's such an awkward number for getting in. We must go two and two, and you might get with some one ever so horrid, and Henry hates not to have me to talk to while we're waiting."

Eleanor shook her head vigorously.

"It is too bad of you, Ada," she declared. "You know quite well that if you had told me I should not have come. I do not wish to make any fresh acquaintances. I shall go back at once."

Ada's eyes filled with tears.

"You'll do nothing of the sort, Eleanor," she declared. "If you do I shall go with you. Do be sensible for once now, dear. I know that we aren't any of us quite your sort, but you've got to live with us for the present, at any rate, and you might just as well make the best of it. You can't stick in at Bearmain's every night, and you can't walk about the streets by yourself."

Eleanor shook her head.

"You mustn't think me unreasonable, dear," she said, "but I really would rather not come. I know that a third person is in the way, and I told you so when you asked me, but you and Mr. Johnson were so nice about it that I think I was a little over-persuaded. But I certainly am not going with a stranger whom I have never met before, and who probably wouldn't let me pay for my own ticket. Besides—"

"That's just it," Ada interrupted triumphantly. "That's what I wanted to tell you. We shan't any of us have to pay for our tickets. Henry's friend, Mr. Chadwick, who is going with us, is a literary gentleman, who writes for papers, and gets orders. He's got passes for four into the Haymarket, and by waiting an hour or so we shall get into the front row of the pit—every bit as good as the stalls, where all the swells sit. Oh, you must come along, Eleanor. He's quite gentlemanly I'm sure, or Henry wouldn't have took up with him, and if you don't like him, you know, why, you needn't have anything more to do with him afterwards. Come along, there's a dear!"

Eleanor suffered herself to be persuaded. They hurried on to the top of the Haymarket, where the two young men were awaiting them. Henry was one of the junior shopwalkers at Bearmain's, and as such a person of some consequence. He greeted Ada with levity, and Eleanor, of whom he was secretly a little afraid, with his best floor manner. Afterwards he begged leave to present his friend, Mr. Laurence Chadwick, a young man on a somewhat expansive scale, who wore a seedy frock-coat, trousers much frayed at the edges, and a silk hat with an abnormally large brim. A waistcoat cut unusually low displayed an uninviting amount of white piqué tie, reposing upon a shirt whose cleanliness was ancient history.

"I hope you young ladies won't mind waiting a bit," Mr. Johnson remarked. "We shall have to stand two and two, you know, like the animals, but there ain't many there yet, and we ought to get in the front row. What do you think, Chadwick, you know all about these places?"

Mr. Chadwick thought that with management it might be done, but proposed an immediate move.

A few minutes later, and they were standing in their places upon the pavement. Mr. Chadwick immediately proceeded to count the people in front with a professional air.

"H'm!" he remarked. "There's a front row ahead of us, and four over. However, the doorkeeper's a pal of mine, and he'll see us right. We'll have to judy some one going in."

Eleanor ventured to remark that the second row was almost as good, but Mr. Chadwick shook his head in a superior manner.

"The front row is the place of the 'ouse," he asserted confidently. "You leave it to me, and we'll get there somehow. Got any smokes, Henry?—that is, if Miss Surtoes has no objection."

Miss Surtoes had no objection to anything. So the long hour of waiting commenced. The cigars were doubtful and smelt rank, the rain and wind were a miserable combination. Eleanor's boots, thin and almost worn through, were powerless to withstand the cold dampness of the sloppy pavements. Before half the time had gone by she found herself choking back the sobs. The drippings from an umbrella behind had worn their way through a weak place in her jacket. Her companion's attempts at conversation jarred every moment upon her overstrung nerves. And all the time the indignity of the thing set her quivering with anger. The passers-by eyed them with blended curiosity and contempt, the women from their cabs and carriages going home from their shopping, or on their way to dine, watched them in languid amusement. A couple behind were peeling and eating oranges, a glass flask of spirits was being passed from hand to hand. She sank at last into a sort of torpor, numbed with cold and the acute discomfort of her surroundings. Her companion had long ago ceased to make any effort to entertain her, and was mostly occupied in trying to maintain a facetious conversation with some friends in the rear. Ada and her escort were standing arm-in-arm, their heads very close together, completely engrossed in their two selves.

The long wait came to an end at last. On the part of the two men there was a rush for the front seats the moment the portals were passed. The girls followed in more sober fashion. Ada looked at her companion with concern.

"You're awful pale, Eleanor. Ain't you feeling well?"

"It was rather a long wait," Eleanor answered. "I shall be better directly we sit down."

They joined the two men, flushed with success, and eager for congratulations. There had been a few words with an old gentleman in front of whom they had slipped, and there were some loud complaints from a stout elderly lady and her two daughters, who for the next half-an-hour made audible remarks to one another as to the undesirable people with whom one was forced to rub shoulders in these democratic times. But on the whole they won their place of vantage cheaply, and settled down to make the most of it. Even Eleanor, to whom the warmth and the rest were inexpressibly grateful, found herself interested in the programme which Mr. Chadwick placed gallantly in her hand.

"It's the usual sort of play, you know," he remarked, in a superior tone. "A woman too many— and all the rest of it. Very smartly done, though. I shall have to make a few notes. I'm not sure whether our people have noticed it yet, but they'll be sure to want to know my opinion."

3

Eleanor eyed him critically. Less than ever in the gaslight did he repay inspection. His shirt was distinctly soiled, his hands and nails were unwashed, his eyes were puffy and weak. What a cavalier! She shuddered as she looked away again into the stalls.

"Like to know who some of the people are?" he inquired. "That's the Earl of G., just come in with Lady C., his sister, you know. The Rothschilds are in that box, and the Arthur Pagets in the other. See that little chap! It's Hertz, the South African millionaire."

"Don't point!" she exclaimed involuntarily.

He looked annoyed.

"I'll look after that, thanks," he remarked. "I should say I'm more used to these sort of places than you are. My eye, there's the Duchess of K. Ain't her diamonds a treat?"

"Your acquaintance with the aristocracy," she remarked, "seems to be most extensive!"

"And a good many of 'em know me," he asserted. "You see, if you've anything to do with a Society paper you're right inside the ropes. All sorts of people pal me up now and again."

She made no remark, but unfortunately for her comfort Mr. Chadwick at that moment made a surprising discovery. This friend of Ada's, whom outside he had set down as a pale-faced nonentity without looks or conversation, was a very different sort of person in the gaslight. Now that the color had come back to her cheeks she was amazingly good-looking; capital style too, Mr. Chadwick decided—and Mr. Chadwick was a judge. He communicated his discovery to Henry in a somewhat audible whisper, and Henry passed it on with a nudge to Ada.

"Chadwick's a clean goner!" he informed her. "Clean bowled over. Nice thing for her, ain't it?"

Ada was doubtful. She knew the meaning of those scornful, tremulous lips, and Eleanor's cold monosyllables were not encouraging. But Mr. Chadwick was not the man to be easily daunted.

"Bit annoyed with me, my boy, because I didn't cotton to her outside," he whispered to Henry. "You leave her to me. She'll come round. I know her sort—high fliers; but bless me, girls are all the same."

Fortunately for the preservation of his self-confidence the curtain went up. After that his whispered asides failed even to annoy her. She passed easily and with delightful readiness into another world, and in it there was no place for Mr. Chadwick.

CHAPTER IV

IT was an ordinary pleasant little comedy of every-day life, brightly written and epigrammatic, leading up, however, to a great situation towards the climax of the third act. Eleanor sat quite still, her eyes bright, her cheeks flushed, drinking in long draughts of delicious enjoyment. It was a chapter from the life for which her heart was faint with longing. Here was everyday existence without labor or vulgarity. She was too absorbed to torture herself with contrasts. With an abandon which was in itself a luxury, she gave herself wholly up to the delight of the moment.

During the intervals the glamour lasted and sustained her. She chatted brightly to her companions, and to spare herself the pain of any jarring note virtually absorbed the conversation. Ada beamed all over with pleasure. She was delighted that her friend should vindicate the superiority which she had bespoken for her. The two young men were amazed. Henry, with the unerring instinct of a born shop-walker, and Mr. Chadwick, who despite his innate vulgarity was gifted with perceptions, recognized that touch of something outside their lives with which Eleanor was certainly endowed. The former became curiously silent, the latter lost a great part of his offensive overconfidence. The first two intervals passed almost gayly.

Then the supreme moment of the play arrived.

The woman of fashion who had chattered her way lightly through a couple of acts found herself face to face with one of the great realities of life. Her well-bred indifference fell away from her like a mask. She stood upon the stage, a white-faced, trembling human being, looking with wide-open eyes which took no account of visible things into a future which the next few seconds must decide for her.

Slowly her lips moved; the words came out faltering, but distinct, quivering with agony, like live things beating upon the air. She spoke her own sentence—accepted a renunciation magnificent, but impossible. She sank into a chair. Eleanor, withdrawing her eyes, hot and throbbing with unshed tears, found them challenged and held. A man from amongst the shadows of a private box was watching her intently.

She recognized him at once. He was leaning up against the wall, looking at her over the heads of the two women who occupied the front seats of the box. His posture and general air was of indifference, as though the play had failed to interest him. Yet when he saw her his expression changed, and as their eyes met he smiled quietly. Eleanor felt her breath die suddenly away from her. She would even have avoided his gaze, but she was powerless. His recognition was courteous enough, even kindly. Yet she felt that beneath it lay a perfect apprehension of her position, of the misery through which she had passed. The telegraphy of thought seemed to her then a very real and actual thing! His lips never moved, his face after that brief smile was almost statuesque. Yet his sympathy made her heart leap, she was conscious of an emotion wholly new, altogether unanalyzed. Every word of their conversation was in

her mind. For the first time she realized that undernote of confidence in all that he had said to her
which had alarmed even Ada. His words were true.
She was the woman for whom he had been seeking.
To him would belong her future. From that moment she was sure of it. Then from the stage rang
out the long-drawn, passionate cry of a woman:

"What does it matter though my measure of days
be long or short, only let me live through them, not
grope my way as one of a herd. Ay, live, whether
it be in sin or in well-being, in joy or in misery.
Life is the one priceless gift, free, vigorous, pulsating.
Break down the walls! Give me a year, a month, a
week, and when it has passed I will take death by
the hand. Yet, O God, how hard to shake the
prison bars."

The passionate, almost shameless cry of the
woman seemed still to echo through the house after
the curtain had fallen. Eleanor sat quite still, her
heart beating fiercely, her whole being in quivering
accord with the words which might almost have
sprung from her own lips. Against her will she
looked once more into the box. He had withdrawn
his gaze, and was talking now to the two women
between whom he sat. She watched him steadfastly,
eager to form a dispassionate and studied opinion of
the man who had come so curiously into her life.
For the first time she realized that he was more
than ordinarily good-looking. His complexion was
very pale, but it was a pallor without any suggestion of ill-health. His features were all good; his eyes
clear and bright, although a trifle sunken beneath a
formidable forehead; his hair, carefully parted, was
dark and glossy. The lines of his mouth were firm,
but not forbidding, the general strength of his face

was almost impressive. In his quiet evening dress he seemed to her to possess more than ever that non-assertive, well-groomed appearance which is the corollary of distinction. She concluded her study of him and touched her escort upon the arm.

"You know every one, Mr. Chadwick. Can you tell me who those people are in the box to the left?"

"Which one do you mean?" he asked eagerly.

"The one next the Pagets?"

She inclined her head cautiously, and his eyes followed her motion.

"Oh, him! That's Sir Powers Fiske. He's quite a big pot."

"Who is he?" Eleanor asked.

"I know a bit about him," Mr. Chadwick affirmed with complacency. "He started life as a doctor, came in for the baronetcy and a pile of money, chucked everything and went abroad for five years. He got lost in Central Asia, and when he came back he lectured before a lot of societies, and he's got half the letters in the alphabet after his name. I don't know what he does now—just enjoys himself, I suppose."

"And the ladies?" Eleanor asked. "Is he married?"

"Don't think so. The old geez—lady with the diamonds is his mother, Lady Fiske. The other's his sister, I suppose. She looks like him."

The curtain rose again. A superfluous fourth act did its best to weaken the general effect of the play. With its fall there was a rush for the door. Eleanor gave one backward glance, but Sir Powers Fiske was helping his womenkind with their opera cloaks. Then again there was a hateful scrimmage, but outside the conditions had improved. The sky was clear of clouds, the stars were shining, and a fresh breeze seemed to Eleanor a delicious change after the stuffy atmosphere of the theatre. They turned up the Haymarket, and as they passed from under the portico, Eleanor was amazed to hear a whisper in her ear:

"I shall write to you to-morrow!"

She walked on, making no sign. Directly afterwards a brougham drawn by a pair of powerful horses passed them close to the curb-stone. A man was sitting on the back seat, and for a moment the gaslight fell upon his still, cold face. He looked steadily at the little party, but without any sign of recognition. The carriage swept round a corner. Ada leaned forward.

"Did you see who that was, Eleanor?" she asked eagerly.

"Yes, I saw him in the theatre," Eleanor answered.

Ada tossed her head.

"Looked as though he's never seen us before in his life," she whispered. "If we were good enough to take out to tea we ought to be good enough to acknowledge in the streets. I don't call it gentlemanly of him at all."

Eleanor made no remark. A certain restraint seemed to have fallen upon their two cavaliers. They walked all four together, Mr. Johnson having resisted an attempt on the part of his friend to detach Eleanor and walk behind. Ada was on the inside and Eleanor between the two. The attention of both seemed fixed upon her.

"I hope that you've enjoyed the play, Miss Surtoes?" Mr. Johnson asked anxiously.

Eleanor withdrew her eyes from the corner round which the carriage had vanished.

"Immensely, thank you," she answered warmly. "Really, it has been a great treat for me. It is very kind of you and Ada to have brought me."

Mr. Chadwick coughed.

"It was lucky," he remarked, "that I was able to get seats. The play is thought a lot of, and there are very few orders being given."

"It was very nice of you to include me in your invitation," Eleanor said absently. "What a sight this is!"

They were at the top of the Haymarket. All around them streams of people were pouring out from the theatres and the music halls. Cabs and carriages full of men and women in evening dress blocked all the thoroughfares. A glare of lights from the restaurants and the Leicester Square music halls turned night into day. The pavements were crowded with wayfarers of all sorts and conditions. It was the nightly pandemonium of the West End, when class jostles class, when the great streams of pleasure-seekers seize upon a few acres of their great city, and seek for relaxation with something of that same feverish absorption with which throughout the day they fight their battle in the greater struggle for existence. To Eleanor, who had seen little enough of it, there was a curious fascination in this brilliant and light-hearted mammon show. Even the dark places were tinselled over. It was early yet for the dregs.

"Cheerful sight, ain't it?" Mr. Chadwick remarked. "You're not a Londoner, perhaps, Miss Surtoes?"

She shook her head.

"No! I have lived nearly all my life in the north of England. Is it like this every night?"

"There's never any change to speak of. No place like it in the world, you know."

Mr. Chadwick, who had never been out of England save once for a day trip to Boulogne, spoke with the bland and insular confidence of his class. All the while he had been feeling surreptitiously in his trousers pocket. What he found was apparently satisfactory.

"Henry, my boy," he said suddenly, "what about a bit of supper, eh? That is, if Miss Surtoes will favor us?" he added, turning towards her deferentially.

"It is my treat," Mr. Johnson declared, with some asperity. "I was on the point of proposing it. We will go to Gatti's—unless Miss Surtoes would prefer somewhere else."

Eleanor glanced across to Ada, who had been walking almost by herself. Neither of the two men had addressed a word to her since leaving the theatre.

"What do you say, Ada?" she asked. "Have we time?"

"There is plenty of time, but Gatti's is a little expensive," Ada answered guardedly. "I don't think that I am very hungry."

"The expense has nothing to do with it," Mr. Johnson declared, somewhat nettled. "Supper we will have, that's certain. I always think it's the proper way to end an evening like this. The only question is, where we shall go to."

Mr. Chadwick had an inspiration.

"What price Frascati's!" he exclaimed. "There's music there, and it's close to Bearmain's. Are you fond of music, Miss Surtoes?"

"I like music very much," she answered, "but I

think, perhaps, that Ada is right. We have had a very pleasant evening, and I am sure supper is quite unnecessary."

The two young men waived aside her remonstrance. Ada, in response to a vigorous nudge from Mr. Johnson, admitted to an appetite. They set out for Frascati's.

CHAPTER V

THE big restaurant was crowded, but Mr. Chadwick, who seemed to have friends everywhere, pre-
vailed upon a waiter whom he called by his Christian
name, and patronized in a lordly way, to show them
to a table at the far end of the room. Eleanor, to
whom had come a brief spell of wonderful light-
heartedness, was the life and soul of the little party.
The cosmopolitanism of the place, the warmth, the
music, and the cheerful hum of conversation, all had
an effect upon her. The event of the afternoon, those
few words which seemed still to linger in her ears,
had touched her imagination. After all, she was
very young. These people were doing their best to
be kind to her. To let herself go on a momentary
wave of enjoyment seemed to her after all a natural
thing. With her sudden access of spirits the change
in her appearance was wonderful. A faint flush of
color brought out the delicate faultlessness of her
complexion, her eyes were brilliant, the feverish mirth
seemed to send the words dancing from her lips. She
took no note of Ada's silence, or of the fact that
both young men vied with one another in their at-
tentions to her. She accepted the champagne which
Mr. Chadwick had ordered with the air of a prince,
wholly unmindful of Ada's barely repressed disapproval. The delight of even these few minutes'
respite from the drudgery of a hated life, of feeling
the blood once more warm in her veins, was like a

spell upon her. After all, it was short-lived enough! When they rose to leave the restaurant and were making their way towards the door, she felt a little touch upon her arm. Mr. Johnson was by her side.

"I say, let's all walk home together," he whispered hurriedly. "Don't go off with Chadwick, will you?"

She was on the point of assenting to a proposition which she herself would have much preferred, when something in his face aroused her to some confused sense of the position. She looked at him in chilling surprise.

"I think it is quite time," she said, "that you made yourself agreeable to Ada. Of course she is expecting you to walk home with her. I shall wait behind for Mr. Chadwick."

"I'm not engaged to her—not properly," he said, in a low, eager tone.

Ada was just in front. Her somewhat dumpy little figure was at its worst in an ill-fitting jacket. She walked with a somewhat mincing and conscious gait, affecting to be busy with her gloves. Between her and the girl at his side, whose natural elegance triumphed over shabby clothes, there could be no manner of comparison. He looked up at her pleadingly. She ignored him altogether. At the door she touched Ada on the shoulder.

"Ada," she said, "will you and Mr. Johnson walk on. I will wait for Mr. Chadwick. He has lost his stick or something."

Henry's look of reproach was wasted upon her. He and Ada moved off together. Mr. Chadwick came out beaming, a big cigar in his mouth and his ill-brushed silk hat set on the back of his head.

"Good business," he exclaimed cheerfully. "I knew Henry's game, so I hung round a bit inside—

couldn't find my hat, you know. Two's company—four ain't. What do you think, Miss Surtoes?"

The momentary light-heartedness had passed away. She looked at him in cold disapproval, from her standard of taste a wholly impossible being, vulgar, devoid of all niceness of person, offensively familiar.

"I have no preference," she answered coldly. "Only as Ada is engaged to Mr. Johnson it seemed to me that they might like to be together. There really isn't the least need for you to come out of your way, Mr. Chadwick. I know my way home, and I can keep them in sight."

Mr. Chadwick looked at her in amazement.

"Oh, come on!" he exclaimed facetiously. "That's a bit thick, isn't it? As if you didn't know I've been looking forward all supper-time to this walk with you."

She was silent. Mr. Chadwick, who was not used to under-estimate himself and his powers of attraction, decided that the change in her manner was one of those feminine wiles designed to enslave him the more deeply. It was by no means her intention to be taken seriously.

"Don't let's hurry," he said. "It's a beautiful night, and you've got till twelve o'clock. Not over-strict at Bearmain's, are they? That sort of thing don't do nowadays."

They met with a stress of traffic. He attempted to draw her arm through his and was promptly repulsed.

"Please do not attempt anything of that sort again," she exclaimed indignantly. "It is most offensive to me."

Mr. Chadwick stared at her. It was obvious that

she was in earnest. She quickened her pace, and he walked by her side in silence. After all, she was scarcely like Ada and the rest. Perhaps his gallantry had been a little premature. Presently he attempted a clumsy apology.

"Sorry I tried to take your arm," he said. "I'd no idea you'd have any objection. I forgot we weren't very well acquainted."

"It is of no consequence," Eleanor answered coldly.

"Haven't offended you in any other way, have I?" he asked. "You seem mighty quiet."

"On the contrary, you have given me a very pleasant evening, for which I thank you," she said.

He coughed. His experience of young women of such aloofness was limited. He began to feel aggrieved. The theatre tickets had been his, and he had paid for the champagne—a prodigality which would seriously affect his meals during the coming week. He was not getting value for his money.

"What about next Thursday?" he asked. "Will you come for a bit of a walk with me?"

"No, thank you," she answered decidedly.

"Why not?" he persisted.

"Because I do not care about that sort of thing at all!" she said.

He threw away his cigar viciously.

"You'd go to the theatre fast enough, I suppose!" he remarked.

She looked at him with some surprise. His ill-humor was incomprehensible to her.

"I should not go with you," she said calmly.

An ugly expression narrowed his eyes.

"Didn't know I was coming to-night, I suppose?" he remarked.

"I did not," she answered. "Ada asked me to go with Mr. Johnson and herself."

"You are quite sure there's no mistake?" he asked, with clumsy sarcasm. "You are one of Bearmain's girls, and not a duchess in disguise."

She vouchsafed him no answer, but turning on her heel crossed the street. He followed, but had hard work to keep up with her.

"I ain't going to be shaken off," he said doggedly. "I can walk as fast as you any day."

She made no remark. He watched her for a moment. The lithesomeness of her walk fascinated him. She possessed the grace of rapid and effortless movement.

"Look here," he said, "I don't know what I've said or done to offend you, but I apologize. I can't say anything fairer than that, can I? I apologize. You understand! Don't go away like this. I tell you I haven't seen any one for years who's taken my fancy so much as you have, and it's stupid to quarrel before we know one another."

"I don't want to know you," she answered wearily. "I am very much obliged for your kindness this evening, but I wish you'd go away now."

He gave vent to an exclamation which closely resembled a snort.

"Well, that's a nice way to talk," he said sullenly. "I shan't bite, anyhow! I suppose there's some one else, eh? Just my luck!"

She made no reply, but still further quickened her pace. Mr. Chadwick remembered that in the textbook of his gallantry was an axiom that women of spirit liked to be treated with spirit. He decided upon bolder measures. He leaned suddenly towards her, and his hand rested for a moment upon her waist. She sprang away with marvellous swiftness, and struck the face which had very nearly touched hers with ungloved hand. Mr. Chadwick, who was altogether unprepared for such a vigorous defence, staggered back with a cry of pain. Eleanor caught up her skirts, and ran with a speed which rendered pursuit hopeless up the dark street. She was on the doorstep of Bearmain's in a moment or two. Ada and Henry were still standing there.

"What is it?" Ada cried.

Eleanor leaned against the wall, panting.

"That beast of a man!" she exclaimed. "Oh, let us get in quickly."

Henry, without a word of good-night, left them. Ada watched him anxiously, but Eleanor was unconscious of his going. The door opened, and she pushed her way inside, ran up the narrow stairs, and into her room. Then she stood quite still, and drew a long sigh of relief.

Slowly she drew off her hat and jacket, and replaced her wet boots with slippers. Then, though the night was cold, she threw open the window and leaned out. Below in the street two men were quarrelling, the hum of traffic still rolled along the Edgware Road. But she took no heed of these things. Her eyes were fixed upon the sky, lurid still with the fire of the awakened city. She drew in long breaths of the pure, crisp air. Here was peace for a little time—and afterwards. What manner of death could this be of which he had warned her?

4

CHAPTER VI

THERE followed for Eleanor a succession of dreary days, differing only from those which had gone before in the somewhat altered demeanor of those around her. Johnson, on whose left cheek was a patch of sticking-plaster where Chadwick's fist had cut through to the bone, seemed to find endless excuses for hovering around her end of the counter. He offered her many small services, few of which she accepted, and was always nervously anxious that no undue share of work should fall to her lot. A few yards away from her Ada stood, pale and heavy-eyed, neglected all the day by her former admirer, who scarcely vouchsafed her a glance. The girls made unkind remarks in Eleanor's hearing. Popular sympathy was with Ada, and it was openly expressed.

Johnson, although he made many attempts, found it hard to see anything of Eleanor alone. One afternoon, however, they came face to face in the passage leading to the tea-room. Instead of avoiding him, she waited. He came hurrying up to her.

"Mr. Johnson," she said, "you are treating Ada very badly."

"Miss Smart is nothing to me," he answered. "I told you before that we were not engaged."

"You were friends, at any rate," she answered. "You spent your Thursday evenings together. You took her out continually. Now without a word of explanation you simply ignore her."

"I cannot help it," he answered simply. "It is your fault."

"My fault!" she repeated indignantly. "What do you mean?"

"I cannot think of her because I cannot think of anybody else but you," he answered. "I know it's presumption. You're different. You're a lady. It's easy to see that. I can't help it, Miss Surtoes; please don't be angry with me. My people are quite well off, and I am only here to learn the business. Will you come out with me to-morrow evening?"

She looked at him with flashing eyes.

"How dare you ask me such a thing," she exclaimed indignantly. "Ada is my friend—the only girl here who has been decent to me. If you say another word of that sort to me I'll never speak to you again."

He looked at her, pale with anxiety.

"I can't help it about Ada," he said. "As long as I live I couldn't care for her now. It's you or nobody, Miss Surtoes."

"Then it will certainly be nobody," Eleanor answered haughtily. "You must be out of your senses."

She swept past him into the tea-room. Ada came and sat by her side.

"You were talking to Henry," she remarked. "Did he say anything about me?"

"He said some very foolish things, dear," Eleanor answered kindly. "Men are like that sometimes, you know, Ada, especially at his age. It will all come right, I am sure."

Ada mopped her eyes.

"I can't tell what's come over him, I'm sure," she said ruefully. "He used to be so sensible. It isn't like him a bit to hang round any one as he does you, and you scarcely civil to him. He must be very fond of you, Eleanor. I've seen him stand and watch you—well, he never looked at me like it."

Eleanor laughed.

"If I were you, Ada," she said, "I should not let him see that it troubled me. If he doesn't ask you to go out to-morrow, couldn't you find some one else to take you—just for one evening?"

Ada shook her head pitifully.

"I couldn't do it," she said. "I couldn't go out with any one but Henry. May I ask you something, Eleanor?"

"Of course!"

"Has he asked you to go out with him to-morrow?"

"He said something about it," Eleanor admitted. "Of course, I shouldn't think of going. You know that."

Ada flushed a little.

"The beast! And only last week he declared that there would never be any one else but me that he'd care to take out. Eleanor, I wonder why men are so much more changeable than women?"

"I wonder!"

There was a short silence. Ada was studying her friend's face.

"Eleanor, may I ask you something?"

Eleanor nodded.

"Yes."

"Were you ever engaged?"

Eleanor was silent. A curious hardness had stolen

into her face. Yet when she spoke her tone was matter-of-fact enough.

"Yes, I was engaged before I came here," she admitted.

"And were you very fond of him?"

"I suppose so—in a way," Eleanor answered. "I don't think that I was very much in love. I was too young. But I felt it terribly when it was broken off. I think that it was my vanity which suffered most."

"Wasn't it your fault, then, that it was broken off?"

"No! It came with the rest of my troubles. I don't think I care to talk about it any more, if you don't mind."

The bell rang, and they hastened back to work. On the way some one handed Eleanor a letter. She glanced at the address, and put it calmly in her pocket. Ada, who was by her side, noticed the thick square envelope and crest.

It was several hours later before she gained the shelter of her room, and had an opportunity of opening it. The contents were brief enough, but to the point :

"131 HANS CRESCENT PLACE, LONDON.

"DEAR MISS SURTOES,—I think you said that you were generally disengaged on Thursday evenings. I should be very glad if you would dine with me to-morrow evening quietly somewhere, and go to a theatre afterwards. I would either call for you, or, if you prefer it, meet you at the corner of Oxford Street and Bond Street. If I hear nothing from you I shall be there at seven o'clock.—Yours sincerely,

"POWERS FISKE."

She replaced the letter in the envelope, and sat

down by the open window. The luxury of a room to herself was only a temporary one. In a week or two at the outside the other little iron bedsteads would be occupied, and these few moments of freedom would be denied her. She told herself that she would make up her mind whether or no to accept this invitation. All the while she knew that she was trifling with herself. Her decision was already arrived at. Only there was so much that was strange in her meeting with this man, so much that was mysterious in his calmly avowed intentions towards her. Ada's earnest warnings she took little account of. She trusted him entirely.

Presently she dragged out from its hiding-place and unlocked a box which she had not opened since her arrival at Bearmain's. She looked it over thoughtfully. The things were a little old-fashioned, but of a different order altogether to anything which she had worn recently. She selected a dress, and fell asleep re-trimming a hat.

All the next day she was conscious that Ada was watching her with nervous anxiety. The hours seemed to drag along, the day was surely the longest she had ever known. At last it was over. She hurried to her room, slipped off her dress, and with beating heart began her transformation. When she had finished, and she surveyed herself in the small cracked mirror, she drew a little sigh of relief. It was the old Eleanor who was smiling at her. Of the shop-girl there was no single trace left.

Just as she was ready Ada knocked timidly at the door. She gave one glance at Eleanor, and sinking down upon the bed, burst into tears.

"My dear child!" Eleanor exclaimed, "whatever is the matter?"

"You are going to him!" Ada sobbed. "I knew it!"

Eleanor laughed a little scornfully.

"I am going out to dinner with him, and perhaps to a theatre," she said. "Why on earth shouldn't I?"

"Because you are too good for any man to amuse himself with—especially that one," she answered. "You think I am a fool, I know, Eleanor, but I've been here seven years, and all the girls who have ever been out with gentlemen have—they haven't stayed here. It's begun by going out to dinner, and afterwards none of the young men about here were ever good enough for them. It's always the nicest girls, too, and the prettiest. Don't go, dear. You may have—Henry!—I—I don't care! But—don't go!"

Eleanor laughed softly.

"It's very nice of you to mind so much, dear," she said, sitting by her side for a moment, and taking her hand. "Now, listen. I am absolutely and perfectly safe, and I am not a silly child to be flattered into doing anything foolish. I want to understand what he meant the other afternoon—you know that I am very miserable here, and if there is any honest means of escape I want to know all about it."

"You're sure you won't take to going out with him regular?" Ada pleaded. "I know I'm foolish, but there was Lyddy Green—she was almost a lady, and such a dear—"

Eleanor broke away.

"I am late already," she said. "I mustn't stay another moment. Sit up for me if you like, and I'll tell you all about it when I come home."

She hurried away, and within a few feet of the

front door came face to face with Mr. Johnson. He was carefully dressed, and smoking a cigarette, which he threw away directly she appeared. He took off his hat with shaking fingers. He was white and red almost at the same time. He could scarcely stand still for nervousness.

"Good evening, Miss Surtoes!"

She looked at him coldly.

"Good evening, Mr. Johnson. You must excuse my stopping, if you please. I am in a hurry."

"I thought perhaps," he faltered, "that you might come for just a short walk—or some dinner."

She stopped short.

"I have an engagement, Mr. Johnson," she said; "and in any case, I have told you distinctly that I do not desire your company."

"It's because of Ada! I know it is!" he pleaded. "I'll make it all right with her. Let me walk a little way with you."

"No!"

"Just to the corner of the street."

"If you do," she answered, "I shall never speak to you again."

He was suddenly pale. He saw a familiar figure lounging against a pillar-box at the corner of the street.

"You ain't going with Chadwick?" he exclaimed.

She shivered.

"Don't ask me such insulting questions."

Mr. Johnson was immensely relieved. He indicated the waiting figure.

"Well, he's hanging about," he exclaimed gloomily. "I suppose he knew this was our evening."

Eleanor stopped short. Mr. Chadwick was watching them with some hesitation. He wore a large flower in his button-hole, and a black shade over his left eye.

"Mr. Johnson," she said, "could I trouble you to call a hansom for me?"

He sighed.

"It's a pleasure to do anything for you, Miss Surtoes," he said. "You really have an engagement, then?"

"I really have."

Mr. Johnson called a hansom, and handed her in. She leaned over the apron.

"Mr. Johnson," she said, "will you do something to please me?"

"Anything!" he exclaimed vigorously.

"Go back and ask Miss Smart to go for a walk. She has a headache, I know, and it will do her good."

He stifled a sigh.

"If you wish it, Miss Surtoes. But I want you to understand there's nothing serious between Miss Smart and myself. We're friends, no more."

Chadwick walked by, and executed a profound salute. Eleanor looked coolly through him. It was a pleasurable moment for Mr. Johnson. The cab was on the point of starting.

She moved her head towards Mr. Chadwick's black shade.

"Mr. Johnson," she said, "did you do that?"

He looked sheepish for a moment, but her eyes compelled answer.

"Yes, Miss Surtoes."

She flashed a brilliant smile upon him and waved her hand.

"Thank you!" she called out.

CHAPTER VII

"YES," he said, smiling across the table at her, "you may ask me any questions you like. But you must remember that I do not promise to answer them."

"Nevertheless," she said thoughtfully, "I have come to-night for information. I must ask you to explain, if only vaguely, your words to me. I must have some sort of an idea as to what is in your mind."

"If you insist," he declared, "I can only answer you in this manner. The service which I may require of you is one which involves a certain risk to your life and health. That risk is very small, but it exists. You will suffer neither pain nor discomfort. You will be removed into another sphere altogether, and it is possible that you may take with you a somewhat cloudy recollection of this portion of your life. Your reward will be an established position in the world and an honorable one. Beyond this I cannot say a single word. In fact, you must consider the whole thing as only a possibility. I do not make you any offer for the present. I simply ask you to accept my acquaintance and give me some portion of your time."

Eleanor leaned back in her chair and slowly stirred her coffee. hey were sitting at a small table in a quiet but fashionable London restaurant. A Viennese band was playing soft music, the room was full of smart and interesting people. Their dinner had been small, but perfect, a great handful of long-stemmed roses had just been presented to her by an obliging head-waiter. Her companion had been most entertaining. For the first time for years she had enjoyed the luxury of conversation with a person of culture and sympathies. A certain coldness which she had noticed in him upon their first meeting had gradually worn away, and he had at times shown signs of a geniality and sense of humor which came as a surprise to her. From whatever point of view she regarded it, their meeting had been a success. She was ready enough, for the moment, to waive all further explanations.

"There is only one thing I should like to add, Miss Surtoes," he said, glancing at the clock. "It would be a great pleasure to me to have you meet my mother and sister, and under ordinary circumstances I should not ask you for your friendship until I had done so. But as it happens, nothing of this sort can happen for the moment, because if we should ever carry out the scheme which I have in my mind, you will be associated with them in somewhat different fashion. This sounds terribly complicated, doesn't it?" he added. "I'm afraid I have not the gift of concise expression."

She laughed.

"You are a very mysterious person altogether," she said. "As for meeting your mother and sister, it is very good of you to suggest it, but of course it would not be possible in my present position. There is one thing more which I am going to ask you, anyhow. What extraordinary chance made you select me as your—what shall I say, victim?"

"I strongly object to the term," he answered, smiling, "and the question itself is not a very easy one to answer. In fact, I cannot answer it. Do you see that it is nine o'clock, and I have seats for Wyndham's? Shall we go?"

She rose at once, and they left the room together. Outside he would have called a hansom, but she checked him.

"It is only five minutes away," she said, "and the air is so delicious. Do you mind walking?"

He too preferred it. They strolled through the crowded streets almost in silence. Eleanor was too preoccupied for conversation. Powers seemed absorbed by his cigarette. But as they neared the theatre she turned towards him.

"It appears to me," she said, "that I am entering upon a sort of probationary period. At least, may I not have an idea as to how long it must last?"

"It need not be very long," he said thoughtfully. "There are two things which I must ask from you : first, your entire trust; secondly, that you tell me the whole of the important features of your past history."

"The first," she said, "I think you already have. The second—is that really necessary?"

"Absolutely."

"I will tell you all that you need know whenever you choose to ask," she said.

They passed into the theatre, and were shown to the box which Powers had engaged. With a little sigh of content, Eleanor drew her chair back into the shadows. The curtain rose almost as they entered.

"I am going to enjoy myself thoroughly," she murmured. "This is the one play of all others which I have wanted to see."

.   .   .   .

Only once did she glance away from the stage.

Once she leaned forward and looked half curiously, half with some faint sense of self-pity, into the pit. She thought of that night of humiliations as of some ugly shadow, a chapter of her life done with forever, She realized and marvelled at her own sufferings. Already she was able to think of the misery of the last few months of her life as finished. What this thing was which would be required of her she had as yet no possible idea, though her acceptance of it seemed to her a thing already assured. It was not until the curtain fell upon the last act that she realized that her emancipation, however near it might be, was as yet a thing of the future. Within three-quarters of an hour she must be back at Bearmain's.

"You have liked it?" he asked, as they passed out into the corridor.

She turned a glowing face upon him.

"The whole evening has been delightful," she assured him.

He smiled. Her enthusiasm was infectious, and he too was conscious that the evening was the pleasantest he had spent for some time. They talked lightly of the play until they reached the street. Then he hesitated.

"What time have you to be in?" he asked.

"In half an hour," she answered.

They turned slowly northwards.

"Shall we have a cab, or would you rather walk?" he asked.

"Let us walk," she begged, "if you can spare the time. There seem to be so many things yet which I want to ask you."

"The forbidden subject, I suppose?" he remarked lightly.

"At least," she said, "you can give me some idea as to how long it must be forbidden?"

He was suddenly grave. He was walking with his hands behind him, and his eyes fixed steadily upon some distant point. When he answered her he spoke very slowly and very seriously.

"After all," he said, "there is no reason for any very long delay. Next time we meet you must tell me your history, and how it is that you are so much alone in the world. Afterwards I will speak to you—about it. I wonder—"

He broke off, looking at her thoughtfully. She seemed to divine something of the nature of the thoughts which were passing through his brain.

"You are wondering whether, after all, I shall be suitable," she exclaimed. "I think," she added, in a lower tone, "that if you were to change your mind—if—"

"We will not consider such a thing," he interrupted hastily. "The drawing back after may be on your part. It is not every one who cares to look, however dimly, into the face of death."

"There is life," she murmured, half to herself, "which is worse than death. And there was a time when I very nearly looked death in the face of my own free will."

"You are very young," he said, "to have known so much trouble."

"I am twenty-one," she answered. "Generally I feel about forty."

"To-night," he said, smiling, "is, I hope, an exception."

"To-night," she repeated, "is an exception."

They crossed the road and slackened their pace a little. They were close to the side street

which led up to the back premises of Bearmain's.

"Next week," he said abruptly, "I will tell you
everything. May I write to you and suggest a meet-
ing-place? Would it be possible for you to come in
the afternoon?"

She thought for a moment.

"I will make it possible," she answered.

A young man brushed rudely against them.
Eleanor looked up and recognized Mr. Chadwick.
There was an evil smile upon his pale face. He
stared at them both insolently. Eleanor's fingers
fell upon her companion's coat-sleeve.

"I am afraid that I must ask you to take me right
up to the door," she said. "There is a young man
there who annoys me."

"I will have a word with him," Powers said quietly; but Chadwick had overheard, and was strolling
away with ill-assumed jauntiness.

"Please don't!" she begged. "Only if you do not
mind coming to the door."

They turned up the side street, passing Johnson,
who cast a single despairing glance at Eleanor, and
a little group of girls home from the theatre. At the
door she held out her hand.

"Thank you so much," she said. "It has been a delightful evening. I shall hear from you next week?"

"I will write you on Monday or Tuesday," he
answered.

Their eyes met for a moment. He hesitated.
There was something else which he would have said,
but Ada and the friends whom they had passed in the
street were already on the doorstep. They stared at
him with covert curiosity. He raised his hat and
hurried off.

CHAPTER VIII

"A PRIVATE box, if you please—and we in the pit!"

"And a baronet! Mr. Johnson's friend, Mr. Chadwick, knew him quite well."

"Looked right at us, my dear, and never turned an eyelid."

Miss Salter, who was a leading saleswoman at Bearmain's, and a person in authority, shook her head and pursed her lips.

"I certainly thought that the girls here," she said severely, "were above that sort of thing, and I must say that I am surprised at Miss Surtoes. I always looked upon her as a particularly quiet and well-conducted young person."

Ada, who had not spoken, looked up.

"And isn't she?"

Miss Salter shook her head dubiously.

"You are, perhaps, not aware of the facts, Miss Smart," she said. "Miss Surtoes was at Wyndham's Theatre to-night, in a private box, with a baronet —a man well known in London—Sir Powers Fiske."

"And why not?" Ada asked. "He is a friend of hers. I know that, for she introduced me to him in Bond Street the other day. I heard him ask her to go to the theatre with him. Why not? We go when we're asked, don't we?"

"We go with suitable companions," Miss Salter answered stiffly.

Ada laughed.

"Well, Sir Powers Fiske might be a very unsuita-

ble companion for any of us," she said, "but with
Miss Surtoes it is a different matter. She was born
a lady."

Miss Salter flushed angrily. She was looked upon
as a very genteel person indeed. Her father was a
coal merchant at Sydenham; she belonged to a ten-
nis club, and went bicycling in the summer in a
patent safety skirt.

"I do not imagine that Miss Surtoes' birth was
much superior to ours," she said with dignity.
"Certainly not so much as to give her the license
to do indiscreet things."

"Miss Surtoes never did an indiscreet thing in her
life," Ada declared hotly.

"You will pardon me," Miss Salter objected. "I
consider that for any young lady employed in this
establishment to show herself at a theatre in a private box with a man of much superior station is
more than indiscreet. It is indecent. I should not
think of doing such a thing myself," she added, with
some asperity, "although there is no mystery, I am
glad to say, about my birth and upbringing."

"You never had the chance," Ada declared bluntly.
"You're insinuating things about Miss Surtoes which
are ridiculous."

"I am insinuating nothing," Miss Salter rejoined.
"I have stated facts. I consider Miss Surtoes' be-
havior reprehensible—reprehensible in the extreme."

Ada turned towards the door.

"Well, I don't suppose she cares what you think,"
she declared, "and I'm sure I don't. I consider such
a remark as yours uncharitable and uncalled for."

Nevertheless, she went straight to Eleanor's room,
and on being admitted, and finding her still dressed,
plumped down on the bed and burst into tears.

5

"Eleanor!" she exclaimed, "oh, why did you do it? Why did you?"

"Why did I do what?" Eleanor asked, laughing softly.

"Go to the theatre with him—alone in a box—and let the others see you."

Eleanor smiled a little thoughtfully.

"They have been making remarks?"

Ada nodded.

"Well, let them. After all, it is my own affair. I have no friends here—except you, Ada. Let them think what they like."

"It's that horrid Maud Salter," Ada continued. "She's such a prig, and she'd give her eyes to know some one a little different from the young gentlemen here. She's as mean and jealous as she can be. I told her that he was a friend of yours, that you had introduced me to him in Bond Street."

"You needn't have troubled—although it was kind of you, dear," Eleanor added hastily. "It really doesn't matter to me in the least what Miss Salter or any of them think."

Ada dried her eyes. She was nervous and ill at ease. Eleanor, on the contrary, who was leaning back in the one chair with her hands clasped behind her head, was perfectly composed. The reflection of her pleasantly spent evening still lingered about her face.

"Eleanor, you're not going out with him regularly?"

"I don't think that I shall say no when he asks me," Eleanor admitted. "Why should I?"

Her calmness was disconcerting. Ada looked at her in despair.

"Eleanor," she said, "remember that I was there

when—when he first spoke to us. I heard him talk. It was a lot of rubbish, wasn't it? You know that. You're not one to be taken in so easily. Of course, it's all very well going out with him now and then, but the girls will talk, and you know what Mr. Bearmain is."

"It is no concern of Mr. Bearmain's," Eleanor said, "with whom I spend my time after business hours."

"No, not exactly," Ada admitted. "Only, the girls exaggerate, and—well, you know as well as I do what they will say. Then Mr. Bearmain will hear of it, and if he does, he will send you away, Eleanor. There, I've told you now. He will send you away, and the only friend you will have will be Sir Powers Fiske."

Eleanor leaned over and took the girl's hand.

"You are a good-natured little thing, Ada," she said. "You needn't look so frightened. I'm not at all offended. Only we girls are all different, you know. We can't all live our lives alike. What might content you wouldn't content me. Another six months here would send me mad. My friendship with Sir Powers Fiske is not a sentimental one. He may be able to help me, it is true; but if so, there would be no question of what you are hinting at between us."

"You don't think so now," Ada cried. "But there is! there is! He is deceiving you if he tries to make you think otherwise. I was in the theatre to-night. I saw him look at you. How could he help admiring you, Eleanor? Don't you know that you are beautiful?"

Eleanor laughed.

"You are mistaken, Ada," she said. "I do not

think that he could tell you even whether I was
dark or fair. He is not at all a ladies' man. Now,
go away, dear. I am tired, and I want to go to bed."

Ada lingered near the door.

"You won't do anything rash," she said, "supposing the girls aren't quite so nice as usual to-
morrow?"

"I can assure you," Eleanor said, bundling her
out, "that it will not trouble me in the least."

.   .   .   .

At the time she meant it, but after a whole day
of studied avoidance on the part of nearly every
young woman who came anywhere near her, after
being the unwilling recipient of at least a score of
slighting remarks and doubtful looks, she changed
her mind. Even the shopwalkers, whom she had
always disliked and treated with studied coldness,
altered their demeanor towards her. She found herself more than once addressed with a familiarity
which was worse than rudeness. She read in their
faces their altered views of her. Mr. Johnson alone
was faithful. He hung about her counter till she
loathed the sight of him. He frowned severely on
those of her persecutors who came within his range,
and lost his temper with one of his seniors to such
an extent that he was told he would hear more of it.
At night Eleanor was wholly unstrung. She had
passed through her long day of indignities with unmoved face, but as soon as it was over, she hurried
to her room and locked the door. She threw herself
upon the bed and sobbed wildly. The last few
months had been like a nightmare to her. This was
the climax. She knew that she had reached the
limits of her endurance.

Presently she dried her eyes, and throwing open

the window, leaned out to cool her face. The breath
of the night wind was wonderfully soothing to her.
She lingered there, her head resting upon her hand.
A wilderness of house-tops stretched away to the
horizon—in the clouds some faint reflection of the
city's myriad lights. The roar of traffic came to her
ears subdued almost into harmony. She suffered her
thoughts to drift away.

She was twenty-one years old. For twenty years
her life had been uneventful enough, the life of hundreds of well-bred, upper middle-class girls. And then
—the thunderbolt of tragedy. She looked back for
a moment—again she remembered its fall. It had
come from a clear sky, it had left her friendless, face
to face, without a moment's warning, with all the
stern realities of life. Friends had melted away; the
meaning of poverty was for the first time brought
home to her. She realized solitude—yet perhaps the
bitterness of it had never presented itself to her with
such terrible poignancy as at that moment. The
humiliation of the last few hours had been the cul-
mination of months of misery. Well, it was at an
end now. No fate could be worse than another such
day. No necessity should force her to face it. She
knew very well the nature of the risks which she had
dared. She laughed softly to herself as she thought
of Ada's pitiful warnings. She was young, and in
her heart remained unstifled the passionate longing
for freedom, for life untrammelled—life with all its
glorious possibilities.

She drew back from the window, and looked
thoughtfully into the glass. By the flickering light
of a candle she studied herself, endeavoring to ar-
rive at some unbiased and impersonal opinion as to
what she saw. It was true, she decided thoughtfully,

that she was good to look upon. Of what account
was it? Her delicate features, her soft coloring, her
long neck with its graceful poise, her glorious hair—
these things were more likely to be a hindrance to
her at a crisis such as this. Yet they gave her pleasure to look upon. They helped her self-respect. She
had one gift at any rate which those other women,
whose ears were deaf now to her sorrows, must envy
her. She passed her long white fingers through the
waving clusters of red-brown hair, and laughed softly to herself. She wondered what manner of death
would leave her beauty most undisturbed. It was a
curious revival of an innocent vanity which had belonged to her earlier girlhood.

An hour later, without permission or farewells, she
left the house.

CHAPTER IX

FISKE, though far from being a sybarite in the ordinary acceptation of the word, possessed a fundamental but crudely developed love of the beautiful. Before all things with him came his devotion to science and scientific investigation. But for his unexpected accession to the Fiske title and estates he would, without doubt, have become a denizen of Harley Street, and made his way without difficulty into the front ranks of his profession. With the passing away of all necessity for work, however, came a curious era of half-doubtful dilettantism, a time during which he read hugely, travelled a good deal, and finally returned to England with the seeds of a great unrest sown in his mind. Mysticism and psychology, which he had dabbled in at first half contemptuously, had become serious studies to him. Dimly he felt the fascination of that unending effort which from the days of the Chaldeans had swayed the lives of a long succession of the world's masters, the effort to establish some sort of communication, however faint, however speculative, between the world of known things and the world beyond. At times he found himself moved to the most profound self-ridicule. He would ask himself how it was possible for a man of science to seriously investigate problems whose very foundation must be an assumption. He looked around his study at his walls lined with books, and he smiled grimly as he realized how little, after all, they had taught him. There was the collected wisdom of the world upon its shelves. The sum of all that he had learned from them amounted to nothing. Yet he remembered what Trowse, a fellow-student, had said to him many years ago after a long day spent in the gloom of the British Museum diving into old folios, making copious notes, seeking for forgotten volumes amongst a wilderness of dead books. They passed out into the street, and, a little befogged with the close atmosphere of the place and their long depressing day, turned westward towards the Park. A few minutes, and they were in Trafalgar Square. They passed along Pall Mall into Piccadilly Circus. The streets were blocked with carriages, the human stream surged on every side of them. Trowse had stopped short, a sudden flush had lightened his thin cheeks, pallid with the ceaseless energy of their student life.

"After all, Powers, I think that we are wasting our days," he exclaimed. "Those ancients whose crabbed work filters through to our intelligence so slowly saw no farther behind the veil than we. I am tired of all this musty lore, this delving amongst cobwebs."

"What then?" Powers had asked. "Modern scholarship has taught us little enough."

"Let us have done with all scholarship," Trowse answered, with a little burst of rare enthusiasm. "It is the laws of humanity we want to understand. Let us study them at first hand. Let us go down amongst the people."

"What can this rabble teach us?" Powers had asked himself, full of the intellectual contempt of the young student for the whole pleasure-loving world.

"Whether their wings be soiled or pure, they are only butterflies!"

Trowse smiled grimly.

"They are the living evidences," he said, "of laws which are worth studying. If we would understand humanity we must not start by despising any part of it."

Powers that night lingered over his wine and dessert, curiously engrossed by certain memories of those earlier days. With characteristic impetuosity the two young men had thrown themselves heart and soul into their new enterprise. They haunted police-courts and places of entertainment, from the West End theatres to the Seven Dials music hall. They lived for a while in a great industrial centre; they listened to the hoarse, tragic undernote of the millions underneath. They made their bow at the reception of a Duchess, and spent a whole Bank Holiday dancing upon Hampstead Heath. The lighter course of their wanderings was strewn with many humorous adventures. They learnt something of the true Cockney wit; they caught a dash of that light-hearted philosophy whose owner, born into the world ill provided with the means of subsistence, feels himself to have a claim upon the goods of all men—and acts up to his principles. The Cockney thief and the Cockney wit are things unique in themselves; these and many other phases of life they had encountered with an amusement, in Powers' case partly genuine, in Trowse's wholly tolerant. For all the time they kept strenuously in view their real end. They were not novelists or journalists seeking to make themselves familiar with life among all classes of people. They wanted to understand the causes of all that they saw; they wanted to discover laws.

The end of their enterprise came suddenly. A disaster in his family left Trowse unexpectedly poor. It was necessary for him to take at once some wage-earning position. The two young men parted, curiously enough, without regret. Nothing but that unquenchable thirst for exact knowledge concerning hidden things, shared by both of them, could possibly have kept them together so long; for Powers had many gifts which Trowse had not himself, and despised in others. Powers, though no sentimentalist, possessed his due share of the affections, had an innate love for the beautiful, and a longing for a catholic and universal understanding of his fellows. Where Trowse would gaze with unmoved face, and pursue his calm calculations, Powers could only peer with barely veiled horror. They held together through those three years of unorthodox study, but towards the end of it they had drawn wide apart. Trowse entered the ranks of his profession a man of steel, without nerves or sentiment or pity. Powers, with his fuller understanding of life, had no longer any desire for a regular career. Possessed of ample means, the necessity for it had never existed. He left England almost at once, and entered upon a somewhat restless but comprehensive scheme of travel.

To-night he was in a curiously disturbed mood. He looked through the blue curling wreaths of his cigarette smoke to his study beyond, where his easy-chair and reading-stand were awaiting him, with an unusual reluctance to enter upon his solitary evening. The perfume of the pink roses upon his table, the bloom upon a dish of unusually fine peaches, the delicate flavor of his wine had brought to his memory the dinner with Eleanor a few nights ago. All the evening she had figured in his thoughts.

She was one of the more tragic figures in that world which he had spent so long and so much strenuous effort seeking to understand. The possibilities in connection with her loomed large in his imagination. He was oppressed with fears which were altogether new to him. Fortune could never have provided him with a human creature modelled more exactly according to his requirements. He knew her life and the ways of it. The confidence which he had expressed as to her ultimate decision was not exaggerated. She would come to him. He was sure of it. She would come to him for an explanation of his words, and she would accept—if ever he made it—his proposition. Yet never since his idea had first begun to loom large in his thoughts did he look upon it with less enthusiasm than at this moment. A few hours ago he had written to her—asked her to spend a day upon the river with him. He knew that she would come. The crisis was close at hand. He hoped to be able to delay it.

He rose at last, and passed through into his study, where coffee was awaiting him. By the side of the little brass pot was a single letter and an evening paper. He took up the former negligently. It bore an Indian post-mark, and the handwriting was familiar to him. He opened it, and read:

"THE SERVICE CLUB, CALCUTTA.

"MY DEAR FISKE:—I have never found it pleasant to ask favors, and I am writing to you to-day with great reluctance, for I am compelled to ask you to do me a great service. I have had offered to me, and accepted, a secret service mission to China which will keep me in that country for at least five years. It is doubtful, in fact, whether I shall ever return, for the post is an extremely hazardous one.

"I have long since given up any idea of ever returning to Europe, but I am forced to admit that I have been seriously troubled lately with the responsibilities which the sole charge of my daughter have imposed upon me. I feel that she ought to have her chance in the Western world, but during the long years of my absence from England I seem to have lost touch with all my old friends, and of relations I have only one alive. My appointment in China helps me at least to a decision. I could not possibly leave Eleanor alone here. We have decided, therefore, that she shall accept the offer of my brother John, made some years ago, and live with him for a time at any rate.

"Now comes the difficulty. John was always a rolling-stone, and I was always a very careless fellow where addresses are concerned. I do not know exactly where to find him, and as I have to leave here next week there is no time for me to start a search for his whereabouts. Eleanor's passage is booked in the *Colombo*, as one of the officers' wives here has offered to chaperon her on that boat. I want some one, you see, Fiske, to meet her on her arrival and put her in the way of finding a quiet home for a few weeks and introduce her to a firm of respectable solicitors who will easily be able to trace my brother from the enclosed papers. Your father, I know, would have been glad to do this for his old friend, and I sincerely hope that you will not think I am making an undue demand upon your good-nature. Eleanor will have a credit at Baring's for all that she requires, and as she is by no means a child, she will not, I think, be much trouble to any one.

"There will, I am afraid, be a very short margin of time between the receipt of this letter and the arrival of the *Colombo*, but Eleanor will explain how it was that I postponed writing to you until so late.

"In haste for the mail, and assuring you, my dear Fiske, of my most sincere gratitude for any kindness which you may be able to show my daughter.—Believe me, yours most sincerely,

"WALTER HARDINGE."

Powers replaced the letter carefully in its envelope and made a note to inquire to-morrow as to the due date of the *Colombo*. The service asked him was slight enough, considering that Hardinge had been his father's greatest friend, and the hospitality with which he himself had been received when in India. His mother would be willing enough to do all this and more. The journey down to meet her would fall to his lot, and would probably remain his sole responsibility. He shook out the evening paper, but he never penetrated beyond the first page. There in big letters, was the appalling news which already loomed large from all the placards in London :—

"Total Loss of the P. and O. Steamer *Colombo*.
Disaster in the Bay of Biscay.
200 Passengers Drowned.
List of the Rescued."

Powers read the few lines breathlessly. The name of Eleanor Hardinge was amongst the drowned.

CHAPTER X

"It is," he said to himself, throwing aside the newspaper, "a tragedy. Poor Hardinge! And her name was Eleanor."

The door was quietly opened. His servant stood upon the threshold.

"There is a young lady asking for you, Sir Powers —the name, I believe, was Surtoes."

In the face of what might prove the greater tragedy, Powers forgot the lesser. He rose slowly to his feet.

"What have you done with her, Morton?"

"I took the liberty of asking her to sit for a moment in the hall, sir. I was not sure—"

"Show her in at once," Powers interrupted.

The man bowed. A moment later he ushered Eleanor in. Her hat was beaten about with wind and rain, even her hair was disordered. She was breathless with rapid walking, her cheeks were wet, and the raindrops hung about her clothes. Powers held out his hand and drew her towards the fire.

"So you have come to see me," he said, in a tone as nearly matter-of-fact as he could make it. "I am delighted! To tell you the truth, I was just looking forward, without much enthusiasm, to a lonely and a particularly dull evening. Allow me."

He wheeled an easy-chair up to the fire, and placed her in it. He saw that she was nervous and embarrassed, and he continued to talk.

"To-night," he said, "is one of the most horrible

instances of our marvellous climate. I had just written to ask you to have a day upon the river with me. Imagine it."

She smiled, and the color began to reappear in her cheeks. She leaned forward in her chair towards him.

"I want you, please, to tell me the exact truth," she said. "My coming here, I know, is very foolish. I want to know whether it inconveniences you in any way—whether your mother or any one else might think it strange?"

He laughed reassuringly.

"Mine is entirely a bachelor establishment," he declared. "My mother and sister live in Berkeley Square. There is no one here to whom your visit would be even a subject of remark."

She gave a little sigh of relief, and leaned back in her chair. The warmth and comfort of the room after that dreary walk through the rain and hail outside were like a strong, sweet sedative. A curious sense of rest, of finality, took possession of her. With the closing of the front door, with the first breath of that air of indefinable luxury which everywhere pervaded her new surroundings, she seemed to pass into a new order of things. Even the man who had let her in had seemed wholly unconscious of her shabby clothes, had taken her poor little umbrella, and had respectfully done his best to make her comfortable during the brief period of waiting. There had been a single moment of breathless excitement, of trembling speculation as to the nature of his greeting, but his welcome had been so easy and natural that her fears had been all dispelled by his first few words.

"You are tired out with the walk," he murmured.

"Please rest for a few minutes while I put away these books. Then we can talk."

She half closed her eyes with a delicious air of relief. Her thoughts became blurred, a sort of mental Nirvana stole in upon her. A drowsiness, brought on by the pleasant heat and the perfume of flowers, soothed her nerves. Presently, however, she roused herself.

"You are very kind to me, Sir Powers," she said. "I am quite rested now. I have come to ask you to dispense with the interval which you said was necessary before you could explain your words to me. I want you to explain them now."

She saw in his eyes as he watched her a gleam of something which she had never seen there before. There came back with a rush the memory of all Ada's dogged warnings, her own fears. It was madness, this visit of hers. It was not possible that from this man could come her salvation. He must think—she shuddered and rose to her feet.

"It is perhaps very foolish of me to be here at all," she said, "but I have never quite forgotten what you said to me in the tea-room. It was probably nonsense. If so, please tell me, and let me go."

He seemed to read her thoughts, for the little gesture with which he invited her to resume her seat was almost ceremonious. He remained at some distance away, and his face now was quite impassive.

"I am much obliged to you for your confidence, Miss Surtoes," he said quietly. "I presume that you have some serious reason for hastening matters, and I will agree therefore to your request. In the meantime, kindly remember what I have told you about myself. You have nothing whatever to fear from me. If, after we have had a little conversation, the thing which I have had in my mind concerning you is not possible, there will be no harm done, and one of my maid-servants will attend you back to your home."

There fell from her at his words every vestige of that sickly fear which for the moment had assailed her. She was even heartily ashamed of it. Her first judgment of him had been true enough. She was at once wholly at her ease. She answered him readily enough.

"You are very kind," she said. "Please forgive me for being so foolish."

He smiled, and coming to the fire, stood there for a moment warming his hands.

"I think you are very plucky," he said, "to trust to your instincts, which I am sure told you to come to me."

A servant entered with coffee.

"I hope that you will keep me company," he said, taking a cup from the tray, and bringing it to her. "It is a fiendish night, and from your boots I believe that you have walked here."

It was upon her lips to tell him that she had not enough money in the world to pay for a cab, but she refrained. He poured some liqueur into a tiny glass and placed it by her side.

"With your permission," he said, "I will smoke a cigarette, and then I am going to talk to you. You must drink your liqueur, please, every drop of it, and your coffee, before I begin."

She obeyed him gladly enough. He stood with his elbow resting upon the broad oaken mantelpiece, smoking leisurely, talking to her with many pauses.

"I must tell you a little about myself," he began. "It may not be interesting, but it is necessary. I

6

was brought up to be a physician, but I have never
been obliged to practise—a fact which has doubtless
conduced to the longevity of my friends. I studied
in Germany as well as in England, and it was at
Heidelberg that I first imbibed a taste for meta-
physics. When I returned I began, like every other
young medical man, by taking up a special branch
of my profession, and devoting most of my time to
it. I chose the brain. You see that I was ambitious
even in my boyhood."

He flicked the ash from his cigarette, and she was
so much at her ease now that she was able to return
his smile pleasantly.

"Well, rather unexpectedly I came into the title
and some money, and I dropped at once all idea of
becoming a general practitioner. It ceased to be
necessary, and the idea had always been hateful to
me. For some time I devoted myself to my favorite
study, until one day I found that I had reached
what was almost a *cul de sac*. Science could only
take me to the borderland of a far greater world of
knowledge into which I have always felt that some
day we shall pass. I reckoned up my exact position,
and I decided for a while to rest upon my oars. I
made arrangements to travel for some time, going in
for sport on a large scale. I tired of it after a bit,
and commenced to read again a little. Then it
chanced that at Calcutta I met a native Indian
doctor to whom I was fortunate enough to be of
some service. My meeting with this man was the
most wonderful thing which has ever happened to
me. I shall never cease to be grateful to him. If
the world knew his name and what he has made
possible to science, he would be the most famous
man of this or any generation."

A faint note of enthusiasm had crept into his tone. He watched the blue cigarette smoke curl upwards to the frescoed ceiling.

"He reawakened all my old interest in my profession. For a year we read together. He taught me the rudiments of the most fascinating science which man has ever evolved from nature. For me he opened one of those hidden gates which leads to the unknown world. He made me ashamed of our Western savants, he showed me where the humble village doctors of a thousand years ago stood nearer to the great secrets of nature than we, with the accumulated knowledge of all the centuries."

He was silent for a few moments. His pale face had become fervid, the bright light of the enthusiast was burning in his dark eyes. He was a changed man. Eleanor felt that she had become once more only a unit in his eyes, a mere atom of humanity, whose interest to him was purely scientific and impersonal. She found herself trembling. What had these things to do with her? She was afraid of what might come. She remembered that he had spoken of death.

"Oh, that wonderful East," he continued, in a low tone. "How puny it makes us feel with our new civilization, our shoddiness, our materialism, which is only another name for hopeless ignorance. What treasures of art lie buried there, what strange secrets sleep forever in the tombs of their wise men. Halkar told me that he was but the disciple of one immeasurably greater who had died, indeed, with many of the primal secrets of existence locked in his bosom because there was no one left behind with whom he dared to trust them."

"Tell me about these secrets," Eleanor asked.

"Were they of the past, or of the future? And what have you or I to do with them?"

"We are children of the ages," he answered, "and it is our heritage to learn. Halkar taught me much. He set me down at the gate of that wonderful inner world. He placed in my hands the key. With your aid it is possible that I may pass inside."

"With my aid!" Eleanor exclaimed breathlessly. "How can that be? I am ignorant—miserably ignorant. What could I do?"

He smiled at her, and Eleanor felt again that vague fear stirring in her heart. Outside in the street a piano organ was grinding out some doleful melody. It seemed to her fantastic—almost irreverent. She knew that they were going to speak of things which savored of death.

"Listen," he said. "One day Halkar took me to a native village. We went to the house of a rich man. We found him at home, just returned from hunting. He was handsome, hospitable, and, it seemed to me, intelligent. But just before we left Halkar asked him a question about the great storm which laid waste the village and the whole country side only a year before. He looked puzzled, answered us courteously, but vaguely. He remembered nothing."

He paused.

"There was an English nurse-girl," he continued. "Halkar took me to see her. She was plump, rosy, and good-natured. She was engaged to be married to a gentleman's servant, and she chattered away gayly, and told me all about it. A year ago a mad fakir had run amuck, had killed a soldier to whom she was to have been married the next day, and both the children who had been in her charge. The

shock had nearly sent her mad. Yet when Halkar
spoke to her of these things, she looked puzzled.
She remembered nothing."

Eleanor moistened her dry lips.

"Well?" she asked.

"Their memory," he said slowly, "was gone.
Their reason was saved. Halkar was the physician."

She shivered, and sat looking into the fire with
eyes full of fear.

"Halkar," he said, "had learned much, but there
was more still. It has taken me many years, but
at last I believe that I have learned the secret
which baffled him all his days. All that I need is
a subject."

She was silent. In the street outside the organ
was playing the music from *The Belle of New York*.
She raised her head and listened idly.

"You," he said, "must be that subject."

CHAPTER XI

THERE was a short, tense silence. Eleanor sat quite still, nervously clasping and unclasping her hands. She kept her eyes averted from his, steadfastly fixed upon the fire. He watched her covertly.

"You know so little of me," she murmured. "I am almost a stranger to you. How can you tell whether I should be suitable—even if I were willing?"

"You will remember the two cases which I have mentioned to you," he answered. "The man was chosen by Halkar because in the great storm he had lost wife, and friends, and children, and in his grief he prayed to God for forgetfulness. The girl was chosen because the tragedy which she had witnessed had driven her far along the road to madness, and this merciful loss of memory was her salvation also. The reason you have been chosen is because I looked into your eyes, and it seemed to me that I saw there more than the ordinary weariness of life. Then I heard you speak, and in your tone, too, was more than the ordinary bitterness of misfortune."

"There are others," she said, "whose misery must be more acute. Why do you choose a stranger? How did you know that my words were not merely peevishness; that I am not merely a discontented girl, who is out of temper with the world because her lot does not please her?"

He smiled and sank into the opposite chair, as though weary of standing. Her eyes were fixed upon the fire. She would not look at him.

"I am a man of science," he said softly; "but science has never blinded my eyes to the other great forces in life which may not be weighed or measured. What I saw in your face I was not able to account for. But I knew that I should not ask this thing of you in vain."

She looked up at him then.

"Halkar," she said slowly, "destroyed memory, and yet his patients lived."

"You, too," he declared, "will live."

"Halkar destroyed memory," she repeated. "You have it in your mind to do more than this."

An extraordinary change came over the man. He sprang from his chair, and resumed his old position upon the hearthrug. His coolness of manner was gone. His eyes were dry and brilliant. He handled a paper-knife with long nervous fingers. A dull spot of color burned in his cheeks.

"No more than this," he answered, "no more. Only I have found a new way. It is as safe as Halkar's, quite as safe. As yet I can do no more than speculate. Yet it seems to me certain that mine is the way which Halkar, and even those others before him, died seeking. Listen, I will tell you more. I will tell you what as yet I have not breathed to a living soul."

She caught his enthusiasm—a fierce compelling thing. Her eyes sought his eagerly. She listened.

"You are a Christian?" he asked.

She was speechless. "I have tried to be," she faltered.

"You believe, at least, in the eternity of human life? You must believe in it. In nature there is no death, no annihilation. All that takes place is transmutation! That is obvious," he declared.

"Well?"

"So in human life! The body rots; the spirit passes—where?"

She was bewildered—unable to reply. He continued with scarcely a moment's pause:

"Down the broad avenues of time, to appear in a thousand different forms and shapes. A king in one age is a serf in another, a savage this century is a scholar in the next. Think! Has there never been a moment in your life when a sense of unreality has seized you? You doubt for a moment your own identity, you are haunted by mirage-like thoughts, beautiful or sad; you are strangely out of touch with your surroundings. Watch a great concourse of people. It is the most fascinating thing in the world. You will see a beggar who has now and then some trick of carriage or gesture or speech which has survived his body's degradation, and which reminds you of a king. Or you will see one of the great ones of the earth, if you watch closely enough, do some small thing, or speak some chance word which has crept out unheeded, very likely exactly repeated, yet which could have no kinship with his present state. There are people who have visited a strange country for the first time in their lives, and found there a street corner, a shop, or by-way which has awakened a peculiar and inexplicable sense of familiarity. They have never been there before, never read of the place, yet the sense of familiarity is there. I have seen a boy fall asleep, and heard him croon an old Mexican war-song, a song of the time of Cortes and the Incas in an almost forgotten language—a boy who awake is a messenger at a draper's, unimaginative, ignorant, stupid. The secret of these things will one day be

yielded up to science. You and I together may become immortal."

He ended with a little laugh. The fierce eagerness
had burnt itself out. Of the two, Eleanor was now
the more disturbed. He lit another cigarette, and
listened for a moment to the rain dashing against
the window.

"I should like to know how it feels," she said
thoughtfully, "to be without a memory, to start
life at twenty-two."

He shrugged his shoulders.

"The things outside your own personal experiences are never lost to you," he said. "They come
back in a perfectly effortless manner. You will find
yourself accepting them as a matter of course."

"How do you know that?" she asked. "One
might have to learn to read and write again. Life
without any background at all would become a
gigantic embarrassment."

He smiled.

"There is no fear of anything of the sort," he
assured her. "Halkar's friend and the girl related
to me their own experiences. They were precisely
similar. It was of events and persons alone that
their mind was swept bare. Their stock of acquired
knowledge remained unimpaired. Sometimes they
even dimly remembered people."

"But there are also many other considerations,"
she said. "What will become of me afterwards?"

"Do you not remember my promise!" he answered.
"I do not ask this thing of you for nothing. It
shall be the other world—the world to which you
belong."

She drew a little breath. No more Bearmain's—
no more of this pitiful poverty, this hideous ser-

vitude. Yet how was it possible? How could he do this?

"I do not understand," she murmured.

"Nor can I explain," he declared. "A certain amount of confidence on your part is necessary. You must trust me."

"And—how long does it take? What do you do?"

"Twenty-four hours," he answered. "There are some drugs—and a slight operation."

"If it should fail?"

"It would be death for you—and ruin for me!"

"There is a risk of that?"

"The chances of failure," he answered, "are about one in twenty. In your case I should say one in thirty. You are perfectly sound, your nerves are magnificent."

"Where would it be?"

"Here!"

"And when?"

"If you like—now," he answered slowly.

She sat quite still, her eyes fixed upon the fire. She talked to herself.

"There would be no more Bearmain's," she murmured, "no more days of speechless mortifications, no more of that hideous unending slavery. It would be freedom, at least—life or death, but freedom."

"It would be freedom," he echoed.

"It is very vague," she said, "this future. I do not wish to be dependent upon any one."

He raised his eyebrows.

"My dear young lady," he said, "I do not ask you to risk your life, however remotely, for nothing. I would give half my fortune, were it necessary, to win your consent. As it is, I promise you freedom and independence. You shall live the life which seems good to you. You shall never again know the taste of slavery."

"I consent," she said simply.

There was a momentary flash in his gray eyes—otherwise he showed no emotion. He had long since taken her consent as a matter of course. Whatever he may have felt concerning her decision he kept to himself. He stood looking down at her thoughtfully·

"There is one thing more which is necessary," he said. "You must tell me who you are, and if you have any friends who would be likely to make inquiries for you. I take it for granted that you have no closer ties. It is imperative that I have this knowledge."

She looked up at him with white face. "Do you mean that?"

"You can surely see the necessity for it yourself," he answered. "You are virtually going to change your identity. The Eleanor Surtoes of a month hence will know nothing of your past. Some one must be intrusted with that knowledge."

"It is a great pain to me," she said wearily, "to speak of it at all. But to-night nothing seems to matter. I will tell you who I am. My name is Eleanor Surtoes Marston. My father was Sir Robert Marston. He was a banker at Hull—Ellifield, Marston & Ellifield. You read the papers. I daresay you remember."

He inclined his head slowly. He showed neither sympathy nor surprise.

"My mother was dead. I had neither brother nor sister, nor any friends save those whom my father's prodigality had brought together. The end of that you know. When exposure came my father killed himself. He left a letter telling me where to find a large sum of money which he had put on one side. He had meant to leave England secretly. I returned the money to the bank. They heard afterwards that I was destitute, and they sent me ten pounds."

He opened his lips, but closed them again without speech. It seemed to be her wish to continue again without interruption.

"I was engaged to be married to a man who was in India with his regiment. I wrote him, breaking off the engagement and forbidding him to reply. He obeyed me. I came to London, and did my best to get a situation, but I was ignorant, ill-brought-up, and uselessly educated. I could do a great many things in a small way, but nothing well enough to teach. With only a few shillings left I wrote to a large firm of drapers in Hull with whom I had dealt. They sent me an introduction to Bearmain's, and I entered their employ as a shop-girl ten months ago. I have done my best, but I left to-night, knowing that whatever happened I should never return."

The man shivered a little—not from sympathy, but at the thought of what he might have missed but for that walk along the Edgware Road. The girl seemed to exist only for his purpose.

"There is no one, then," he asked, "who is likely to make inquiries about you? No one who could trace you here?"

She shook her head bitterly.

"There is no one," she answered, "to whom my disappearance will cause one iota of uneasiness. There was a girl there who did her best to be kind to me—she was my companion when you met us. I managed to offend her—I think that was the last straw. She will only be too glad that I have left."

"Do you mind telling me the name of the man to whom you were engaged?" he asked.

"Captain Angus Hood," she answered.

He nodded thoughtfully. "And he is still in India?"

"I suppose so," she answered. "In any case, what does it matter? Our engagement is broken off. He would be more likely to avoid me than to seek me out."

Powers looked at his watch.

"I am going to leave you alone for a quarter of an hour," he said. "I do not think that it will make any difference, but I should like you to have that time for unbiased reflection."

"As you like," she answered. "I shall not change my mind. I am ready."

.   .   .   .

She sat before the fire, her head buried in her hands, her eyes fixed upon the burning coals. She heard muffled voices in the hall, she heard Powers enter an adjoining room, and close the door behind him. Her fingers clutched the sides of her chair, her eyeballs were hot. For the first time a spasm of physical fear seized her. He had gone to make ready. What if it should be death? She had spoken boldly of it but a moment before. Yet she was young, for good or evil her life was as yet unlived. Then with a rush came back the memory of the last ten months. The hopeless weariness of those days behind the counter, the miserable humiliation of it, the web of bitter despair drawn so closely and inevitably around her. All the petty tyrannies to which she had been subject, all the fettering restrictions which had gone to turn servitude into slavery were suddenly fresh in her mind. A hideous vista of dreary days and lonely nights—nowhere a ray of hope, the same yesterday, to-day, and all other days. The fear passed away from her. Death might have its terrors, but a return to Bearmain's would be a living hell. She heard the door open without a single tremor. She even smiled as she saw Powers standing upon the threshold.

"You have not changed your mind?" he asked.

"There was never any fear of that," she answered. "I am quite ready."

He held open the door. "Will you come this way?" he said.

She rose at once without reluctance or fear—even gladly. Her feet seemed scarcely to touch the carpet. He was beckoning her into a new life.

CHAPTER XII

"REALLY, my dear Powers, you have completely taken my breath away," Lady Fiske exclaimed. "I never heard quite so extraordinary a story in my life!"

"Extraordinary is the mildest of words," Marian Fiske remarked, pouring herself out some tea. "You are quite sure, my dear brother, that you have not been addling that poor little brain of yours with a course of Baron Munchausen! You know that I am a practical person, and I must confess that the whole thing seems to me to savor of the miraculous."

Powers leaned back in his chair and smiled.

"I agree with you both," he said. "The whole affair is most extraordinary, as Marian puts it—miraculous! Hardinge's letter, in the first place, was a huge surprise, for I had never had the faintest intimation from him of anything of the sort. Then within a moment or two of reading the letter I see her name in the list of drowned, and almost before I had time to recover she was brought round from the hospital."

"She is actually at Hans Crescent now, then?" Marian asked.

"She is at this moment in my best bed-chamber, with a hospital nurse in attendance," Powers answered. "You can see her for yourself in a very few days."

Lady Fiske set down her cup, and looked thoughtfully across at her son.

"I must really consider, Powers," she said, "whether I ought not to send you a chaperon. One cannot be too careful nowadays. People do talk in such ridiculous fashion. By-the-by, I presume you have no doubt as to her identity. All her letters and things are in order, eh?"

"I have not as yet cross-examined her," Powers answered. "As she is still unconscious, it would be a little premature. There is no room for doubt on that score, however. I should have recognized her anywhere, and she had a further note from her father addressed to me in her pocket."

"Her name," Marian remarked, "has appeared in every list of the drowned."

Powers nodded.

"Yes! I have cabled her father with the news of her safety. It was a marvellous escape."

"You do not know the details yet?" Lady Fiske asked. "They must be very thrilling."

"Not yet," he answered. "I do not suppose that we shall know them until she is well enough to talk!"

"It will be most interesting," Lady Fiske declared. "I shall look forward eagerly to her narrative. When do you suppose, Powers, that she will be able to talk to us?"

"I wish that I could tell you," he answered gravely. "There has evidently been some injury to her brain. It will pass off, no doubt, but for the moment she is in a curious, and from a medical point of view a most interesting, state of coma. She has not spoken a single intelligent word, and she is obviously in a condition which precludes any questioning. I am as curious as you can be to hear the story of her adventures."

"You have a nurse, of course, Powers?" Lady Fiske asked. "I trust that you have selected a thoroughly respectable and capable person."

"I have the best I could get," Powers answered. "She was at Guy's when I was, and has saved more lives than any doctor."

"How did she reach London?" Marian asked. "In her condition I should have thought that she was scarcely fit to travel."

"She may have had a relapse," Powers said. "She has rather that appearance."

"I noticed in the paper this morning," Lady Fiske said, "that a boatful of survivors were landed at Dover on Thursday. It is possible that she was amongst them."

Powers nodded. "We shall know very soon," he said.

"At any rate, I am surprised that they let her leave the hospital," Marian interposed. "They are generally so careful."

"She was perfectly fit to be moved," Powers answered. "She is suffering only from the wound in her head and severe shock. I don't see why she should not pull round at any moment now."

"And when she does," Marian asked, "what are you going to do with her?"

"My dear Marian!" Lady Fiske exclaimed reprovingly. "Your brother has explained to us the position exactly. She must come here, of course. It would be better for her to come as soon as possible."

Powers nodded.

"It is very good of you, mother," he said. "Of
7

course, her uncle might turn up at any moment; in which case I should be relieved of any further responsibility. If he does not, I certainly am afraid that I must ask you to help me out."

Marian took up a book and paper-knife, but paused before settling herself down to read.

"Mr. Hardinge was an old friend of father's, was he not?" she asked.

"A very old friend, dear," Lady Fiske answered. "They were boys together. Your father knew him before he knew me. I remember hearing tales of their school-days."

"It seems odd that he did not write to you instead of to Powers," she remarked.

"Bless you, my dear, I did not know the man," Lady Fiske declared. "He lived always in India. So far as I know, he has never been back even for a visit."

"He was very hospitable to me," Powers said. "No one could have been kinder when I was in India, and he certainly earned the right to ask so simple a favor as this from me."

"You saw a good deal of the young lady also, perhaps?" Marian asked.

Powers laughed dryly.

"She was about fifteen years old," he said, "and she wore print gowns and a pigtail. I saw very little of her indeed."

"Yet you remembered her?"

"Without an effort," Powers answered, rising. "I have a good memory for faces, and Miss Hardinge is by no means an ordinary-looking girl. Well, I think that I must go. I felt obliged to come and tell you the news, or I should not have left my patient for so long."

He rose, and stooping over his mother, kissed her on the forehead. She was a remarkably well-preserved old lady, with a figure and complexion which were still the envy of many younger women. She had large, restless eyes, and a wonderfully animated manner. She dressed most extravagantly, and had two weaknesses only—her son and Society.

"Good-by, Powers," she said. "You are quite sure that you will not dine here? Hallam can fetch your things, you know, and we can drop you afterwards on our way to Chester House. We are quite alone, and I have a new cook, who is a treasure. She is a perfect artiste in cold savories. Let me ring for Hallam!"

He shook his head.

"I must not think of it, mother," he declared. "I have been longer away from my patient now than is altogether wise. You must ask me another evening."

Lady Fiske sighed.

"My dear boy," she said, "I do not know when it will be. Really, I find my friends more exacting every season. I do not think that we have an evening at home for a fortnight, have we, Marian?"

"You know more about it than I do, mother," Marian answered, looking up from her book.

"I believe that I am right in saying not for a fortnight," Lady Fiske repeated. "It is really almost slavery, is it not? We will come and see Miss Hardinge as soon as you send us word. By-the-by, I suppose there is no chance of seeing you at Chester House this evening? I know that you have a card, and the Countess always inquires most kindly after you."

"It is very good of her," Powers answered; "but

you know that I never go to these sort of gather-
ings. Good-by, Marian!"

She laid down her book and looked at him
curiously.

"Good-by, my knight errant! I am dying to see
your protégée. Bring her round as soon as you can."

.   .   .   .

Powers walked slowly home, his eyes upon the
pavement, a heavy frown upon his forehead. He
was uncomfortable and ill at ease. He had committed himself to a course of deception naturally
revolting to him, and concerning the wisdom of
which he already began to have grave doubts.
Numberless complications began to present themselves to him. The thing which had seemed so
simple at first presented itself now in a different
light. He would have given anything to have recalled the events of the last half-hour. There would
be always the danger of meeting Anglo-Indians who
had known the Hardinges. Her story, as recounted
by himself, was too extraordinary to be kept altogether secret. He saw himself cross-examined,
badgered with ceaseless questions, forced to commit
himself deeper and deeper as the thing went on.
And after all, for what satisfaction? So far as
Halkar had gone, he felt certain of success. But
beyond! It was, after all, an unknown land. He
could do nothing but experiment. The result might
be absolutely futile. He could destroy, but he could
never create. There would be no laws to guide him,
no precedent. He must stumble along in the dark.
Success, although the bare thought of it still thrilled
him, seemed at that moment wholly an illusionary
thing.

He let himself in with a latch-key, and went softly

towards his study. A hospital nurse met him on the landing. A little unnerved by this new phase of life upon which he had entered, he fancied that she looked curiously at him.

"Well, nurse," he asked, "and how is the patient?"

"About the same, sir. Her pulse is almost normal."

"She has not spoken?"

"Not a word, sir."

He deliberated for a few moments.

"What about her temperature?" he asked.

"It is a shade higher, sir."

"I will go in and change the bandage," he said, turning away from the study door.

"It is not necessary, sir," the nurse added. "I have just attended to it."

Powers flashed a sudden keen glance upon her. The nurse's face was inscrutable. He controlled his rising anger with a strong effort.

"That is against my orders," he said. "How came you to disobey me?"

The nurse looked at him with a surprise which he felt could not be wholly assumed.

"It slipped, sir, and when I went to replace it I found that it was hot. I had a fresh one ready, so I changed them."

"It was against my orders," he repeated.

"I am sorry, sir," she said. "It seemed to me to be within my discretion. The patient was under my charge in your absence, and I only did what was necessary."

Powers was silent for a moment.

"Did you notice the condition of the wound?" he asked.

"Yes, sir!"

"It was healthy?"

"Yes, sir."

There was a further uneasy silence. Then he asked a direct question.

"Did you observe anything special in connection with it?"

"Yes, sir."

"Well?"

"It had not the appearance of being the result of an accident," she said. "I understood that the patient was suffering from concussion owing to a blow received whilst in the water."

"Go on."

"There is no sign of anything of the sort," she continued. "The wound was evidently the result of—"

"Well?"

"The operating knife."

"It was the conclusion I came to myself," he said. "It is singular, too, that the wound should be in that precise spot."

"I thought so, sir," the nurse agreed.

Powers looked her teadily in the face. Her expression was unchanged.

"May I ask, sir," she inquired, "from what hospital the young lady was brought?"

He waived aside the question.

"Nurse Endicott," he said, "I have known you for a good many years, and believe you to be a woman of good sense and discretion."

"I believe so, sir," she admitted.

"Are you willing to continue this case, asking no questions and without curiosity? It may present to you some strange aspects. Are you able to ignore them? If so—I shall remain your debtor."

She hesitated for the fraction of a second.

"It is my professional duty, sir," she answered. "I am not a curious woman."

He drew a little breath. He understood the person with whom he had to deal, and he was satisfied.

"Very good, nurse," he said. "I rely upon you. I think that I will go in and see the patient."

He opened the bedroom door and passed on tiptoe to the bedside. Eleanor lay there, quite still, though apparently awake. Her eyes met his without any sign of interest or recognition. He looked into them steadily, and taking her hand from the coverlet, felt her pulse. Then he bent closer over her.

"Miss Surtoes!"

No answer. No sign of hearing.

"Miss Surtoes—Eleanor!"

Still no answer—no change in that blank, expressionless stare. Powers stood upright again. A gleam of triumph flashed in his keen gray eyes. He moved to the window and stood looking out.

"So far it is very well," he said to himself softly. "The memory is dead. Eleanor Surtoes exists no longer. There is only the sanity for which I fear. With that pulse and her nerves, she should stand the strain."

He left the room presently. The nurse was upon the threshold.

"You are satisfied with her condition, sir?" she asked.

"Quite," he answered. "See that her strength is kept up. She takes nourishment freely?"

"She takes whatever is given to her, sir."

Powers nodded.

"If she should speak or attempt to speak, nurse," he directed, "send for me."

"Very good, sir."

He turned away and met his servant, who was waiting for him in the hall.

"There is a young man wishing to see you in the study, sir," he announced. "He has been waiting for an hour or more."

Powers nodded. "Any name?" he asked.

"He gave me this card, sir."

Powers entered the study.

CHAPTER XIII

POWERS looked from the card to the young man in some perplexity. The latter's face seemed dimly familiar. He stood in the middle of the room, nervous, yet defiant, holding a silk hat in one hand and a pair of light yellow kid gloves in the other. His ready-made frock-coat, inked at the seams, and shiny in places, had seen service. His boots were not all that they should have been.

"I am Sir Powers Fiske," Powers said. "I understand that you wish to see me, Mr.—Johnson!"

"Yes! I have come here to know what you have done with her! You've got to tell me."

The suaveness of Mr. Johnson's manner, which, combined with his dulcet tones and ready address, had won him such speedy promotion at Bearmain's, had altogether deserted him on this occasion. He spoke in an odd, jerky tone, and his weak little mouth was for once firmly set. Powers, to whom as yet no light was vouchsafed, regarded the young man in genuine amazement.

"Have you come here to ask me riddles?" he answered curtly. "What have I done with whom?"

Mr. Johnson was huskily indignant.

"It won't do!" he exclaimed. "You know whom I mean. You spoke to her and Ada, and you took them to tea. They'd no right to go! I'll never forgive Ada for it. And you'd no right to ask them. They were flattered, I suppose, because you're what's called a gentleman. I hope to God you are one."

Powers remained for a moment speechless. He recognized the young man now as one of the little party at the theatre. The meaning of his confused words was suddenly clear. It was Eleanor for whom he was asking. But what had he to do with her? What was the meaning of his dishevelled appearance and disjointed words? Powers looked at him steadily.

"You are not mad, are you?" he asked quietly. "You know what you are talking about—and whom you are talking to?"

"I am not mad, and I know quite well whom I'm talking to," Johnson answered fiercely. "I'm talking to the man who spoke to two respectable girls in the street, and talked a lot of high-falutin' rot to Miss Surtoes—a lady, if ever there was one. You asked her to come to you! Ada understood what you meant, if she didn't. Where is she? You've got to tell me. I'm not going away until I know."

Powers walked to the sideboard, and opening a box of cigarettes, selected one and lit it. Then he drew up an easy-chair and sat down. All the time he was thinking hard. This was a wholly unlooked-for annoyance.

"You are a little peremptory, my young friend," he said, "and not altogether coherent. Do I understand that you are related in any way to the young lady in question?"

"No, I am not related to her," Mr. Johnson answered. "I am her friend. I want an answer to my question. Where is she?"

Powers smiled faintly as he settled himself down in his chair.

"You will forgive my resting," he said. "I am a little tired. Pray sit down yourself, if you care to.

No? Just as you like, of course. Now, do you really expect me to answer your absurd question?"

"You've got to," was the blunt response. "I'm not going to leave this room until you do. No more are you."

Powers frowned upon him.

"Do not be foolish, young man," he said sharply. "You will leave my room in a few minutes whether you wish to or not, for my patience has limits. If it will expedite your peaceful departure, however, I have no objection to telling you that I know nothing whatever about the young lady of whom you are in search."

Mr. Johnson dropped his silk hat upon the floor, and doubled up the hand which still clutched his kid gloves. He was very white. He scarcely knew the sound of his own voice.

"It's a damned lie!" he said.

Powers turned slowly round in his chair. "What?"

"It's a damned lie! She came here! She'd nowhere else to go. She hadn't a friend in London, and Ada had turned against her something cruel!"

Powers leaned forward, and his finger rested upon the bell.

"You'd better go," he said. "You're not quite yourself."

Mr. Johnson planted his feet firmly upon the floor.

"If you want a scene," he said, "ring that bell. I tell you I won't go. If you throw me out, I'll sit upon the doorstep. You've got to tell me where she is."

Powers looked him over. A wonderful earnestness had transformed the young man. His acquired manners had fallen away. White and desperate as he was, there was something of the man about him. Powers answered him no longer superciliously.

"I can assure you," he said, "that I know nothing about the present whereabouts of this young lady. But supposing for a moment that I did. Where do you come in? What have you to do with her?"

The young man was dogged—pathetically in earnest.

"That's nothing to do with you. If you want to know—I was fond of her. Smile away if you like. You think she wasn't my class. I don't care! I just want to know that she hasn't come to any harm—to help her if I can find her."

"I can assure you that you won't find her here," Powers said. "This is a bachelor establishment."

"She's been here! You know where she is!"

"If you'll excuse my bluntness," Powers said, "you're getting a shocking nuisance. If you won't go, I shall have to ring this bell after all."

Something strange flashed into the young man's face. His hand fumbled in his tail-coat pocket.

"If you won't speak without, I shall make you. It is life or death to me. It may be the same for you."

Powers looked up. It was an old-fashioned-looking weapon, but ugly enough. The shining barrel was pointed straight at his head, behind it the eyes of the little shopwalker were lit with red fire. A · curious note of tragedy had suddenly crept in upon a scene which a moment before had savored of pathos. The young man's words were true enough. For the moment he controlled the powers of life or death.

"Put that thing away," Powers said sternly. "I

will talk to you only so long as you behave like a reasonable being. You will gain nothing by trying to frighten me. Put it away at once!"

It was the tone of a conqueror, and the weaker man went to the wall. Then Powers swung round in his chair and faced him.

"You must be out of your mind," he exclaimed, "to come here and make such an ass of yourself. I know nothing whatever of Miss Surtoes. So far as I am concerned, she does not exist. Is that sufficient for you?"

"No!"

Powers rose to his feet. The other fell back a little, but his hand crept into his pocket. Powers cursed himself inwardly for not having possessed himself of the pistol a moment since.

"We are at a deadlock," he remarked coolly. "I repeat that I know nothing whatever of Miss Surtoes. What more can you want? You have not the slightest evidence that she came here."

He made this statement tentatively, but the young man's gloomy face confirmed it.

"There was nowhere else for her to go," he said. "You have been going out with her. You can't deny that! Ada heard you pressing her to come to you. She had no friends and no money. You took advantage of her! You villain!"

Powers shrugged his shoulders.

"If it affords you any relief to call me names," he said, "pray go on. Only if you want to find Miss Surtoes, can't you see that you are wasting your time. She is not here. So far as my knowledge goes, such a person does not exist."

Mr. Johnson was visibly both affected and depressed. He remained for a moment without speech.

Then he picked up his hat and made a movement towards the door.

"I suppose you must be speaking the truth," he said. "Ada was so sure that she had come to you."

"If she does," Powers said, "I will certainly assist her in any possible way—if you like I will send you word. Your address, I suppose, is care of Messrs. Bearmain's?"

"I don't know," Mr. Johnson admitted ruefully. "I've been off my head the last few days. I expect I'll get the sack. A letter there will find me, though."

"I will write if I hear anything," Powers promised.

Mr. Johnson was on his way to the door, and Powers had turned towards the bell. Suddenly an evil cry of triumph rang through the room. Powers looked round sharply. His visitor had snatched some dark object from the top of a small bookcase and was holding it out towards him. Powers recognized it at once. It was Eleanor's hat.

After that first shout—silence. The young man had turned very pale, but his undersized form seemed to swell with a new and threatening dignity. For a moment his eyes, weak, expressionless things enough as a rule, seemed lit with fire. There was a space of time, brief enough, but existent, during which he dominated the stronger man.

Then Powers shrugged his shoulders. He had hated the lie. Now that it was over he was more at his ease.

"Well?"

The monosyllable was like fuel to hungry fire. The dignity of silence forsook the little shopwalker. The pistol was in his right hand again. He raved.

"You liar! Give her up to me. You hound! You thought she was just a shop-girl. You could amuse yourself! She ain't! She's a lady. If you've done her any harm, I'll shoot you though I swing for it. Oh, you damned coward, if you've done her any harm . . . if she's believed all that deceitful rot! Let me see her! Quick! Where is she?"

Powers had faced death coolly in more than one different form, but he had a profound disinclination to end his days in such ignoble fashion. To be shot by a little shopwalker mad with jealousy seemed to him ridiculous and humiliating. He edged towards the bell.

"Miss Surtoes is perfectly safe, and perfectly well able to take care of herself," he said. "If I answered your questions falsely you have only yourself to thank for it. You are meddling in what does not concern you in the least, and you are not in a fit state to discuss the matter reasonably."

Johnson was swaying upon his feet. His cheeks were deathly pale, his burning eyes seemed to be the only live things in his face. He was mumbling to himself, but he did not utter a single intelligible word. Powers drew a little breath of relief. He was beginning to think that the danger was over.

"Put that thing away," he ordered, pointing to the revolver which his visitor still grasped. "Listen! I am in a position to help Miss Surtoes, and you are not. I am not a libertine. Go away now, and I promise you, upon my word of honor, that Miss Surtoes will never come to any harm through me."

Johnson raised his head.

"I cannot trust you," he said quickly. "You lied to me once. Besides, you are a gentleman—damn you!"

He raised his arm, and fired point-blank with no other warning. A vase just over Powers' head fell shattered to pieces. The room seemed full of smoke and the smell of gunpowder. The little shopwalker was dancing about like a mad thing.

"Say your prayers," he cried, "quick! I've five more barrels all loaded. 'In the midst of life we are in death.' Say it after me. We had it in chapel last Sunday. 'In the midst of life—' Don't you want to pray?"

He fired again—more blindly this time, and the bullet buried itself in the wall several feet away. Powers took up a chair and hurled it with all his force at his assailant. It struck him on the chest and knocked him over. He fell in a heap, catching his temple on the edge of a bookcase. The blood streamed down his face. Nevertheless, he still held his pistol, and balanced it upon the legs of the chair. Powers could see his face, white, blood-stained, yet with an evil smile upon his lips.

"Say your prayers, you fool!" he cried. "I don't trust you. You've lied to me. She's not safe while you're alive. You'll have to die. She wouldn't look at me, wouldn't speak to me. I was the dirt beneath her feet—and I loved her. No one else shall have her. You shan't! You beast! She was all right till you came. Now you're going to die."

At last the door was thrown open. A girl pushed aside the astonished servant who was hurrying into the room, and sprang to where the little shopwalker was crouching.

"Henry! Henry!" she cried. "Get up! Are you mad?"

She threw herself upon him, the weapon fell from

his nerveless fingers. Then she flung her arms
around his neck, sobbing.

"Henry," she cried, "what have you done? Oh,
how could you be so wicked?"

The young man stared at her with dilated eyes.
Then suddenly he gave a little gasp and fainted
away. Powers recognized his preserver at once. It
was the girl who had been Eleanor's companion in
the Edgware Road, and at the theatre.

8

CHAPTER XIV

POWERS, having first carefully secured and locked away the still smoking revolver, bent over the prostrate man and applied a few of the ordinary restoratives. In a minute or two he opened his eyes and stared wildly about him.

"Shall I send for the police, sir?" Mason asked, in a low tone.

"Police, no!" Powers answered contemptuously. "The asylum would be the proper place for him. Are you any relation?" he asked the girl.

She shook her head tearfully. She was crouching upon the floor by his side, and had taken his hand in hers.

"No, sir! I was engaged to him—until that night," she answered, with a little sob.

"What night?"

She fished out a pocket-handkerchief from the front of her jacket, and dabbed at her eyes.

"We all went to the theatre, Eleanor and I and a Mr. Chadwick and—him," she explained, looking downwards. "It was the evening we had tea with you. Eleanor was very quiet at first, but presently she began to talk to both of them, and you know how pretty she was, and elegant in her ways. Henry had never taken much notice of her before, though he'd heaps of opportunities, but that night he seemed to go right off his head. It was just as though she had bewitched them both, sir, for they neither of

them took their eyes off her. She said such clever
things, and she had such a beautiful color. Then
Mr. Chadwick tried to kiss Eleanor going home, and
when Henry knew it he rushed away after him, and
they fought in the street, and Henry, though he was
much smaller than Mr. Chadwick, he gave it him
awful.''

Powers looked with a trifle less contempt at the
slowly reviving figure.

"But what made him come to me in this mad
state?" he asked.

She dabbed her eyes again vigorously. They were
already red and swollen.

"He's been like a creature unsettled in his mind
ever since that evening," she answered, with a little
catch in her throat. "All day he was hanging round
her counter instead of attending to his work, and the
more she sent him away the more he followed her
about. I heard Mr. Bearmain himself speak sharply
to him more than once, and as for Eleanor, she was
so mad she wouldn't speak to him at all, but looked
right over his head all the time. She came to me at
night, and she was very white and her voice shook.

"'If you can't keep him away, Ada,' she said, 'I
shall go mad.'

"I was a beast, but I had had a miserable day
too, seeing him as I was engaged to following another girl about, and him being spoken so sharply
to. He'd always been so proud of his position at
Bearmain's, but all of a sudden he seemed to go
quite reckless, and to care nothing about it at all.
I answered her sharply, and I said that it was
partly her fault, which it wasn't at all. I don't
think she forgave me for that, though I did my best
to make up for it afterwards. Then the next evening

she was at the theatre with you in a box. Some of
our girls were there in the pit, and they didn't like
it. Afterwards they made remarks to her; so e of
them are just as jealous and spiteful as cats, and the
next thing we knew was that she had left without
permission or anything. Henry seemed to go like a
corpse when he heard about it. I knew he'd do something desperate."

"He did his best to murder me," Powers said
dryly; "but for your arrival I do not know what
would have happened."

Ada shivered.

"In his right mind," she declared, "he wouldn't
hurt a fly."

Mr. Johnson sat up. He was rather a pitiable
object, with the wound on his temple and his dis-
arranged hair and dress.

"She is here, Ada," he whispered hoarsely. "I
have seen her hat."

Ada looked at Powers with deep distrust.

"Well," she said, "if that's so we can't help
it, Henry. She came of her own free will. We
couldn't stop her, and there's no one can help her
now."

Powers looked from one to the other with a faintly
satirical smile upon his lips.

"You both seem to look upon me as a sort of
Mephistopheles—or something pretty black in the
way of libertines," he remarked. "Listen, both of
you. Miss Surtoes is here, but she is dangerously ill.
She is being properly taken care of, and as soon as
she is well enough she is going to stay with my
mother, Lady Fiske. As to what that young madman has got into his head—it is perfectly ridiculous."

"You hear that, Henry?" Ada exclaimed.

He staggered to his feet. "Yes, I hear," he said quietly.

"If I did my duty," Powers continued, "I should have you locked up, Mr. Johnson. However, for the sake of the young lady I do not wish to be severe, and if you will promise not to molest me again, or to call here without permission, you can go."

"You hear, Henry," Ada said, passing her arm through his. "Promise, dear. After all, it is no affair of ours, you know."

"I promise," Mr. Johnson declared, in an odd, stifled tone.

"One word more—to both of you," Powers said. "I think I may assu e that you are well-wishers of Miss Surtoes. It is in your power to do her a great service or a great injury. When she has recovered from her illness she is going at once to Berkeley Square as my mother's guest. That should dispose at once of your suspicions. I am desirous of befriending Miss Surtoes, but not if I am to be subject to this sort of thing. You understand me, I hope. Miss Surtoes has finished with her past life, and everything connected with it. She would not, I am sure, wish to be ungrateful, but she is suffering now from brain-fever, and I do not wish her ever to be reminded in any way of her life at Bearmain's, or of anybody connected with it."

Johnson remained dumb. Ada drew herself up with some show of dignity.

"I'm sure that I don't wish to intrude where I'm not wanted," she said. "So far as I am concerned, I have finished with Eleanor. I only hope for her sake that you are speaking the truth. If you are not, it is too late for either Mr. Johnson or I to help her."

"I have spoken the truth," Powers assured her, "and you are a young lady of common sense. Good evening."

They passed out together. Powers gave a little sigh of relief as the hall door closed behind them. He rang for Mason, and together they straightened the room.

"You will see that this absurd affair is not talked about," Powers said, when they had finished. "The young man is out of his mind, and quite irresponsible."

"Certainly, sir !"

There was a tap at the door. Nurse Endicott entered.

"I beg your pardon, sir," she said, "but there is a change in the patient."

Powers sprang up at once. His eyes questioned her eagerly.

"She has been asking questions, and she wanted to sit up in bed, sir," the nurse explained. "She is talking quite distinctly."

"What has she said?" Powers asked.

"She wants to know where she is, sir."

"Anything else?"

The nurse coughed.

"She seems to have forgotten her own name, and where she came from, sir. She is a little confused just at first, perhaps."

Powers drew a quick little breath between his teeth. The nurse, who was watching him keenly, was amazed at the gleam of triumph which flashed in his steel-gray eyes.

"What did you tell her?" he asked.

"I remembered your orders, sir," the nurse answered. "I told her nothing except that she must keep quiet. I came at once for you."

"What she said was intelligible?" he asked.

"Perfectly, sir. She spoke very nicely, and quite distinctly."

Powers went on his way.

"You have done very well, nurse," he said. "Leave me alone with the patient until I ring."

CHAPTER XV

POWERS permitted himself the luxury of a rare emotion. His patient had come back to life. The faint flush of recovery was upon her cheeks, the light of a dawning intelligence was in her eyes. The first stage of his great experiment had been successfully reached.

"So you are better, I see!" he remarked, standing by her bedside.

She answered him a little weakly, but distinctly enough.

"I suppose I am. I feel quite well enough to get up. Only—"

"Well?"

There was trouble in her eyes as she looked up at him.

"It seems as though I must be dreaming. I can't remember anything. I can't remember what has happened to me—why I am here!"

He smiled at her reassuringly.

"I wouldn't bother about it," he said. "You are with friends, and you must try and get well quickly. I daresay when you are stronger that it will all come back to you."

She looked at him reflectively.

"You are a stranger to me," she said slowly. "Is there no one here whom I have ever seen before?"

He felt a sudden chill. Yet, after all, it was what he had expected.

"I do not suppose that there is," he answered. "You see you are in London now. I thought, perhaps, that you might have remembered me. I was in India, and came to see you when you were a little girl."

"In India!" she repeated vaguely. "Why, what can have happened to me? I do not remember anything about India."

She raised her hand to her temples. Her eyes were full of an undefined fear. The words came from her lips in a broken stream.

"You are my doctor, they say, and this is your house. Tell me what it means—tell me. I try to think, and there is nothing. Something has happened to my head. Have I been ill for long? Who am I? Where did I come from? Why am I here?"

"I will answer all your questions," he said quietly, "but you must please not excite yourself. Your name is Eleanor Hardinge, and you were shipwrecked on your way from India here. Your father is an old friend of mine, and you were coming to England to visit my mother. You met with a very unusual accident. You will notice that your head is still bound up, and no doubt it will affect your memory for some little time. You must try and make the best of it. You are amongst friends, and we shall all do our best to look after you."

She felt the bandage around her head.

"I can't even remember the accident," she said. "I suppose it will all come back some day."

"There is no doubt about it," he answered. "All that you have to do now is to keep as quiet as you can. The less you try to think, the better."

The nurse entered with a tray. Eleanor sat up and smiled with the satisfaction of a child.

"You are hungry!" he remarked.

"I think so," she answered. "I should like some chicken, please. No more beef-tea."

"You remember what chicken tastes like, then," he said. "That is a proof, you see, that your memory still lives. Let me ask you another question. Who is your favorite author?"

"Shakespeare!" she answered promptly.

He nodded approvingly.

"You see that you need have no fear," he said. "Your loss of memory is only partial. Now I am going to leave you to have your dinner. Do not talk too much, and try to sleep as much as you can."

Her eyes sought his fixedly, pathetically. She seemed suddenly moved by a new fear. Her large eyes, a little sunken now, were dilated.

"I—I have forgotten my name again," she cried. "It is horrible. What is it? Tell me quickly."

"You are Eleanor Hardinge," he said. "You are perfectly safe, and you will soon be quite well."

"But I am afraid," she cried, with a sudden shrill note of terror. "My head is going round. I cannot think clearly."

He took her hand in his. There was something soothing in the touch of his firm, cool fingers.

"You have no cause for fear," he said reassuringly —"none whatever. You are getting better and stronger every hour."

She raised herself a little from amongst the pillows. Her eyes sought his eagerly. Her hands refused to let his go.

"I am afraid," she moaned. "There are shadows everywhere amongst my thoughts. Tell me. Have I been mad? Am I going to be mad?"

His fingers strayed to her pulse. He smiled upon her as one smiles upon a child.

"Nonsense! Look at me."

His eyes held hers. He spoke, and his voice dominated her. The sense of a commanding influence was
inexpressibly soothing to her. His words seemed to
come from a long distance.

"You have not been mad! You are not going to
be mad. There is really nothing the matter with
you except that you are suffering from a great
shock. By-and-by everything will be clear to you.
You must not be impatient. I promise that you will
soon be well."

She gave a little sigh—the moment of excitement
had passed away.

"It is very strange," she murmured. "I do not
understand it at all."

"Some day," he said cheerfully, "it will be quite
clear. You must be content to wait. Dinner, nurse.
That is good. You must try and get your patient
to eat as much as possible. If you want me I shall
be close at hand."

He talked himself out of the room. On the landing
he stood and wiped the dampness from his forehead.
He knew that she had been on the verge of brain-
fever, that even now she was scarcely safe. The impulse which had taken him into her room was an
irresistible one. He felt that he must see her. He
had looked into her opened eyes, he had heard her
speak. The change, which he alone could understand, which he alone was responsible for, appalled
him. He was bewildered by a feeling of personal
loss. The soul of Eleanor Surtoes seemed to have
passed away with her sense of personal consciousness. It was another woman who lay there in his
guest-chamber.

Afterwards she slept. He dined mechanically, and

without the ghost of an appetite. The rest of the night he spent with a pile of medical books and a note-book kept during his stay in India open before him. In the early morning he looked out upon the gray dawn-lit streets, haggard, and with a gnawing fear at his heart. He was unnerved. The ordinary sounds of the waking household, the street cries outside, the rattling of carts, jarred upon him. He glanced in the looking-glass, and was startled at his own reflection. Softly he opened the door, and made his way into the room where Eleanor lay.

It was still in semi-darkness. From the threshold he could hear with immense relief her regular breathing. He drew up the blind a few inches, and moving to her bedside, stood looking down upon her.

Her deep brown hair lay about the pillow in some confusion. One long white arm, thin but graceful, hung over the coverlet. Her face, notwithstanding its pallor, was like the face of a little child. A certain, almost pathetic, sharpness of outline, which in the days of his first acquaintance with her had been only too noticeable, seemed to him to have faded away. Her closed eyes were no longer windows through which shone the tragical misery of her bitter life. The lines about her mouth and forehead had all been smoothed away. And with these things— something else. He found himself struggling with a sense of unfamiliarity. After all it was still Eleanor. If only he could persuade himself of it.

He looked at her long and steadily. Then he left the room and entered the library. For a time he sat at his desk irresolute. More than once he drew note-paper toward him and dipped his pen in the ink. He was wholly unaccustomed to this indecision. Yet the way before him, which had seemed so clear only a short while back, seemed now beset with anxieties. It was not technical skill or knowledge that he needed. So far as these were concerned his self-confidence was unimpaired. Only a new sense of responsibility, a strange new web of fears, seemed suddenly to have paralyzed his enthusiasm. For the first time in his life he felt the need for advice—the stimulus of sympathy. Yet for hours that note remained unwritten. He was unable to account for his hesitation. The man whom he was about to summon would approve of all that he had done. He was sure of that. Yet he was oppressed by the shadow of some nameless fear, some instinct which seemed to be doing its utmost to warn him against this course which, from any ordinary point of view, was both natural and advisable. Afterwards those hours of hesitation ranked as history with him. At the time he was ashamed of them.

The note was written at last, and despatched by an urgent messenger. He bathed, changed his clothes, and ate some breakfast. Just as he had finished, a small brougham stopped at the door. Dr. Trowse was announced. It was the man for whom he had sent. Even at the moment of his entrance Powers found himself struggling with an insane desire to abandon his purpose, to invent some trifling excuse and to keep silence.

The two men shook hands silently. Powers pointed to the breakfast-table, but the new-comer shook his head.

"You forget that I am an early riser," he said. "What is wrong with you?"

"Nothing," Powers answered.

Dr. Spencer Trowse was a clean-shaven, well-groomed man, with strange light-colored eyes and

weak eyebrows. His figure was spare, one shoulder
was a trifle higher than the other, and he walked in
a shambling manner, like a man whose eyes were forever glued upon the pages of a book. He looked ten
years younger than his age, which was forty-five,
and he was the greatest known authority upon
diseases of the brain. He had been lecturer at St.
Thomas's when Powers had been a student, since
which time an odd, spasmodic friendship had existed
between the two men. He eyed Powers curiously.

"You sent for me," he reminded him, "and if you
waste my time you'll have to pay for it. These are
my busiest hours."

Powers came back to the present. It was too late
now for hesitation. He smiled grimly.

"You won't want payment," he said, "when you
have heard why I sent for you."

A light, like the flashing of fire upon polished
steel, lit up for a moment those strange-colored eyes.
Yet in other respects the man was unmoved. Not a
muscle of his face twitched.

"You have found a subject?" he said.

"I have."

"You are going to attempt the operation, or you
want me to?"

"It is done."

Trowse set down his hat, and deliberately selected
a chair.

"You've pluck!" he remarked. "Dead or alive?"

"Alive."

The absence of any sentiment of triumph in
Powers' face or tone made its impression upon the
older man. He decided at once that the thing had
gone wrong.

"Alive! In what condition is he?"

"It's a she," Powers answered.

"Better subject, perhaps. Go on."

"She has recovered consciousness. So far everything has gone according to calculation."

"You administered your Indian drug?"

"Yes. I was going to tell you. She is conscious, and physically unhurt."

"The memory?"

"Gone!"

Trowse rose briskly.

"Let me see her," he insisted. "Then we will talk."

Silently they made their way to the bedroom. Eleanor was having breakfast. She had made a somewhat fastidious toilet, and wore, with the air of one who has been used to such things all her life, a dressing-jacket trimmed with lace, which was amongst the things which Marian Fiske had sent. Her hair was tied up with ribbon, and skilfully arranged to hide the bandages on her head. The delicacy of her face and hands seemed heightened by the faint spot of color which flushed her cheeks as the two men entered the room.

"I have brought a friend of mine," Powers said, after a few words to Eleanor and the nurse, "to congratulate me upon my case. This is Dr. Trowse, nurse. I know that he considers me a dangerous amateur, and I want to convince him that I am nothing of the sort."

Trowse moved a little forward, and Eleanor turned her head to meet his earnest gaze. Almost immediately there was a change in her expression. The color faded from her cheeks, she shrank a little away, a curious troubled light filled her eyes. Trowse, if he noticed her agitation, ignored it. He bent over the bedside and touched her fingers, asked a few apparently careless questions, and let his hand rest for a moment upon her head. Then he turned away and addressed the nurse.

"Sir Powers has justified himself," he said, with a faint smile. "Your patient is going to have the good sense to get well very quickly."

Eleanor drew a little breath as though immensely relieved. She turned her head a little so as to leave him altogether out of her range of vision. Powers, who to some extent misunderstood her action, exchanged quick glances with Trowse. The desire for life was there once more, then.

"I am glad to hear it, sir," the nurse answered quietly. "She seems to be going on very nicely."

Without turning her head towards him, Eleanor addressed Trowse.

"Will you please tell me something?"

"If I can."

"When shall I remember things?"

He looked at her thoughtfully. She kept her eyes averted, but she seemed to be shivering a little.

"Perhaps to-morrow," he answered. "Perhaps not for a year. It is one of those things which science is powerless to determine."

"But I shall—remember—some day?"

He felt her pulse idly.

"Some day—certainly. Let me ask you a question."

"Well?"

"Are you very anxious to remember?"

"It is so puzzling," she answered. "Sometimes I want to very much, sometimes I am content."

There was a moment's silence. As though against her will, she turned her head and looked up at him standing over her bedside. Again there was the faint shrinking away, again her troubled eyes seemed held by his against their will.

"I will give you some advice, young lady," he said. "Let things go. You have made a marvellous recovery. The completion of it is in your own hands. Accept the present. If the past eludes you—let it. You will remember this?"

Eleanor remained speechless, though her lips seemed to move. Every word, though easily spoken, seemed to come to her charged with a precise and serious meaning. His tone was unemotional, his manner was not even earnest. Yet she never forgot.

The two men left the room. By common consent they turned into the study. Trowse eyed his friend curiously.

"I wonder," he said, "what the devil made you send for me?"

9

CHAPTER XVI

POWERS did not immediately reply. The two men stood side by side upon the hearthrug. Trowse, who seemed to have forgotten his hurry, lit a cigarette, and threw the match into the fire.

"I scarcely see," he said, "where I come in. You have had your chance, you have taken it, and you have succeeded. Very well! What do you want with me? If it had been before the risk was over I could have understood it. At present I must admit that I cannot."

Powers answered as one who makes a confession.

"I have lost my nerve," he said.

Trowse looked at him oddly.

"I might believe that of some men," he said, "not of you. Besides, the risk is over. The girl will live. You know that as well as I do."

"She will live," Powers answered, "yes! That is certain. And yet, since she opened her eyes, since I heard her speak, I have felt myself nothing less than a murderer. That is what I am. A murderer, Trowse."

Trowse stared at his friend for several moments without speaking — a cold, deliberate inspection. Then he sighed.

"You are not the man you were, Powers," he said, speaking softly, and as though to himself. "It isn't drink, and you don't smoke much. What has happened to your nerves?"

Powers looked steadfastly and gloomily out of the window.

"I cannot tell you," he answered. "You know me better than most men, Trowse. You have never seen me turn a hair at any operation yet. Together we have watched death come to strong men and to beautiful women. We have seen it come to those who have welcomed it, and we have seen men work themselves into a frenzy in that last struggle against extinction. These things have never troubled me. I have never felt anything more than curiosity. Yet there is a weak spot somewhere. I have learned what fear is."

Trowse eyed his friend with genuine interest. He was puzzled.

"If the girl were dead," he remarked meditatively, "it might have turned out awkwardly for you. As it is, you seem to have stumbled across a very nearly perfect physical creature. She is less likely to die than you or I. In a fortnight she will be recovered."

Powers frowned impatiently.

"You have not made a study of this thing as I have, Trowse," he said. "Yours is the purely scientific point of view. You do not see—what lies beyond."

Trowse shook his head.

"I do not understand you," he said simply.

"I want you to understand," Powers declared. "We have talked of this thing many times until it has grown to seem a simple thing. We forgot!"

"Forgot what?"

"Forgot that the continuity of life after all is purely physical. Behind—there is a woman slain—up there a woman created."

Trowse for a moment was bewildered. A searching glance into the other's face showed him that Powers was in earnest. He became contemplative.

"I am not sure that I understand you, Powers," he said slowly. "In fact, I am sure that I do not. We have watched operations together when, to our certain knowledge, the knife has gone a little deeper, has gone a little more to the left or right, in order that some addition might be made to the sum of human knowledge. You have never blenched. We have seen men die whose lives might have been prolonged, if not altogether spared, that the race to come might benefit. Tacitly, you and I have always recognized the principle that the individual must be the servant of humanity. Therefore, as I say, I do not understand your present attitude."

"I am not sure, Trowse, that I can make you understand," Powers answered. "Only remember this. Our point of view is probably not the same. You are a materialist, pure and simple. I am not!"

"Proceed!"

"In the cases which you have mentioned it is the body only which has suffered. In this case the body has survived, but something else—has been destroyed. You know the danger which still exists."

Trowse nodded.

"Lunacy! That, of course, is a possibility."

Powers shivered slightly.

"It is a possibility," he admitted. "Even if she remains sane, will you tell me this? What connection can there be between the mind of the girl of a month ago and the woman of a month to come?"

"It is an interesting psychological problem," Trowse answered, "which we shall know more about shortly. I must admit, though, that your position is inexplicable to me. Fortune has given you a marvellous opportunity. I cannot conceive how you could have acted differently. I cannot understand your present hesitation. If you wish for any sort of co-operation on my part, tell me how you first met this young woman, and under what circumstances you persuaded her to become your patient."

"It is told in a few words," Powers answered. "She was a shop-girl, born a lady, friendless and miserable, with just sufficient self-respect to make the usual means of emancipation impossible for her. I cultivated her acquaintance, and offered her freedom and a life amongst our own class if she would submit herself to this experiment, which I carefully explained to her. I don't suppose she did more than accept the thing in its crude form, and the loss of memory presented no terrors at all to her."

"And what," Trowse asked, "will be your future course with regard to her?"

"Circumstances have presented me with an excellent opportunity of keeping my word to her strictly," Powers answered. "You read of the foundering of the *Colombo*, of course?"

Trowse nodded.

"Well, on that ship was a young lady of exactly Miss Surtoes' age, who was coming to my mother from India on a long visit. She was unknown in England, she had no relations here, and her father, who is almost her only surviving relative, has gone on a secret mission to China, and has announced his intention of never returning to Europe. There were a few survivors from the *Colombo*. Their names were never clearly given. Eleanor Surtoes will recommence life as Eleanor Hardinge."

There was a short silence. Trowse was regarding his friend with cold surprise.

"All that you tell me," he said, "makes your present hesitation the more extraordinary. Your scruples are unworthy of you. They would be unworthy of you even if you belonged to that sickly order of sentimentalists who would shrink from killing a poisonous snake because the reptile had been given life. According to your own showing, the girl was in an intolerable position. She enters upon her new life with every prospect of happiness. Believe me, Powers, the hand which struck away the bridge between her past and future was the hand of a benefactor."

"I suppose you must be right," Powers murmured.

"Right! It is hopelessly obvious," Trowse answered. "If this hesitation is anything more than a passing mood with you, I shall be amazed. You probably saved the girl from moral shipwreck—you have transported her into a life which she could certainly never have reached by any other means. Where I find fault with you is that you have borrowed instead of inventing an identity for her. I look upon that as a blunder which may give you a good deal of trouble. What if her father should come back to England?"

Powers shook his head.

"It is very unlikely," he said. "When I last saw him he told me that he had sworn never to set foot in England again."

"Still, it was an unnecessary risk. There may be Indian acquaintances, too, turning up at any moment. You will never be quite safe."

Powers admitted it.

"You must not forget," he pointed out, "that the situation presented difficulties. I had to keep my word and transport her into the position which I had promised her. Further, I had to provide a home which should be absolutely free to me, and where I could see her at any time. It was inevitable that this should be amongst my own people. My mother is kind-hearted, but most rigidly conventional. A story with the girl I was bound to invent —and I am a clumsy liar. It was easier to have it founded upon fact."

"I hope that it may not lead to complications," Trowse remarked coolly. "Your proper course would have been to have married her."

Powers turned upon his adviser a face of blank astonishment.

"You are joking, Trowse."

"I never, to my knowledge," the other answered, "made a joke in my life. A sense of humor is not amongst my accomplishments."

Powers laughed shortly.

"I thought that you and I agreed years ago that we were not marrying men," he remarked.

"That is quite true! But what is a trifle like marriage compared to a vast thing like this? You have lost your sense of proportion, man. I would have married her myself without a moment's hesitation, for the slightest chance of a future such as you may be able to command."

In his tone, and in his face, were signs of a rare and intense enthusiasm. The eyes of the two men met. Trowse continued, with a gesture stiff but almost dramatic:

"Man, it is wonderful! I could kill you as you stand there, for envy. It is amongst the possibilities that you, a dilettante, a dabbler, may solve the secret of all the ages past and to come. It may be that she will sing to you the songs that Pocahontas sang to the great god of the Indians, or you may wake in the night to hear the wail of one of those daughters of Judah led captive into Egypt. Perhaps she was a priestess in the time-forgotten cities of Africa, gone before our history crept into being, swept who knows where off the face of the earth. Oh, damn your luck, Powers !"

Powers was shaking with excitement. This sudden eloquence from the one man on earth whose cold self-restraint had become a by-word moved him strangely.

"Well," he said, "for good or for evil, the thing must go through as it has been arranged. I am glad that you are interested, Trowse. It may be that I shall need your help."

"Likely enough," Trowse answered shortly. "It seems to me that you have let go some of the old ideas. Believe me, they were the safest. The man who has work to do in the world has no greater enemy than this shifting sentimentalism. May I come and see your patient to-morrow?"

"You may see her as often as you like," Powers answered, "so long as you let me know beforehand that you are coming."

"I thank you," Trowse answered, with a cold smile. "You need have no fear that I shall attempt any single-handed experiments. Only if you want my advice, do not send her to Lady Fiske, and, above all things, do not attempt to have her launched upon society as Eleanor Hardinge. The thing is too great to run any risks about."

Powers was thoughtful.

"There will be difficulties," he said, "but I must make the best of them. It is too late to alter my arrangements. I have already spoken to my mother."

Trowse frowned.

"Why on earth don't you keep her quietly to yourself here?" he asked. "What do you want to go publishing her to the world at all for?"

"It was her side of the bargain," Powers answered. "I promised."

"Promised whom?" Trowse demanded.

"Eleanor Surtoes!"

"The shop-girl! She doesn't exist. The girl whom I have just seen knows nothing of it. To all effects and purposes she is a different being. You must be reasonable, Powers. A thousand things may happen if you carry out this hare-brained scheme of yours. She may even want to marry. She is good-looking enough. You might easily lose her altogether."

Powers was suddenly pale. There were, indeed, many possibilities which he had not seriously considered. Yet he never hesitated.

"I must keep my word to her," he said. "I shall do it at all costs."

"You are a fool," Trowse declared bluntly. "Make her your wife, your mistress—anything. Bind her to you. Make sure of her."

Powers walked to the door with his visitor.

"It is useless to argue with you," he said. "We look at the matter from different points of view. The girl risked her life to gain a certain end. She has won, and she shall have her reward."

"Even," Trowse said, "at the risk of losing her."

"At any risk whatsoever," Powers answered firmly.

CHAPTER XVII

THE girl was weary. For two hours they had waited in the quiet street, and still there was no sign of life in the house. She leaned up against the railings.

"Don't you think that your friend must have made a mistake, Henry dear?" she said timidly. "It's long after three o'clock, and I'm dead tired."

"You can go," he answered shortly. "I shall wait."

"She won't come to-day now. We've been here since one, and people are beginning to look at us. It seems so odd to be here all this time."

"You can go," he repeated. "I didn't ask you to come. I think I'd rather be alone."

The girl's eyes suddenly filled with tears. It was less his ingratitude than his surprising tenacity of purpose which distressed her. Commonplace, colorless, egotistical, there had seemed no room in his character for such a vigorous growth as this.

"You ain't fit to be about alone, Henry," she said reprovingly. "And after all, what is the good of it?"

"I shall see her," he answered drearily. "I shall speak to her if I can. I want to know that he is treating her kindly—that she is there of her own free will."

A momentary impatience flared up in her.

"Of her own free will! Such rubbish! Do you think that she was drugged? Why, I saw her put on her things myself, and walk out of the place."

"You never told me that," he muttered.

"What was the good of telling you? You won't listen to reason—you won't, or you wouldn't be here."

"I want to see her," he said. "She can't help but speak to me for a moment. That's all I want."

She looked at him critically—for once with the keen, illuminative gaze of one who understands. She saw his cheap overcoat, of which the velvet collar was already bare, his linen frayed and only moderately clean, his boots thick and clumsy, over which his trousers hung in uncertain folds. Upon him was the ban of the ready-made—even illness and anxiety had not improved the weak features and characterless face. She saw him for the moment as he was— no longer glorified by that little halo of romance which had softened down all his shortcomings in her sight. And she laughed sharply.

"I never thought that you were a fool, Henry," she said. "Can't you understand why she hated us all and the life at Bearmain's?"

"You girls were beastly to her!" he declared.

"It wasn't that! She was brought up as a lady. It makes a wonderful difference. We weren't her class—none of us. That's why she's gone and made a fool of herself."

He eyed her with dull, resentful anger.

"It's as much your fault as any one's," he said. "What call had you to take tea with a gentleman you'd never seen before—to let him speak to you in the street?"

"Me! I was nothing but a puppet," she answered. "They just looked at one another, and then they began talking as though they had known one another all their life. I just didn't count."

A carriage drove past them, and pulled up at the door of the house which they had been watching. He caught hold of her sleeve in his excitement.

"There!" he exclaimed; "I was right! Look! They are coming out. Let me go!"

He flung aside the hand which had clutched at his coat-sleeve, and stood in the middle of the pavement. From the door of the house came Eleanor, leaning on the arm of a nurse in plain black uniform. She was dressed becomingly—as they had never seen her —and though she was pale she walked with a light, springy step. Behind came Powers. The gate swung open. They were all face to face.

"Miss Surtoes! Miss Surtoes!"

The light in Powers' eyes was murderous. The little man stood within a few feet of Eleanor, his lips trembling, his eyes fearfully intent upon her. Despite his utter commonplaceness, he was a pitiful, almost a tragical figure. Eleanor looked at him without interest, almost without curiosity.

"Who is this?" she asked, turning to Powers, "and why does he call me by that name?"

Johnson interrupted. Ada gave up the attempt to hold him back. They were all in a group upon the pavement.

"You remember me, Miss Surtoes," he exclaimed. "Henry Johnson! Will you let me say a few words to you alone? You left Bearmain's without giving any of us a chance to say good-by. There is something important I want to ask you. You won't turn your back upon me!"

Powers drew a sharp, quick breath. He restrained his first impulse, which was to throw Johnson to the other side of the street, and faced the situation. After all, he had faith in himself and what he had accomplished. Sooner or later this meeting was inevitable. Better to have it over.

"This young man is evidently not in his right senses," Powers said to Eleanor. "He cannot possibly know you. You see he does not even know your name. Stand out of the way, sir!"

His hand fell like a vise upon Johnson's shoulder, and he turned to hand Eleanor into the carriage. But for once in his life those flaccid muscles stiffened, and Johnson stood his ground.

"It is a lie!" he said. "She remembers me quite well. What have you done to her to make her look like that? You beast! Miss Surtoes, you remember me at Bearmain's? I have left now. I can offer you a home. Ada, you speak to her."

A moment's tense silence. The nurse's clasp upon her charge grew tighter, for Eleanor was showing signs of uneasiness. There were all the makings of a tragedy in the little scene. But Powers, unmoved, smiled at her reassuringly.

' "Eleanor, these good people have lost their senses," he said contemptuously. "Look at them. Do you think it likely that they were ever friends of yours?"

She obeyed. Her eyes appraised them. She realized the shabby insignificance of the man, unredeemed even by his great earnestness—the ordinariness of the girl in her cheap clothes and hat, and with her tear-stained, homely face. She looked at them steadily, but without a gleam of recognition.

"You are quite mistaken," she said. "I do not remember ever having seen either of you in my life before, and my name is not Surtoes. I am Miss Hardinge, and I have only just arrived from India. You must please let me pass."

Johnson was speechless. Ada tightened her clasp

upon his arm, her little round face on fire with indignation.

"Well, I never !" she exclaimed. "Do you think
we're both silly? If you don't want to have no
more to do with us you've only to say so, and I for
one wouldn't never trouble you again, Miss Surtoes.
And it's none of my doing we're here to-day, that I
can tell you. Only seeing how Henry's put himself
out about you, I think it's disgraceful to stand
there and tell us such stories. I only hope it'll show
him what sort of a friend you are. Come right
away, Henry. I shan't stop another moment."

He shook himself free. He stood before Eleanor,
and he trembled from head to foot.

"Do you mean this?" he pleaded. "I only want
to know as you're here of your own free will—that
there's nothing a friend can do for you. I can't see
you go away. I can't give you up !"

Eleanor looked him up and down in undisguised
contempt.

"I suppose," she said to Powers, "that they are
crazy, both of them. Thank you !"

He handed her into the carriage, and turning
round faced them both.

"If you persist in annoying either myself or this
young lady again," he said, "you will find that my
patience has its limits. I am in earnest, mind."

He took his seat by Eleanor's side, but Johnson
flung himself upon the carriage door.

"You fiend !" he cried. "It's a lie, all of it. It's
a plot ! Give her back to us ! You've been practis-
ing some cursed doctor's tricks upon her."

Powers leaned over and wrenched the frenzied fingers from the side of the carriage. The horses
sprang forward, and Johnson would have fallen but

for Ada's clutch. She held him to her, breathless and pale to the lips with passion. So they stood together, and watched the carriage pass out of sight.

"There's the end of your fine young lady," Ada exclaimed bitterly. "She's a pretty one to go mad over, I must say."

But her words fell upon deaf ears. The lines about his mouth were more dogged than ever. He was muttering softly to himself:

"They were his words, not hers. Next time—she will recollect!"

.   .   .   .

She clutched his arm as the carriage swept round the corner.

"Those people," she said. "I want you to tell me that they were impostors. The man's face worries me. It seems to me dimly familiar, as though I had seen it in a picture or a dream. But they were so impossible."

"They were either impostors or lunatics," he said coolly. "I am not sure which."

She drew a little breath of relief.

"I am delighted to hear it," she said. "I hope that I shall never see either of them again."

The nurse, who sat on the opposite seat, looked across the Park with a faint smile upon her lips. She had never had a more interesting case.

CHAPTER XVIII

MARIAN FISKE lowered her lorgnettes and sighed. She met her neighbor's gaze and shrugged her shoulders.

"Are you too amongst the fallen, Dr. Trowse?" she exclaimed. "I am overwhelmed already with reproachful looks from the men whom I could not send in with Eleanor, or place at her table."

Trowse smiled quietly.

"My years, dear Miss Fiske," he said, "should preserve me from such an imputation. Your charming guest might very well be my daughter."

Marian passed an entrée, and leaning back in her chair, became contemplative.

"I have known many men," she said, "who were devoted admirers of girls young enough to be their daughters."

"If not my years, then my habits—my reputation," he murmured.

"I know very little of your habits, and I have no faith at all in a blameless reputation," she answered.

"That sounds either paradoxical or immoral," he declared.

She laughed.

"Don't try to bewilder me. Of course, I mean that it is the man with the blameless reputation whom I distrust. It generally means an evil talent for concealing things."

"What hideous pessimism," he said gravely. "Besides, it was only last week that you called me a woman-hater."

"I am not sure," she said deliberately, "that I believe in woman-haters. They are usually the men who are hated of women."

"That may be true," he admitted. "Upon reflection, I am almost sure of it. I can't remember any woman who ever took the trouble to make herself decently agreeable to me."

They laughed at one another after the fashion of old friends. He glanced thoughtfully around the softly-lit dining-room, transformed by the latest fad of the moment into the similitude of a West End restaurant. The long table had been replaced by half-a-dozen smaller ones—at the one farthest from them Eleanor and a little party were seated. He watched her again for a few moments. Then he looked back at Marian Fiske.

"I am a very poor judge of such matters," he said, "but is not Miss Hardinge more than usually good-looking?"

She laughed derisively.

"You poor man!" she exclaimed. "I wonder if that is affectation or genuine ignorance. Eleanor is the most beautiful girl in London. The Society papers have said so, and all the men are raving about her."

He played with his wine-glass for a moment.

"The most beautiful girl in London!" he repeated. "H'm!"

"You disagree?"

"I should not presume to differ—from the Society papers and your assertion," he answered. "Yet I was wondering just now whether an artist might not detect a certain—what shall I say—lack of spiritual-

10

ity in her face. It is the face of a beautiful child on
the shoulders of a woman."

She looked at him curiously. She was a little surprised at his criticism.

"After all, Eleanor is only a child," she remarked.
"At the first little lesson which life teaches her the
rest will come. Her coloring and features are something marvellous, and her hair is glorious. I can
assure you that I am beginning already to feel the
responsibility of having such a paragon under my
charge."

"You may very soon be relieved of it," he remarked.

"Perhaps! She is rather an odd girl, though!
She has a great deal of attention which delights her
—collectively, but she does not seem to care in the
least for any one in particular, however good they
are to her. I do not think that she will lose her
heart easily."

"Provided," he remarked dryly, "that she has
one."

A peal of light, sweet laughter rang out above the
babel of conversation. They all looked towards
Eleanor's table. She was leaning a little forward
in her chair, her lips parted, her cheeks flushed, her
eyes alight with enjoyment. A single row of pearls
encircled her long, graceful neck, her shoulders and
bare arms were dazzlingly soft, her hair gleamed like
burnished gold in the shaded lamplight. It was as
though a magician had touched her face, and there
had passed away from it all sense of trouble, all evil
memories, every trace of suffering. The troubled
mouth seemed ever ready to break into laughter,
the faint lines and wrinkles had faded completely
away. She was years younger. The light of past

sorrows had gone from her eyes, they remained only the mirror of the brightest and gayest things in life. In her youth, her beauty, and her almost assertive *joie de vivre*, she seemed like a child amongst the little company by whom she was surrounded.

"Did you ever see any one more beautiful?" Marian Fiske asked.

"From a purely pagan point of view, no," he answered. "I still hold that there is something missing. But then you must remember that I am the worst judge in the world of a woman's looks."

"I know what you mean," Marian answered thoughtfully. "Yet I believe that nineteen men out of twenty would prefer her as she is. She is no trouble to talk to, she is ready to be amused at anything; she is never serious for a single moment."

"All of which qualities," he remarked, "should endear her greatly to schoolboys—and Lord Winandermere."

She laughed softly.

"And yet," she said, "there is absolutely no accounting for things which happen sometimes. I have known the very cleverest men attracted by the most frivolous women. I shouldn't be in the least surprised if she married a professor."

"She might be useful," he remarked, "as an antidote. But even if the wise men were willing—what of the girl?"

Marian shrugged her shoulders.

"Those things with women," she said, "go so often by caprice. At this rate she will soon be surfeited with adulation of the ordinary sort."

He followed the motion of her head, and glanced around again. Powers had left his seat at the farthest table. He was leaning over Eleanor's chair, talking to her. Trowse watched him narrowly. When he looked away there was a rare smile upon his lips.

"Your brother," he said, "must be very proud of Miss Hardinge as a patient. To look at her one would not imagine that she had ever had a day's illness in her life—or a day's unhappiness. India must be a pleasant place to live in."

Marian was suddenly meditative. "It was a marvellous recovery," she said.

He bent a little closer to her.

"There were a few days," he said, "during which Powers was a little uneasy. You know perhaps that he sent for me?"

She shook her head. "No! He never told us!"

"At that time," Trowse continued, "her memory seemed to be somewhat affected. Is there any change in that direction?"

"None whatever," Marian answered. "I thought you knew all about that. It is the most extraordinary position. She remembers absolutely nothing about the accident. It is some injury to her head, Powers said, and he will not have her questioned. You can't imagine how foolish it seems to go about continually explaining to people."

"Ah!"

There was a short silence. Marian Fiske was studying her companion's immovable face. She leaned a little closer towards him.

"I wonder," she murmured, "whether you will answer me a question?"

"My dear Miss Fiske!" he protested.

"Have you ever known a similar case to Eleanor's?"

He did not immediately reply. Marian's eyes never left his face.

"Exactly similar—no," he admitted.

She nodded.

"I should think not. Now tell me this, will you? If you had not this case before you, should you have believed such a thing possible?"

"Possible—yes; likely—no," he answered deliberately. "You see, in our profession we are bound to place the limits of possibility very far back indeed. But why do you ask me this? The subject is one to which your brother has given far more time and thought than I have. I believe that he came across several very interesting cases of the sort in India."

Their eyes met for a moment. Marian was studying him keenly. Somehow, she felt that under his measured talk there was at least some shadow of the knowledge which she desired to gain.

"You do not think it possible," she said, "for Powers to have been in any way—it is a hateful suggestion, but I cannot help it—in any way dsceived?"

"I am not in a position to form any opinion," he answered. "On the face of it, it does not seem possible, does it? The young lady, I understand, had letters addressed to your brother; she was expected, and he recognized her."

"You are right," she admitted, with some shadow of a mental reservation in her tone. "On the face of it, it does not seem possible."

Almost immediately Lady Fiske rose from an adjoining table, and the room was filled with the soft rustling of silk and lace as the women passed out. Trowse, tall and ascetic-looking in his evening clothes, stood back amongst the shadows behind the small table at which he had been sitting, and steadfastly watched the girl of whom he and Marian Fiske had been talking. Prosperity had indeed had a wonderful effect upon Eleanor's looks. The light of perfect health had flushed her delicate cheeks, her figure had filled out; she carried herself with a grace and confidence which took no count of those days of slow torture through which she had passed. Yet there was about her beauty some faint note of peculiarity which had puzzled others before Trowse. He asked himself what it was as she passed out, a queen running the gauntlet of a court of admiring eyes, fresh, exquisitely natural, the living embodiment of light-hearted gayety. When at last the door was closed and the men drew nearer together, he smiled quietly to himself.

"It is like one of those pictures," he murmured, "which come near to breaking the heart of the painter. It is perfect in color and form, it is beautiful—and yet it does not live. There is no background."

He took up his wine-glass and moved to a table nearer the centre of the room from which he could watch his host. The heavily shaded lights were kind enough to the faces of the men who sat laughing together over their cigarettes, but Trowse was a keen watcher, and he saw things which were hardly apparent to a casual observer. Powers had altered during the last few months. There were curious lines about his mouth, his eyes were a little sunken, his geniality was a trifle forced. Trowse smiled grimly.

"Conscience!" he muttered to himself. "Powers was never quite free from the sentimentalities of life. What a fool to trifle with such an opportunity!"

He waited for his chance, and moved up presently to his host's table. Powers welcomed him, but without heartiness. It happened that for the moment the two were virtually isolated. Trowse lit a fresh cigarette and leaned over towards the other.

"How does the great experiment go?" he asked, in a low tone.

Powers visibly flinched. He glanced around him nervously.

"So far," he said, "it has turned out much as I expected."

"You have not attempted—"

Powers stopped him with a quick gesture.

"As yet," he answered quickly, "I have attempted nothing. Be careful. I will talk to you again about this. The women are expecting us in the billiard-room. There is to be a pool and some bridge."

He rose. Almost at the same moment the butler approached him with a card upon a salver.

"This gentleman is in the library, sir. He wished me to apologize for disturbing you, but he would be much obliged if you could spare him a few moments."

Powers took up the card and read it:

"Captain Angus Hood,
2d Staffordshire Regiment."

"Don't know him," he muttered. "Trowse, take my place for a moment. If I am more than a minute or two, Winandermere, will you fellows go into the billiard-room. You know the way."

He crossed the room. At the door he suddenly stopped short. Trowse looked at him curiously. He was suddenly livid. He called out to a man in the more distant part of the room, and his voice sounded harsh and strained.

"Morton, do you happen to know where the 2d Staffordshire's are?" he asked.

The man addressed looked up.

"Don't know exactly," he answered. "Somewhere in India!"

CHAPTER XIX

"SIR POWERS FISKE, I believe?"

Powers, who during his few minutes' respite had regained his self-control, bowed, and eyed his visitor inquiringly. On the whole, he was relieved. Captain Hood was a clean, fresh-looking young man with clear blue eyes and a fair moustache. He was admirably typical of a class for whom Powers had but scant respect.

"Yes, I am Sir Powers Fiske," he answered. "I understood that you wished to see me urgently. You must forgive my asking you to be as brief as possible, but I am entertaining guests to-night."

"I must apologize for coming to you at all at such an hour," Captain Hood answered. "The matter is one, however, of great moment to me. To be as brief as possible, I have been told that you might be able to give me some idea as to the present whereabouts of a young lady of whom I am in search."

"A young lady!" Powers repeated slowly.

"Yes! Her name is Eleanor Marston."

Powers shook his head.

"I do not know any one of that name," he said. "My mother or sister might perhaps be able to help you. My own acquaintances are few, and the name you mention is strange to me."

"You are quite sure? Eleanor Marston is her real name. I understand that she has been in a situation

in London under the name of Surtoes.   Perhaps that
is more familiar to you."

Powers faced the latent hostility in the other's
manner with indifference.

"I can only repeat," he said, "that both names
are strange to me. May I ask why you have come
here to ask me such questions?"

"I have been told," Captain Hood repeated, "that
you could give me the information I desire—that her
whereabouts, in fact, was known to you."

"I regret," Powers answered stiffly, "that you
have been misinformed. I am powerless to assist
you in any way."

He made a movement towards the door, but his
visitor intercepted him.

"One moment, Sir Powers," he said gravely. "I
do not wish to trouble you with another visit, but
you must give me a moment or two now. I will
try to be as brief as I can. I was engaged to Miss
Eleanor Marston when she lived in Yorkshire, and
my regiment was stationed in York. I was ordered
out to India, but we corresponded regularly, and
were to have been married next year. Last May
twelvemonths I was given the command of a particularly troublesome little hill station out at Dar-
jeeling, and while I was there a lot of my letters
went wrong. Amongst them was one from Miss
Marston, telling me of her father's death, and of a
great change in her fortunes. She was going to
London, she said, to take a situation, and she
wished to break off our engagement. This letter
reached me eighteen months after it was written.
In the meantime, all my letters to her had been
returned, and I had only learned of her father's
misfortune from the newspapers. Immediately I re-

ceived it I got leave and left for England at once. After a lot of inquiries, I found that Miss Marston had taken a situation with Bearmain's, drapers, in the Edgware Road. I went there this afternoon, only to discover that she had left several months ago."

Powers was listening with an air of strained courtesy.

"You must really excuse me," he said, "but do you mind coming to the point. At any other time I should be perfectly willing to hear all this. Just now it is inconvenient, and I cannot see how I can possibly be interested."

"I am coming to that," Captain Hood continued doggedly. "At Bearmain's they recommended me to make inquiries of a young person called Ada Smart. From her I learned that just before Miss Marston's disappearance you spoke to her and Miss Smart in the street, took them to tea, and made some proposition or suggestion to Miss Marston which involved her coming to you. Shortly afterwards she disappeared. This Miss Smart and a young man named Johnson seem to have been much interested in Miss Marston, and they have laid the facts before me."

Powers turned impatiently away.

"I must absolutely decline to neglect my guests any longer," he said, "for the sake of listening to matters which cannot possibly interest me. The whole thing is ridiculous."

Captain Hood barred the way to the door.

"Sir Powers," he said, "I should be sorry to make a scene here, but I decline to go until I have finished what I have to say."

Powers shrugged his shoulders.

"If you think it worth while, then," he said, "pray go on."

"The young man Johnson and Miss Smart laid these facts before me," Captain Hood continued. "Johnson came to your flat in Hans Crescent a few days after her disappearance, and saw her hat in your study. Further, they are both of them prepared to swear that they saw Miss Marston in your company a few weeks later. Come, Sir Powers, the long and short of it all is this : I am informed that Miss Marston is living in your house under the name of Miss Hardinge, and I have come to ascertain the truth of that report."

Powers breathed a sigh of relief.

"At last, then, he remarked, with a grim smile, "you have arrived at something definite. I will try and answer you in fewer words. You have been made a fool of. Your whole story is a farcical delusion. At the same time, I believe that you have been imposed upon, and I will not adopt the obvious course of ordering you out of the house. You shall be amply satisfied, after which I will expect your apology. In the first place, then, I can assure you that I am not in the habit of accosting shop-girls and inviting them to tea, and you will forgive me if I add that you seem to have amazingly little confidence in the young lady if you take it for granted so readily that she would have accepted such an invitation. I certainly received a visit from a young madman of the name of Johnson, who was under the same impression as you seem to be, and I am inclined to regard that young man as either a practical joker of the first water or a dangerous and exceedingly annoying lunatic. The only young lady who ever visited me at my flat is at present under this roof, and you are welcome to see her, and if you choose, to interrogate my whole household. At present my flat is closed, and I am residing here with my mother and sister. Is there anything more I can say?"

"You deny, then, that Miss Marston ever came to your flat in Hans Crescent?"

"Deny it! I have never even heard of such a person," Powers answered.

"Then who was the young lady," Captain Hood asked, "who left your flat with you one day about four months ago, and whom the two persons I have spoken of saw in your carriage and accosted?"

"The young lady in question was Miss Hardinge, my mother's ward."

"And where is that young lady at present?"

Powers raised his eyebrows.

"I believe that you are in earnest, Captain Hood," he said, "and I am very sorry for you; but you must forgive my pointing out that your questions are becoming impertinent."

"I am informed," Captain Hood persisted, "that Miss Marston is at present living under your roof and is known as Miss Hardinge."

"I cannot be responsible for any mad story which you may hear," Powers said stiffly. "The fact that this is my mother's house, and that Miss Hardinge is my mother's ward, should, I think, be sufficient for you. I have reached the limits of my patience."

He moved towards the door, but his visitor blocked the way. Powers confronted him haughtily.

"Sir Powers," Captain Hood exclaimed earnestly, "this is a matter of life or death to me. If I am

wrong I shall owe you the most profound apologies.
But I must tell you that my information bore the
stamp of truth, and I shall not rest until I have
tested it. I am bound to repeat my question. Where
is the young lady whom you call Miss Hardinge at
present?"

Powers hesitated for the fraction of a second. Then
he shrugged his shoulders.

"I agree with you," he remarked dryly, "that you
will owe me all the apologies your eloquence can
command. However, I will continue to treat you
like a rational being. Miss Hardinge is at present
assisting my mother and sister in entertaining
their guests."

Captain Hood was silent. Powers leaned against
the mantelpiece with his hands behind him.

"You will probably admit," he continued, "that a
young lady who has come to us from an old friend
of my father's, whom we have known since her girlhood, and who is now in the position of a daughter
of the house, is scarcely likely to be connected in
any way with a runaway shop-girl from the Edgware Road. However, since you have shown yourself so hard to convince, the matter had better be
settled finally. I will present you to Miss Hardinge."

"Now?"

"Precisely. I presume that there is a likeness
between her and the young lady of whom you are
in search, or I should not already have been sub-
jected to the annoyance which I have experienced
from your crazy informants. I shall expect your
apologies to take the practical shape of an attempt,
at any rate, on your part to convince these people
of their error."

"It is a fair offer," Captain Hood said quietly.
"I accept it."

He glanced downwards at his clothes, but Powers
shrugged his shoulders.

"I shall explain that you have just arrived from
abroad," he said. "Come this way!"

CHAPTER XX

THE two men passed out into the hall. Through
the open door beyond came the click of billiard balls
and the sound of a babel of conversation. Powers,
who had recovered his nerve, led his visitor in without hesitation. Eleanor was not at once visible,
but Lady Fiske was standing just inside the room.
She turned round as they entered.

"I want to present to you an old Indian acquaintance who has just returned to England, mother,"
Powers said. "Captain Angus Hood—Lady Fiske."

Lady Fiske held out her hand with a pleasant
smile.

"My son has spoken so often," she said graciously,
"of the many hospitalities which he received in India
that I am sure it will give me very much pleasure to
know any of his friends from there."

"You are very kind," Captain Hood murmured.

"You have been seeing some active service, have
you not?" Lady Fiske continued. "Your name is
quite familiar to me. Were you not in command at
Malika when the rising took place?"

"I was very fortunate," Captain Hood answered.
"I had been there only a week."

Lady Fiske nodded approvingly.

"I know that those frontier affairs are very tiresome," she remarked. "My father, General Hyslop,
was an old Anglo-Indian. Are you on long leave?"

"A year," he answered; "but I am not sure
whether I shall go back at all."

"I hope that we shall see more of you," Lady
Fiske said graciously. "I must go and talk to Mrs.
Penwick. She is one of those tiresome people who
won't do anything, and are always thinking themselves neglected."

An old brother officer came up and greeted Hood
warmly. They all three stood talking together,
then the psychological moment arrived. Eleanor,
who had been standing with her back to them,
studying the marking-board, came suddenly across
the room, cue in hand. Powers fell a little back
with a quick indrawn breath and clenched teeth.
The end of a half-spoken sentence died away on
Hood's lips. He stood and watched her like a
statue. Her eyes were bright with laughter. She
was superbly beautiful.

"Sir Powers, do come and play with me," she
begged. "Take Lord Winandermere's cue. He is
quite hopeless. We cannot even make a game with
those two."

Her eyes rested carelessly upon the bronzed young
officer in morning clothes, who was regarding her
with such strange fixedness. Powers turned towards
him.

"Let me introduce my friend, Eleanor," he said.
"Captain Hood—Miss Hardinge!"

She smiled and bowed. She was quite unconscious
of his barely repressed emotion.

"Are you very great at billiards?" she asked him.
"I do so want to find somebody for my partner who
can really play. Sir Powers is awfully good, but so
lazy."

Captain Hood answered her like a man in a
dream.

"I am only a very moderate performer," he said,
11

"and I am afraid that our partnership would involve defeat."

She shrugged her shoulders.

"Then I won't ask you to play with me," she said, "for I am quite tired of being on the losing side. Lord Winandermere has deceived me grossly. From what he told me at dinner-time, I thought that he was a scratch player at least, and I really don't believe that he made any more than I did."

Lord Winandermere, who had turned round at the sound of his name, strolled up to them.

"'Pon my word, Miss Hardinge, that's rather rough," he declared. "I can assure you that I didn't have a thing left. Come and try again. They will give us twenty."

"If they beat us this time," she said, laughing, "I shall never speak to you again."

They went off together, and Powers, glancing quickly at Captain Hood, was alarmed at his appearance. He was white to the lips, and in his eyes was the frightened look of a man who has received a shock. Powers took him by the arm.

"Come into the next room and have a brandy and soda," he said, in a low tone.

Hood followed him without a word. They were separated from the billiard-room by a thick curtain only. Powers poured out some brandy and forced him to swallow it.

"You look done up," he remarked. "Better rest here quietly for a few minutes."

Hood sat for a while with his face half-hidden in his hands. When he looked up he was still unnaturally pale, and there was a strange, scared look in his eyes.

"I am very sorry to be such a fool," he said huskily. "I cannot tell what came over me."

"It was the likeness, I daresay," Powers suggested.

"There is a likeness, I suppose?"

Hood shuddered.

"It is more than a likeness," he said slowly. "It is something—altogether beyond explanation. I could have sworn when her eyes first met mine that it was Eleanor. And then she looked and looked, and there was nothing behind—no life! It was her body, but it was not Eleanor. No! No!"

Powers felt a momentary shiver pass through his veins.

"You are over-tired and over-excited," he said. "You shall talk to Miss Hardinge again presently, and then you will find the likeness less startling. If it is really so striking as you seem to have found it, I suppose I must make allowance for those crazy young people at Bearmain's who have been causing me so much annoyance."

"It is more than startling," Hood said slowly. "It is unearthly."

Powers lit a cigarette and strolled down the room. When he returned, Hood was more composed.

"If I may trespass upon your hospitality a little longer," he said, rising, "I should like to take my chance of a few more words with Miss Hardinge."

"By all means," Powers answered. "You are looking quite fit now. We will go back into the billiard-room."

Trowse joined them as they entered. Powers introduced him, and the three men talked together for some time. Then Hood, on some pretext, left them, and remained in a small recess from which he could

watch Eleanor. His eyes followed her every movement. Trowse and Powers exchanged glances.

"Your friend came—from India?" the former asked.
Powers nodded.

"He was engaged to—Eleanor; has been to Bearmain's in search of her. I was driven to risk his
recognition of her. She has altered—so much, that
I thought it safe."

Trowse raised his eyebrows. "It was a risk," he
remarked.

"It was inevitable," Powers answered. "You can
appreciate how altered she is. I can. The worst
is over now. He speaks already of the likeness—
nothing else."

"There was the risk—on her side!" Trowse said.
Powers shook his head.

"Too soon after the operation," he declared. "It
will be years before we need fear that. Look!"

Hood had found his opportunity. Eleanor, who
had lost her second game, turned her back upon her
partner and sat down in the recess close to where
Hood was standing. He moved at once to her side.
Her face was clouded and almost childish in its disappointment.

"I am afraid that you have been unlucky again,"
he said.

"Lord Winandermere is so stupid," she exclaimed
pettishly. "He can't play a little bit. I'm sorry I
ever played with him. He is a shocking partner."

Hood looked at her in some surprise. She appeared to be genuinely angry.

"It is a long time," he remarked, "since I have
seen a billiard-room like this. I have just got home
from India."

She nodded, but failed to show any interest.

"I used to live there," she remarked carelessly. "I have forgotten all about it, though."

Hood drew a little breath. His vague disquietude was fading away.

"You came to Europe when you were quite young, I suppose?" he remarked.

She shook her head.

"No, I came quite recently. Only I have had a very bad illness, and I find it difficult to remember anything clearly."

He was properly sympathetic. It was impossible to doubt her sincerity. Yet at that moment something in the languid poise of her head as she leaned back sent the blood rushing through his veins. It was a veritable torment, this.

"Do you know," he said suddenly, "that you remind me of some one, of a friend, so powerfully that I have to keep on looking at you to assure myself that I am not dreaming."

She laughed softly. "How amusing! Was she— a great friend?"

"I was engaged to marry her," he said simply. "Her name was Eleanor Marston."

He was watching her. There was not even the flicker of an eyelid, not the faintest sign of anything beyond a polite but somewhat bored interest.

"And where is she now?" Eleanor asked.

"I have lost her," he answered. "I have come to England to try and find her."

She looked at him sideways, and discovered that he was handsome. Further, she saw that Lord Winandermere was watching them, and looking very cross. Her manner softened suddenly.

"I hope very much that you will succeed," she said. "You must look upon it as a good omen that you have found some one who reminds you of her."

"Thank you!" he answered. "I mean to find her. It is fortunate for you, Miss Hardinge, that I met you here knowing who you were. If I had come across you in the street, or I think anywhere else, I should have thought my search ended—and have greeted you accordingly."

She laughed gayly.

"That would have been most embarrassing for me," she exclaimed, "and for you afterwards."

Lady Fiske came up to them, and after her others. Hood slipped quietly away. He left the room as though reluctantly, with his eyes still following Eleanor's movements. Powers spoke to him for a moment in the hall.

"You are satisfied?" he asked quietly.

"To the extent of offering you my most humble apologies—yes," Captain Hood answered. "But— you will laugh at me, I know," he added, after a moment's hesitation, "and yet it seems to me that the likeness is something—unholy. I feel as though I had come into contact with something I can't understand."

Powers smiled genially. "Try a good night's sleep!" he said.

CHAPTER XXI

ELEANOR held out her hands and thanked him with a brilliant smile.

"How lovely, Powers! Thanks ever so much."

She lifted the great cluster of deep red carnations to her face, and rested them for a moment upon her cheek. Then she tossed them carelessly on one side and yawned.

"How dull it is indoors," she remarked. "I cannot think what has become of Lord Winandermere. He promised to come and take me to Hurlingham. He was so sure that his sisters were going to-day."

Powers frowned, and watched the carnations, for which he had given a special commission to Gerard's, torn to pieces by a delighted little dachshund. He looked from them to Eleanor. She was gazing out of the window moodily.

"Why don't you play polo, Powers?" she asked suddenly.

"Why should I?" he answered.

"How stupid! Don't you see that if you played, or were even interested in it, I should have some one to take me there without depending upon other people."

He turned away impatiently. He was a fool to have provoked the answer which he could quite well have foretold.

"It would be a convenience for you beyond a doubt," he remarked, with wasted irony. "Are you

not afraid, Eleanor, that some day you will grow
tired of amusing yourself?"

She looked at him with wide-open eyes.

"No! Why on earth should I? What else is
there to do?"

"What about amusing other people sometimes—by
way of a change?"

She smiled—delightfully.

"How dull! I suppose you mean follow Marian's
example, and have a night class for boys, or get up
concerts to send ragged children to the seaside."

"Why not? Such things are kindly enough; they
do good! They are excellent things for a girl to
interest herself in."

She looked at him in manifest and amazed wonder.

"But it wouldn't amuse me at all, Powers! I
should be bored to death. I call it a most horrid
suggestion!"

"And are you going to think of nothing but
amusing yourself all your life?" he asked slowly.

"Why not? I must do something to keep my
thoughts occupied. You forget that I am not like
other girls."

"What do you mean?" he asked.

"How ridiculous!" she exclaimed. "Of course
you know what I mean. Am I always to grope
through life asking questions, and knowing nothing
of my past beyond what you choose to tell me. Will
it ever come back to me, Powers?"

"I believe that it will," he answered, "but you
must be patient."

"You are supposed to be a clever physician," she
said, "but you keep on doing nothing but tell me
to be patient. I am quite tired of it. I shall have

to ask Dr. Trowse for his advice. Everybody says
that he is wonderful."

Powers winced.

"I beg that you will not do anything of the sort,
Eleanor," he exclaimed. "I can assure you that
time only is of the slightest avail. Trowse would
not understand. He might attempt things which
would be dangerous."

She leaned forward and looked at him, her beautiful face clouded, her eyes still full of a moody dis-
content.

"He might say that you do not understand," she
retorted.

"He probably would," Powers admitted. "Yet
the fact remains that Trowse, if he had the opportunity, would attempt experiments with his own
daughter—if he had one. Eleanor, I wish that you
would promise me to have nothing whatever to do
with that man. Believe me that it is for your own
good I ask this."

"Why should I promise?" she asked carelessly.
"They say that he hates women, and that sounds
so interesting. I meant to talk to him the other
night, only I couldn't get the chance."

Powers rose up hastily.

"You must not forget, Eleanor," he said, "that I
am for the present your guardian, and that I have
some claim to be heard by you on such matters as
these. I am not likely to be arbitrary. I do not
approve of your sudden intimacy with Captain
Hood, but I have not interfered in any way. But as
regards Trowse, I have special reasons for asking
you most emphatically to have as little to do with
him as possible."

She shrugged her shoulders.

"Bother Dr. Trowse!" she said. "By-the-by, Powers, you have just reminded me that you are my guardian. I want to ask you a few questions."

It was characteristic of her that she abandoned the subject with a perfectly unassumed indifference. She made no promise, no attempt to allay his palpable anxiety.

"Some questions? Well!"

"I want to know why I was sent over to you and Lady Fiske. You could scarcely have known my father when he lived in England. Lady Fiske told me that he went to India forty years ago."

"You forget," he answered, "that I was in India for several years. I saw a good deal of your father then—and of you."

She laughed—and broke off suddenly in the middle of it. Powers felt his heart stop beating. There was a look in her face which he had never seen there before—a vague, questioning trouble in her deep, soft eyes.

"Of me? Oh, how I wish—"

She stopped short. Her eyes grew suddenly thoughtful almost to dreaminess. Her voice dropped to a monotone.

"If ever I do remember anything, Powers," she murmured, "I think that it will be of you. I woke up last night, and I had a curious sensation. I seemed to be in some great trouble, and I was holding out my hands for help, and I saw you stoop and grasp them. It was you, Powers, but not as you are to-day. That must have been a glimmering of memory. Perhaps it will grow stronger. Tell me that you think it will!"

"I do think so," he answered. "I am sure of it."

She leaned back with half-closed eyes.

"Sometimes," she said, "when I cannot sleep, or when I wake in the night, I have tried to get to the other side of that black wall. Do you know, it always terrifies me. I seem to be groping in a thick darkness, and the faces of the men and women whom I see are like shadows, and they are hidden from me. They come and go, and mock at me, for just as I seem on the point of realizing them they fade away. Last night I woke suddenly. The whole house seemed full of music. It was the strangest, wildest air, with deep, long undertones in a minor key—an organ, I thought at first, but afterwards it was like a multitude of people singing together very slowly—very wearily. I sat up in bed, and I cried out to myself that it had come at last. It seemed to me that in a moment I should see the faces of the people and hear the words of their song. And then it all faded away quite suddenly. I was alone in my room, and the house was quite still. I could hear my watch ticking and the policeman in the street below. The rest had gone. There was a horrible sense of emptiness everywhere— and the black wall was higher than ever."

"It was a dream," Powers said huskily.

"A dream!"

She repeated his words, and smiled wearily. The delicate freshness of her beauty, so suggestive of childhood, seemed in those few minutes to have become a crumpled thing.

"A dream," she murmured, "does not set strange voices whispering in your ears, does not mock you with phantom faces. Powers, I have a fancy that some day when this thing happens to me again I shall go mad."

Her eyes were filled with terror. He took her hands into his. They were hot and dry.

"Eleanor," he said earnestly, "you must not have such fancies. Do you hear? You must not! There is no reason for them. You are as well as I am. Be brave, and they will pass away."

"You do not understand," she declared impatiently. "All the time something goes thumping in my head like a sledge-hammer while I am struggling —to remember."

"You must not struggle," he said firmly. "Your memory, when it does return, will return naturally. It will not be forced."

She laughed hardly.

"Not struggle. You might as well ask me not to breathe. When—that—comes—I feel myself changed—a different person. And I scarcely know whether I long for it or dread it the more."

She rose up—her face was drawn, her wonderful beauty seemed to have passed away from her; she was haggard, and her eyes wandered restlessly about as though seeking ever some elusive thing. And Powers, who watched her, found his own eyes dim, and his heart beat thickly with the sense of coming trouble. He caught her hand in his. She snatched it away.

"I wish you wouldn't do that!" she exclaimed pettishly. "You know I hate it."

She turned her back upon him and stood at the window.

"Powers, how much money have I?"

He was startled. "Money?"

"Yes! I suppose I have some, haven't I? I should like to know how much. Your mother and sister always seem to think that I am terri-

bly extravagant when we are out shopping together."

"I will speak to them," he said slowly. "You have
money sufficient for anything you require."

She nodded. "Is Captain Hood well off?" she
asked.

He looked at her wonderingly.

"Captain Hood! I know scarcely anything about
him, but I believe that he has very little beyond his
pay. Why do you ask me that?"

She shrugged her shoulders.

"I think," she said, "that he will ask me to marry
him."

Powers sprang to his feet. "What!" he exclaimed.

She looked at him over her shoulder as though
surprised at his vehemence.

"He tried to ask me yesterday, but I stopped
him. He was almost eloquent—and so clumsy."

"Why, you have only known him a few weeks."

"That is quite true," she admitted. "And yet do
you know, I have something the same feeling about
him as about you. I seem to have known him before. Sometimes I could fancy that he feels the same
about me."

"You would not think of it, Eleanor?" he asked
hastily.

"I do not think so," she said deliberately. "I
should not dream of marrying a poor man."

Her words were at once a relief and a shock to
him.

"You do not care for him, then?"

She seemed to be weighing something up in her
mind.

"I like being with him," she said. "There is the
sense of familiarity I spoke of, and he is a very

pleasant companion. But I should not think of marrying any one who had not a good deal of money. It is so terribly important to be rich. Everything worth caring for at all is so expensive. And then there is Lord Winandermere."

"I wonder," he muttered, "have you any heart at all?"

Her old laugh rang out. She half looked round at him, and at the sight of his face, white with pain, laughed more merrily than ever.

"What a tragedy—and what a question! I don't suppose that I am very different from other girls in caring for the things worth having in life."

"And the things worth having in life," he asked slowly—"what are they?"

She accepted the question seriously, and moved across the room with a soft silken rustle, her brows faintly contracted in thought. Every movement was perfectly graceful, every trifling detail of her toilet seemed carefully and deliberately chosen towards a harmonious whole. To Powers for a moment the four walls of the room fell away. Once again he seemed to hear that bitter cry of hers in the wind-swept streets, where the hideous white lights were flashing, and the men and women flitted along the rain-washed pavements like haunted creatures. This was his promise—the consummation of her desire. The echo of her cry beat again upon his ears.

"The things worth having in life," she murmured. "For a woman, they seem so obvious. Unlimited power to possess beautiful things, to live amongst beautiful surroundings, to be free from pain, and to have pleasant people about one, who are always cheerful and gay. I really believe that that includes everything."

"What about marriage?" he asked.

"Oh, one must marry, I suppose," she answered carelessly. "Perfect liberty seems impossible without it. I should like my husband to be young and good-looking, and, of course, devoted to me."

"Do you ask nothing more from life than this?" he cried hoarsely.

She looked at him and laughed.

"Nothing! With these things granted, I should be perfectly happy."

"It is paganism, pure and simple," he muttered.

She was unmoved—perfectly complacent.

"You can call it what you like," she answered. "It is good enough for me."

Her eyes, full of soft, tantalizing laughter, maddened him. He caught her by the wrists fiercely.

"Listen," he cried, "these are the words of a selfish child, who sees no more in the world than one vast playground. It cannot be possible that you have no sense whatever of the things beyond—the things which beauty only represents. I have seen you engrossed by pictures—the Madonna at the National Gallery, the Monk whose head you copied; the Huguenot who mocked death with the sword at his throat. You went out on the balcony alone last night; you were watching the stars, you turned your face to the breeze—I saw you close your eyes and listen to the music. Those things are the voices and the sign-posts of life. It is not possible that they speak to you in vain."

She wrested her hands from his, and smoothed a red mark upon her wrist with soft, delicate fingers.

"I hate you when you are rough," she exclaimed petulantly, "and I haven't the least idea what you are talking about. The things which you have mentioned were all beautiful, and so of course I liked them. I wish you wouldn't get so terribly in earnest about nothing. It wearies me."

She moved towards the door. He made no effort to stop her. Sure of her retreat, she looked around upon the threshold.

"You seem dissatisfied with me, Powers," she said, readjusting one of her bracelets. "I am sorry, but I cannot help it. Don't you think it would be better if you left me alone. It would be much more comfortable for both of us. Good-by!"

Her bracelet came together at last. She looked up at him, nodded, and left the room. The unuttered words died away upon his lips. The utter hopelessness of all protest laid an icy hold upon him. He heard her moving blithely up the stairs singing to herself.

CHAPTER XXII

"Is it anything serious?" Trowse asked quietly, preparing to rise from his writing-table.

Powers flung himself into a chair with a groan. "No! I want to talk to you."

A short silence. Trowse eyed his visitor narrowly. On the whole, Powers was a surprise to him. Such a nervous breakdown in such a man was beyond his comprehension. Powers was looking very ill indeed.

"The young lady," he inquired, "is well, I hope?"

Powers raised his head.

"I have come to talk to you about her, Trowse," he said. "I can't expect your sympathy, and you can't help me—you nor any other man. But I've got to talk to someone—or go mad."

Trowse nodded with the air of a Sphinx. "Well?"

"She is so horribly changed. Can't you see it?"

"You forget," Trowse remarked, "that I had not the pleasure of the young lady's acquaintance before—your little experiment."

"Of course you can't judge," he said. "Trowse, I feel like a man who has created a monster, who has breathed life into some evil thing and let it loose upon the world."

Trowse smiled grimly.

"Personally," he said, "I admit that I am no judge. I understand, however, that society in gen-

12

eral scarcely takes the same view of Miss Hardinge. Isn't she supposed to be rather a beauty?"

Powers beat impatiently with his hand upon the table.

"You know that I am not talking about her looks, Trowse. She's beautiful enough to bewitch every man who comes near her—and she does it."

"It must be a little inconvenient for you," Trowse remarked. "Beyond that, I scarcely see your point."

"Man, you have eyes," Powers exclaimed, with subdued passion. "I have seen you watching her, studying her closely when you fancied yourself undisturbed. You can see what I see. She is like a marvellous piece of mechanism. The working of it is perfect, but it isn't human. She is only alive upon the sensuous side. Damn it, Trowse, don't look at me like that. She has no soul. There is. nothing alight inside."

"You want a tonic, my friend," Trowse said coolly. "You want it very badly. Don't swear at me again like that, because I don't like it. I know nothing myself about souls. From what I have heard I should think that they are very troublesome things, and that Miss Hardinge is just as well off without one—for your purpose, better."

Powers looked at him with a strange, shuddering curiosity. There was a long pause.

"I was a fool to come to you, Trowse," he said despairingly. "I cannot make you understand. I never could. And there is nobody else in the world to whom I can speak of this."

Trowse rose up and stood over him. The shadow of a sneer lingered still about his thin lips. His cold gray eyes flashed with a steely light. He spoke slowly—there was emphasis in every syllable.

"It is very clear to me, Powers," he said, "that you are utterly unworthy of your good fortune. You have committed what amongst us is the one unpardonable crime. The girl should have remained to you always a patient and a subject. Your experiment should have left you free from any personal bias whatsoever. It was nothing more nor less than a solemn charge accepted by you on behalf of science, and bringing with it certain distinct and absolute obligations. It is easy to be deceived in men. I have been deceived in you. I held you far above such callousness to great interests, such sickly sentimentality as you are now pleading guilty to. What has happened is perfectly obvious. You have conceived some sort of affection for the girl. In the language of those men to whose ranks you have sunk, you have fallen in love with her. Ugh!"

Powers was doggedly silent. The other's contempt stung him like a lash. Yet he made no attempt at denial.

"I can scarcely find patience to speak to you calmly," Trowse continued, "and I am a man not easily moved. You are a traitor to our great mistress—the only mistress in the world worth serving. Unless you can recover yourself, and I am beginning to doubt the possibility of such a thing, you will be unable to complete the most wonderful experiment which it has ever been the lot of man to undertake. Now I do not know altogether with what purpose you came to see me, but I myself was on the point of opening this subject with you."

Powers looked up. There was a note of apprehension in his tone.

"What do you mean? What concern is it of yours?"

Trowse seldom laughed, and when he did no sound could be less suggestive of mirth. He laughed then, and Powers watched him with a new anxiety in his eyes.

"It is very much my concern," he said calmly. "If you saw an ignorant lunatic seeking to destroy through simple wantonness some priceless work of art, I presume you would consider it your duty to intervene. So I, who see a man sink to the level of a lunatic, trifling with an experiment which bids fair to open one of the locked gates of science, feel a similar responsibility. I appeal to you, Powers, for the sake of our past friendship, to rid yourself of this gigantic folly. There are women enough in the world if you want to play the lover. Be a man, and accept your destiny."

Powers rose up. A certain doggedness had crept into his face—showed itself in his tone.

"Argument between us," he said, "is futile. Our point of view is wholly different. I yield to no one in my reverence for science, but I'm a human being, and I can't alter it. When I tell you that I love Eleanor I can't expect you to understand. I don't understand it wholly myself. But it is best that you should know the truth. I have no longer any desire to use her as a blind and soulless instrument for experiments, which at any moment might cost her her reason. We both of us know that mentally she is not in a healthy state. I have only one desire— to undo the past."

"You talk like a fool," Trowse answered. "How can you do that?"

"I want to lead her gently back to the state in which I found her," Powers said. "Her present condition is a torment to me."

"What about her present admirers?" Trowse asked. "Hood and Winandermere follow her everywhere like sheep—and she encourages them. I have not noticed that she regards you with the same favor."

Powers was white to the lips.

"She is nothing but a child," he said. "For the moment she does not understand."

"Yet they are there. How will you deal with them? There are rumors of an engagement already. She would accept either of them in preference to you."

Powers flinched. His persecutor's words had cut him like a lash.

"She is nothing but a child," he said, "and the people who please her most just now must be young and gay. But I have watched her, and I know. Her present state is not permanent. Before long there will be a crisis. I shall help it on. It is Eleanor Surtoes whom I love. Of her I have no fear."

There was a short silence—broken by Trowse.

"I am to take it, then," he said coldly, "that you abandon the experiment. In your present condition it is, I suppose, inevitable. You have lost all influence over her. It would be hopeless to expect her to respond to your will."

"I have already abandoned it," Powers answered. "I curse the day and the thought which made me ever attempt it."

"It is as well, then," Trowse answered, "to give you fair warning. I do not propose to stand by quietly and watch your folly."

"What do you mean?" Powers demanded.

"This! That if you do not carry this thing through—I shall!"

Powers sprang to his feet, his face was dark with passion.

"If you should dare to interfere," he cried, "if you should make the slightest attempt to—"

"Stop!"

The monosyllable came like a pistol shot, incisive, compelling! There was a breathless silence. Trowse continued, and his words were cold and hard.

"Do not threaten me," he said. "You should know better than that. You should know exactly of how much account I hold my life when it comes to a question of adding to the sum of human knowledge. I shall do as I say. My decision is unalterable."

Powers rose up. He was a man again.

"It is well to be prepared," he said. "I thank you for your warning. Take mine in return. I have as little fear of death as you, and I think that my love for Eleanor is a passion as strong as your devotion to science. I tell you that I will not have her made the subject of your experiments. I will not have her life or reason imperilled, even to solve the greatest of all mysteries."

Trowse shrugged his shoulders as he leaned towards the bell.

"I think," he said, "that we understand one another perfectly."

CHAPTER XXIII

"I MUST confess, Powers, since you ask me, that I am not altogether charmed with your protégée," Lady Fiske declared.

Powers looked away from his mother's face into the ball-room. Almost within a few feet of them Eleanor floated by, a delicate vision of muslin and silk, her face radiant with pleasure, her movements the perfection of effortless grace. She was wholly absorbed in the delight of the moment. Powers felt a little stab at his heart.

"I am sorry, mother," he answered. "You must remember that she is very young—and all this is new to her. I am anxious that you should make allowances for her."

Lady Fiske shrugged her shoulders. She was silent for a moment, during which her eyes rested thoughtfully upon her son's face.

"I have been always anxious to do so," she said, "but I am afraid that her character is too obvious to be misunderstood."

"She is young," he repeated, "and after her quiet life all this attention has perhaps turned her head a little. I can assure you, mother, that I have known her when she was a very different person."

Lady Fiske appeared unconvinced.

"I fancy that you must have been a little misled in those days, Powers. Her absolute selfishness and total indifference to the feelings of others are glaringly apparent. She appears to possess neither gratitude nor consideration, and for a young girl she is ridiculously extravagant. I never understood that Colonel Hardinge was a rich man, did you?"

"She has a considerable credit," he answered. "I have spoken to her about her expenditure."

"That, of course, is your concern," Lady Fiske continued. "So far as her chaperonage is concerned, I could not possibly undertake to look after her beyond Goodwood. Marian and I are going to Homburg the last week in July with the Fitzallans, and it would be impossible for her to accompany us. I hope that that is understood, Powers."

"It must be as you say, of course, mother," he answered. "I am expecting to hear from her uncle every day now. You will probably not be burdened with the care of her much longer."

She passed them again. Captain Hood was her partner, and there was a look in his eyes which no woman ever misreads. Lady Fiske sighed.

"I am really sorry for that young man," she said. "I knew his mother quite well. He is far too nice to be fooled as Eleanor is fooling him."

Powers frowned darkly. "I do not think that she encourages him," he said.

She raised her eyebrows. She was an even-tempered woman, but there was asperity in her tone.

"Rubbish! Even you should know better than that, Powers. A girl is always perfectly aware when a man is in love with her. If she does not intend to accept him, it is positively wicked to keep him dangling after her. That is what Eleanor is doing. I consider it—indecent!"

"Perhaps—she intends to accept him!"

Lady Fiske smiled scornfully.

"Captain Hood has two hundred a year besides

his pay," she said. "You are positively futile to-night, Powers. Why don't you go and dance? At least, let us abandon Eleanor as a subject of conversation."

"There is one thing more I want to say about her, mother. You will find it hard to understand. Still, I want to tell you the facts. You know, of course, that her memory is still entirely unawakened?"

"Yes!"

"Some day I believe that it will return—perhaps quite suddenly, perhaps by degrees. But when it does, I confidently believe that there will be a great change in Eleanor. A great deal that puzzles and disappoints us now will, I am sure, pass away. It is virtually the corollary of her numbed sensibilities. I can assure you that the Eleanor I knew was most unlike the Eleanor of to-day. She was high-minded, brave, fond of pleasure perhaps, but with plenty of imagination and generosity."

"The change, then," Lady Fiske said dryly, "is indeed wonderful. You cannot seriously tell me, Powers, that you believe her altered disposition to be in any way due to her illness?"

"I am quite sure of it," he answered firmly. "The brain is the most wonderful thing in the world, and responds to accidents and changes in its structure in the most extraordinary manner. I could give you a German book to read on the subject which would amaze you."

Lady Fiske shook her head.

"I am content," she said, "to give her the benefit of the doubt. I hope that your theory may account for a good deal which has disappointed me in Eleanor. Here she comes!"

They were in a delightful little alcove, looking out upon the ball-room, and which for the last quarter of an hour had been unoccupied save by themselves. But with Eleanor's entrance all that was changed. Lord Winandermere had followed them across the room—several other men at once made their appearance.

"I have come to plead for at least one other waltz, Miss Hardinge," Lord Winandermere said. "Please let me have your card."

She shook her head.

"It is quite impossible," she declared. "You see, it is absolutely full. There are the Lancers after supper. You must be satisfied with them."

Lord Winandermere looked anything but satisfied.

"Then may I have an extra dance at the Castletons' Thursday night?"

There were other claimants for the Castletons' dance. Powers waited for his opportunity, and leaned over to Eleanor.

"Have you kept me my dance, Eleanor?" he asked.

She shook her head.

"You waltz so badly, Powers," she said, "and I am sure you don't care about it. Besides, to tell you the truth, I forgot all about it."

She was talking to some one else almost at once. Powers turned away with immovable face. Suddenly a fresh arrival paused upon the threshold and entered. Powers recognized him with a little start of amazement. It was Trowse.

He talked for a few moments with Lady Fiske. Then he turned to Eleanor.

"I am almost afraid to put such a tax upon your good-nature, Miss Hardinge, but I cannot resist asking if you have still a dance you can spare me."

She shook her head, looked for a moment into his eyes, and hesitated.

"I—am afraid not, Dr. Trowse," she said, with much less than her usual confidence. "You are very late."

"It was my misfortune to be detained at the last moment," he said quietly. "I can see that you are hesitating, Miss Hardinge. Be merciful!"

Powers, who was watching her closely, was perhaps the only one who noticed the change in her. The exuberant life seemed suddenly to die out of her face—for a moment an uneasy light flashed in her eyes, she was almost haggard. Trowse was leaning forward, his gaze riveted upon her as though anxious for her decision.

"You can have the next waltz," she said, in a low tone. "Captain Hood will forgive me, I am sure. I never really promised it him."

Powers drew a quick little breath. He could scarcely believe his ears. Then Trowse, after a word of thanks, turned away, and Eleanor was herself again. Only to Powers it seemed that the brilliancy of her eyes was almost feverish, and her laugh a little strained. She was combating a storm of jesting reproaches—some of which were not jesting at all.

"'Pon my word," Lord Winandermere declared, "you are absolutely heartless, Miss Hardinge. I would have given half my kingdom for that dance."

She laughed at him. "You never offered it."

"And it was mine, not his," Hood declared ruefully. "What have I done to be treated so cruelly?"

"You trod on my train," she declared. "But for the interposition of Providence, I should have been a wreck—and the first dance, too."

"It wasn't my fault," he protested, "and what you call the interposition of Providence was simply my marvellous skill in avoiding a catastrophe. I deserve credit rather than blame."

She made a little grimace.

"It is done!" she exclaimed. "How can I atone?"

"Three dances on Thursday night instead of two!" Captain Hood suggested.

"And four for me," Lord Winandermere echoed.

She laughed. "Indeed. Why four?"

"It is as many as I dare ask for!"

"Without fear of my chaperon," she said. "I do not think that I will give you any, Lord Winandermere. You are too timid. Besides, I have not robbed you of a dance to-night. Captain Hood is the only one who has the right to complain."

"I would to God I had the right!" he murmured, under his breath.

Her eyes mocked him. A wave of music swept in upon them. Trowse drew near.

"Consideration for the aged," he murmured, as he bowed before Eleanor, "is the most charming attribute of youth. It is delightful of you to have spared me this dance."

Powers thought it significant that Eleanor, who thoroughly enjoyed talking nonsense, made no answer whatever. She laid her hand upon his sleeve, and they passed out together.

CHAPTER XXIV

POWERS left the ball-room early and walked home. All his life a man of subdued emotions, of plentiful self-restraint, the abyss into which he had fallen was intolerable. All the scientific aspirations, the quiet culture, and the easy, pleasant days of sybaritical studentship which had filled his life were suddenly things of the past. His passionate love for Eleanor was predominant. He was like a man afflicted with a strange fever of unknown origin, which no physician could prescribe for, and which he himself was powerless to resist. His judgment of her remained unbiased. He knew that she was behaving like a spoiled and selfish child, that she treated him without even the courtesy due to her host, that she lived only for her own pleasure. But he thought of those days before, and his heart ached with the pain of it. Even then he had seen this thing coming. He knew quite well that her presence affected him as no other woman's presence had ever done. And he put the thought away from him in contempt. Women had never taken any place in his life—he thought himself invulnerable. What folly it seemed to him now! A little patience then, a little kindness, and her heart had been so easily won. He could have answered her cry with a full hand. He could have unlocked the gates of her promised land, and himself have been the guide.

The cool night air blew softly upon his heated face. He had left the dance in a moment of almost ungovernable rage. As he walked he grew calmer and more composed. He had no right to be angry with Hood and these others who had become almost her blind slaves. She was beautiful for them as for him. But Trowse! Again his face darkened, again the fierce anger swelled in his heart. Trowse, at any rate, was not fascinated by her beauty. His object in entering the ranks of her admirers had been boldly declared, and Powers' defiance was no idle threat. There should be no more tampering with her life and reason. If Trowse persisted, there could be but one end to it all. Powers contemplated it without even aversion. A strong man, the whole current of whose life has been diverted into strange channels, looks upon death with a certain curiosity, the solution of a mighty problem, a dignified ending after all to an existence more or less purposeless. A certain vein of fatalism in Powers' temperament came to his aid in these weary days.

As he passed across Berkeley Square, he was suddenly aware of a familiar object loitering on the pavement near his mother's house. He stopped short, extended his hand, and caught by the shoulder the man who was on the point of slinking away.

"What are you doing here?" he asked sharply.

Johnson straightened himself as soon as he found escape impossible. The change in him was wonderful. He was no longer smug or dapper, no longer would he have been described even by those partial young ladies who had submitted to his mild authority as gentlemanly. He was a strange, unprepossessing-looking creature, with a thin, straggling beard and unshaven cheeks, dressed in seedy black, with a manner half-nervous, half-dogged. He answered Powers' question after a moment's hesitation:

"I want to see—Miss Surtoes!"

Powers was exasperated.

"You unmitigated ass!" he exclaimed. "Can't you understand that the young lady who is living here with my mother is not Miss Surtoes?"

"So you say—so she says," Johnson muttered; "and you both lie."

"You have spoken to her then—without my knowledge?"

"You have no right to prevent me," Johnson answered stolidly. "It is true that I have spoken to her."

Powers mastered his anger. The creature, after all, was in an abject state.

"Well! She told you, I suppose, that her name was Hardinge. She did not encourage you in your folly, I am sure."

"She told me that she was not Miss Surtoes. She —laughed at me."

"And yet you hang round here to see her!"

"I cannot help it," Johnson muttered. "I have tried to go away. I cannot. I must be where I can see her."

Powers was not hard-hearted, and the pathos of the thing was suddenly borne in upon him.

"My poor fellow," he said, more gently, "can't you see that this is the most consummate folly? You are wasting your time, and making yourself miserable absolutely to no purpose. Come, be sensible. Walk on with me to my flat. I may be of service to you if only you will try and rid yourself of this madness. You are being made miserable by a chance resemblance. I know no more where Miss Surtoes is than you do."

"It is a lie!" Johnson said quietly. "It is not

worth while talking like that to me. If every one from Bearmain's, if every one of her relations, and every one who had ever seen her were to say the same thing, it would be no use. You are a gentleman, and you shouldn't tell lies, even to such as me."

Powers was silent for a moment. He looked meditatively at the creature before him.

"Well," he said, "supposing for a moment that you were right. The young lady declines to talk to you; she is well and happy, and amongst friends. Where do you come in? What possible good can you do yourself or her by this amazing conduct?"

"There is a mystery," Johnson answered, "which bewilders me. Something evil has come to her—and I believe through you. She herself may realize it some day. I want to be on the spot to help. I want her to know that she has one friend—who would die for her."

Powers sighed.

"I can see that there is nothing to be done for you," he said. "Take one last word of warning from me, though. I am a physician, and I know what I am talking about. Go on as you are doing, and the asylum gates are open before you. You are not quite sane now. Take care of the little reason that is left."

Johnson shuddered.

"You may be right," he said hoarsely, "but if Hell was yawning before me—the real Hell, you know, with burning fires for everlasting—I could not step aside. I must be where I can see her sometimes. I've given up Ada, got the sack from Bearmain's, my father has turned me out of doors, because he thinks that I have taken to drink. I never think of these things. They don't seem to matter. It is as though her fingers had closed upon something inside me, and she was holding me to her. I couldn't escape—if I would. It will be like this till the end!"

"What end is there to wait for?" Powers asked.

"Death or madness—or the solution of the mystery which has changed Eleanor Surtoes into Eleanor Hardinge!"

He slunk away, and Powers let him go. The creature was surely no longer dangerous? Yet the echo of his last words struck home with a chilly premonition of evil, revived almost as soon as Powers reached his flat, and looked through the letters which were awaiting him. The first which he opened was from a firm of bankers:

"DEAR SIR,—We understand that Miss Eleanor Hardinge, daughter of Colonel Archibald Musgrave Hardinge, of Calcutta, is a resident at present under your roof. We have a considerable credit in favor of this young lady, but were under the impression that she was amongst the passengers who perished in the unfortunate accident to the *Colombo* in the Bay of Biscay. We have made the most careful inquiries, and have failed to find her name in any list of survivors. Under these circumstances, we should esteem it a favor if the young lady in question and you, who are named as her guardian, would pay us a personal visit, so that this matter may be cleared up, and in the event of satisfactory evidence of Miss Hardinge's identity being forthcoming, her account with us duly opened.

"We beg to remain, yours faithfully,
"BARNARD & BARNARD, Ltd."

The second letter which Powers opened bore an
13

American post-mark, and was typewritten. It was
dated from Boston, U. S. A. :

"DEAR SIR,—I have to-day received a delayed letter
from my brother, Colonel Hardinge, of Calcutta, in
which he advises me that he has found it advisable
to send his daughter Eleanor to Europe, and begs
that I will ultimately assume the care of her. He
mentions your name as that of an old friend, who
will be glad to give her a home in London for the
present, and where I may hear of her.

"I should be glad, sir, to hear from you by cable
as to whether my niece is at present domiciled with
you, and if that is the case, I will arrange for a trip
to Europe without delay.—I am, sir, yours truly,
                              "JOHN HARDINGE."

Powers sat with pen and paper before him for fully
an hour. He realized now the folly of which he had
been guilty. The future would be beset with difficulties. He resolved at last upon his course of action. He wrote to the bankers a few formal lines
acknowledging their communication, and begging
them to allow the matter to remain over for the
present, as Miss Hardinge's health did not permit
any allusions to the unfortunate occurrence to which
they referred. And he sent the following cable to
John Hardinge :   ·

"Regret to inform you Miss Hardinge was drowned
in *Colombo* shipwreck.
                              "FISKE."

CHAPTER XXV

POWERS had scarcely finished breakfast the next morning before a visitor was announced. Captain Hood followed so closely upon the footsteps of the servant who had let him in that denial was impossible.

Powers found himself committed to a *tête-à-tête* with the one man whom he was most desirous to avoid.

"I am an early visitor, Sir Powers. You will forgive me, I hope. I could not rest until I had seen you."

Hood was carefully groomed and dressed, but the healthy tan seemed to have left his cheeks. He was pale, and there were deep lines under his eyes. His manner was restless, almost to nervousness. He looked like a man who had known no sleep.

"I am quite at your service," Powers said quietly. "Have you breakfasted?"

"Long since, thank you."

"Then what can I do for you? Sit down—will you smoke? There are cigarettes at your elbow."

Hood helped himself, but the fingers which held the match trembled painfully.

"I have come to speak to you—about Miss Hardinge."

Powers raised his eyebrows.

"About Miss Hardinge?" he repeated coldly. "I don't understand."

"Understand! Good God, no more do I!" Hood

exclaimed. "I haven't slept a wink all night. I couldn't even keep my eyes closed. Sir Powers, I am beginning to realize what a man feels like—when he is going mad."

"You are talking very strangely, Captain Hood."

"Strangely! Listen! I told you when I first saw Miss Hardinge that her likeness to Eleanor Marston was a wonderful thing. You will remember how powerfully it impressed me that night. Well, I have seen a good deal of Miss Hardinge lately—and Sir Powers, sometimes I have to pinch myself to be sure that I am sane. She's so different—and she's so—hellishly like. And she says things sometimes which startle me. Last night I told her of a great friend of mine—a girl to whom I was once engaged—who lived in a little village in Yorkshire. For the moment I had forgotten the name of the place, and while I was hesitating she repeated it softly—as though to herself. When I asked her how on earth she had heard of it, she did not know, could not repeat the name, did not remember having uttered it. And she was telling the truth! Beyond a doubt she was telling the truth. And again I was speaking of the house. I called it the Hall. She shook her head. 'The Grange,' she murmured, and, Sir Powers, she was right. She knew nothing about it, she said. She had never been in Yorkshire, she had known no one of the name of Marston. And yet she corrected me twice, and both times she was right. What in God's name does it mean?"

His eyes were burning with anxiety—he was positively haggard. Powers looked at him curiously.

"I am afraid, Captain Hood," he said, "that you are suffering from an attack of nerves. You have let your imagination run away with you. It is easy enough if once you are a little run down. You must use your will-power. It was, after all, not possible for Miss Hardinge to have corrected you in the way you tell me. Try to convince yourself of that."

"I cannot!" Hood said. "I heard her!"

"You thought that you heard her," Powers said coolly. "You were in an overstrung and excited state, and this likeness you speak of had evidently got upon your nerves. At such times the evidence even of one's senses is not to be relied upon. Now Miss Hardinge's history is known to me. Positively she has never been in Yorkshire in her life. Think of that, and realize what it means. She has never been in Yorkshire in her life. Therefore what you thought you heard was impossible. Dismiss the memory of it at once."

Hood rose up.

"Let me hear you say it again—repeat it after me," he demanded. "Miss Hardinge and Miss Marston are two different persons. There is no connection between them."

"It is ridiculous to doubt it for a moment," Powers declared. "They are two utterly different persons. There is no connection between them."

Hood sat down again. He wiped the perspiration from his forehead.

"You must think that I am mad, Sir Powers," he said apologetically. "I can't help it. There are times when—but enough of that. I want to try to forget it if I can. I had another object in coming to see you."

Powers sat with stony face. "Indeed!"

"Yes! I understand that for the present you are —her—guardian?"

"Miss Hardinge is temporarily in my care," Powers admitted.

"I am going to see her—this morning," Hood said. "I am going to ask her to marry me."

Powers made no sign. He had had ample warning.

"My guardianship," he said, "is scarcely sufficient to warrant my direct interference in such a matter. But I understand that you are almost dependent upon your pay."

"I have only two hundred a year outside it," Hood admitted. "I am a poor man."

Powers smiled faintly.

"You know that Miss Hardinge has little or no money?"

"Yes!"

"Then what do you propose to live on?" Powers asked.

"My uncle will give me a secretaryship if I leave the army," Hood said. "It will not be much to start with, but it will be better than my pay."

"Do you seriously suppose," Powers asked, "that Miss Hardinge would contemplate marriage—upon such prospects?"

Hood winced a little.

"She has been used to different things, I know," he admitted, "but if I am lucky enough to find that she cares for me—at all—I do not think that she would mind."

Powers smiled bitterly.

"I am afraid," he said, "you do not quite understand Miss Hardinge."

"On the contrary," Hood retorted, "I think that it is you who fail to understand her. You and she never seem to get on—do you?"

"I suppose—not."

"She is fond of pretty things, of course," Hood went on. "All girls are. And then she has been very much admired, and she is very young. •It is a wonder that she has not been completely spoiled. But she hasn't. She is just as simple and natural as a child. I am quite sure—that if she cared for any one—she would not consider money at all."

"I trust," Powers said, "that you have not been mistaken in your estimation of her character."

"You don't agree with me, then?"

"I do not," Powers admitted. "I should strongly advise you to defer your proposal for the present. If you are determined to go on with it, I think that you will be disappointed."

Hood rose up.

"She may refuse me," he said simply. "I don't know why she should do anything else. But if she does, I am quite sure of one thing. It will not be because I am a poor man. Whatever you may say or think of her, I am convinced that she is not mercenary."

Powers did not reply. He walked to the door with his guest.

"You will wish me luck?" the latter asked, holding out his hand.

"I cannot even do that," Powers said gravely. "I do not consider you suited for one another. I do not think that there is one chance in a thousand that she will accept you."

Hood turned away, white and determined.

"I hope," he said, "that I shall be able to surprise you."

.   .   .   .

He asked for Miss Hardinge, but was shown into

the drawing-room, where it chanced that Lady Fiske
was busy arranging some flowers. She greeted him
pleasantly, and chatted for a few moments about
the ball.

"I suppose—perhaps, I am a little early for Miss
Hardinge?" he asked.

She looked at him quickly—and sighed. Hood was
not equal to the task of concealing his purpose.

"No. I think that Eleanor is down!" she answered. "Shall I ask for her?"

"If you would be so good!" he begged.

He attempted no excuse. Rightly he felt that it
was useless. And Lady Fiske, who had risen as
though to leave the room, checked him as he sprang
up to open the door.

"One moment, Captain Hood!" she said, looking
at him kindly. "You will forgive me, I am sure.
Your mother was a dear friend of mine, and though
you won't remember me, I knew you when you were
a little boy. Am I right in supposing that you wish
to—speak seriously to Eleanor?"

"Yes! I daresay you can guess—you must have
seen. I want to ask her to be my wife."

She let her hand fall upon his, and looked up at
him earnestly.

"Don't!"

He started and changed color. The emphasis of
that monosyllable was disconcerting.

"You think—that I have no chance?" he murmured.

"I am sure that you have not."

He went very white. For several moments he was
silent.

"You will not think me unkind, will you?" she
went on. "I only want to save you pain. I am sure

that Eleanor has no idea of marrying you. If she
has encouraged you at all, and I know that she has,
it has been simply because she likes having for her
companions those who can give her the most pleasure. That sounds rather a cruel thing to say, I
know, but I am afraid that Eleanor has not been
brought up to have much consideration for the feelings of others."

He raised his head. She saw how her words had
scarred him.

"Your son," he said, "has been telling me the
same things. Perhaps I have been mistaken in Miss
Hardinge—but if so, it is my own fault. I am sure
that she would not wilfully have misled me. Lady
Fiske," he added, with more decision in his tone, and
a sudden straightening of his back, "I am bound to
believe in her. I do believe in her. I am not afraid
to stand my chance."

She smiled at him wistfully. No woman likes to
see a man suffer.

"It will be best, perhaps," she said. "Eleanor is
in the morning-room writing a letter. You can go
in to her."

.   .   .   .

Ten minutes afterwards she heard the hall door
close. Eleanor came out from the morning-room
with a frown upon her face.

"You have had a visitor?" Lady Fiske remarked,
looking round with her foot upon the stairs.

"Only Captain Hood!" Eleanor answered petulantly. "He has annoyed me very much. He
wanted me to marry him."

"Annoyed you?" Lady Fiske repeated.

"Yes! It is too ridiculous. He is shockingly poor

—he had no right to think of such a thing. He was
so useful, too, and now, I suppose, he will go away
or do something stupid. Men are so selfish."

Lady Fiske continued on her way upstairs. She
made no remark.

CHAPTER XXVI

CAPTAIN HOOD found a visitor waiting for him at his rooms, a seedy-looking little man, with a manner half nervous, half obsequious. He had been dubiously offered a seat in the hall, and he rose to his feet eagerly as Hood let himself in with his latchkey.

"You don't remember me, sir," he began eagerly. "My name is Johnson—Henry Johnson. You came to Bearmain's, in the Edgware Road, to make inquiries about Miss Surtoes, and they sent for me. It was my last week there. I have had the sack since then."

Captain Hood nodded.

"Yes," he said, "I remember you. What do you want with me? Come inside if you've anything to say."

He led the way into his sitting-room. Johnson followed him closely.

"I wanted to know—about Miss Surtoes, sir," he said timidly. "You found her, after all."

"How do you know that?" Hood asked.

"Because I have seen you with her, sir," Johnson answered promptly.

Hood shook his head.

"You have been deceived," he said, "by a most remarkable likeness. I do not wonder at it. I was almost deceived myself. The young lady was not Miss Surtoes."

"It's a lie, sir," Johnson said stolidly. "They

may have made you believe it, but it's a lie all the same.",

There was a moment's silence. Hood realized the convincing note in the other's words. Here, at least, was a man who believed in what he was saying. A thrill of the old wondering mistrust stirred in his blood. He felt his pulse quicken.

"What do you mean?" he asked sharply.

"What I say. I tell you that I traced her from Bearmain's to his door. I found the cabman who drove her there. I saw her come out of his house after her illness. I mean this: As God hears me it is the truth. The young lady who is living to-day with Lady Fiske as Miss Hardinge is our Miss Surtoes from Bearmain's, and no other."

Again there was silence. Hood was confused. His brain was in a whirl. He walked restlessly to the window and back again.

"It is impossible!" he exclaimed.

"It is God's truth," Johnson said doggedly.

"Do you happen to know," Hood said impressively, "that I was engaged to Miss Surtoes?"

"I am not surprised," Johnson admitted. "I guessed it."

"And do you mean to tell me that I should not have recognized the girl whom I saw constantly for months—the girl whom I was going to marry?"

Johnson peered at him shrewdly.

"I can't believe," he said, "as you didn't sometimes feel that you recognized her. She was altered, of course, by her illness, and there was a queer, childish look about her sometimes. All the same, I can't believe that you haven't had your doubts. They've done their best, all of 'em, to throw dust in our eyes. They never fooled me, though. Don't you let 'em come it over you either, Captain Hood."

Hood struggled with the crowd of suspicions which suddenly beset him.

"It is impossible!" he exclaimed. "What on earth reason could a man in the position of Sir Powers Fiske have for such an outrageous tissue of falsehoods and misrepresentations? Besides, there is his mother, Lady Fiske. She would never lend herself to anything in the nature of a conspiracy. The very idea is absurd."

"Lady Fiske may have been deceived," Johnson said. "I have heard a few strange bits of gossip. They say that the young lady has lost her memory —can't remember anything about India, where she was supposed to come from, or any part of her past life."

Hood nodded. "That is true," he admitted.

"It's rot!" Johnson broke out. "She can't remember about India, because she never was there."

"You must not forget," Hood said, "that all this is a serious reflection upon the young lady."

"It's him that's responsible," Johnson asserted fiercely. "She's no way to blame. Captain Hood, you listen to me. You're a gentleman, and, of course, I ain't. You've got some sort of claim upon her; I haven't, and never could have. You may ask me—why do I worry about her? I can't answer you. It's damned foolishness, and I know it. But I'll never rest till I've found out what it all means. She's been ill-treated somehow, and by that villain Fiske. I don't care if he's a baronet twenty times over. I'll find him out. I'll expose him!"

A luminous moment came to Hood. He saw the

pathos, the futility of this man's suffering. He was a good-hearted fellow, and he forgot for a short space of time his own sorrows. He laid his hand upon the little shopman's shoulder kindly.

"Look here," he said, "take my advice and drop it. Go back to your situation, if they'll have you, and forget all about Miss Surtoes. You see after all it isn't your affair, is it? She was not even your friend."

Johnson shook his head.

"I know all that," he said mournfully. "I've tried hard to drop it. I can't! It's like the fever. I believe it's turned me a bit crazy. They all say so— Ada and the rest. I can't help it."

Hood shrugged his shoulders. What sort of argument could he use to a creature like this?

"I didn't come here to waste your time," Johnson continued. "I've got something to say to you!"

"About this matter?"

"Yes."

"Well, what is it?"

"I am going to prove that the young lady living with Lady Fiske is not Miss Hardinge."

"How are you going to do that?" Hood asked.

Johnson looked furtively round. A gleam of cunning was in his eyes.

"There's a friend of mine," he said, "has put me on to a private detective office, who have a branch at Calcutta. We've sent out there, and we've a photograph and full description of Miss Hardinge on the way to us now. It'll be here next week. When it comes, I shall hand it to you."

"I shall have nothing whatever to do with any

inquiry made through a detective office," Hood declared. "Besides, I cannot see—"

Johnson interrupted. He had sunk unbidden into a chair as though exhausted, but his eyes were strangely lit, and his cheeks flushed.

"Look here, sir," he protested; "there's nothing mean or underhand about this. Sir Powers Fiske has told you, and has published everywhere, that this young lady is Miss Hardinge, daughter of Colonel Hardinge, of Calcutta, and that she was saved from the wreck of the *Colombo*. I've made every inquiry, and no young lady was landed at Dover or picked up anywhere, except those whose names were given. Now listen here again. When this photograph and description arrives, it will prove beyond a doubt that the young lady living in Lady Fiske's house is not Miss Hardinge or any one like her. Now, you tell me the truth, sir. You've had your doubts, because you've admitted them. When Sir Powers Fiske's story is proved to be a lie, when it is certain that she is not Miss Hardinge, won't you begin to believe then that I am right? She is not Miss Hardinge! Who is she, then? Why, Eleanor Surtoes!"

Hood was thrown into a strange confusion of thought. His own barely smothered suspicions were alive again. All those bewildering similarities which from the first had been almost a torture to him, rushed into his mind. Yet what could be her share in such a deceit? How was it possible for her or any woman, however consummate an actress, to carry it through so perfectly? He recalled the many hours they had spent together. Never once had she uttered a syllable, or thrown a single glance which he could interpret as having the slightest bearing upon their common past. Yet—there were those corrections, given, however, with utter unconsciousness. Hood could see no light anywhere.

"You will let me bring you the photograph?" Johnson begged nervously.

Hood roused himself with an effort.

"Yes, you can do that," he said. "I make no promise to act upon it, but I will see the photograph, and hear what your correspondent has to say. By-the-by!"

"Yes, sir!"

Hood hesitated.

"Well," he said, "if I were making these inquiries about Miss Hardinge, I think that I should have appealed to her father."

"I wrote him a month ago," Johnson answered. "From what I can hear, however, it is doubtful whether he will ever get the letter. He has gone on a secret mission into China. I saw it in the papers. May I ask you a question, Captain Hood?"

"Certainly."

"You have seen Miss Surtoes lately?"

"I have seen—the young lady this morning," Hood answered.

"She is quite well, sir?"

"Quite."

"And happy?"

"She appears to be."

Johnson sighed.

"She ain't!" he declared, picking up his hat from the floor. "It's all outside show."

"I hope not," Hood said gravely.

Johnson moved towards the door.

"I saw her in the Park the other day," he said. "She was laughing with the rest of them—as gay as you please. But all of a sudden, when no one was looking, the smile flickered away from her face, and I saw her pale and drawn, looking everywhere about her, searching for something she feared—and yet was anxious to find. It wasn't the look of a happy woman, Captain Hood. Good-day, sir!"

14

CHAPTER XXVII

FROM his chair Hood looked gloomily out upon the throng of passers-by, rebelling alike against the sudden impulse which had prompted him to accede to Johnson's request, and the infatuation which had brought him to this particular spot at this particular hour. For it was a bright Sunday morning, and the Park was crowded. Everywhere was the music of soft feminine laughter, of rustling dresses and well-bred voices. On all sides people were greeting friends and saluting acquaintances, standing about in little groups talking over the follies of the past week, and the vanities of the week to come. Hood, who had enjoyed all this only a very short time ago, found himself now curiously out of touch with this gay, light-hearted flood of people. For him the whole world was changed. There was no longer any sunlight, any joy in this phantasmagoria of pleasure. The past week was fast becoming a nightmare to him. Always he was oppressed with the same memory—the shadow of it brooded over him, chilling all his thoughts, wrapping him in a cloak of ceaseless depression. He remembered his sudden declaration, the crowd of words hot from his heart, the eager hope with which he had taken his fate into his hands. Powers' warning had shaken him not a jot, he had believed wholly and loyally in Eleanor. How breathlessly he had waited for that faint soft-ness, the nameless change which he had hoped and

prayed that his words might awaken! Then her
eyes had met his—cold, bored, a little indifferent,
empty of all those things which he had longed so
passionately to see there. What a chill her words
had given him! How completely she seemed to
have destroyed all hope! She was heartless, miserably heartless! She had shown no remorse at his
disappointment, had given utterance to no single
word of sympathy. After all, it was best, he told
himself. He would have no excuse now for lingering,
for nursing the shadow of a hope. Then a woman
laughed softly, and he sprang to his feet.

"What a rueful face, Captain Hood! Do come
and tell us what is the matter with you."

He stammered a few barely comprehensible words.
She had come upon him so suddenly, was smiling at
him so graciously, that he was scarcely master of
himself. By her side stood Powers.

She motioned Hood to join them, and turned to
her companion.

"You, too," she said softly, "seem plunged in
melancholy. You are tired, I know, of this prom-
enading and meeting people. You are to go away
now, please, and Captain Hood will take care of me.
I mean it."

"On the contrary," he assured her, "I find it very
amusing. I am not in the least anxious to escape."

She leaned over towards him.

"Please to go away, Powers," she said, in an
undertone. "I want to speak to Captain Hood."

He hesitated. He would very much have preferred
remaining by her side, but in view of her dead halt
and imperious little gesture, he had no alternative.

"There are some people on the other side I want
to speak to," he said. "I daresay I shall come

across you again. In case I do not, remember that there are guests coming to luncheon, Eleanor."

She did not answer him, and he walked away with tightly-compressed lips and a dull pain at his heart. Hood found himself walking by her side. He was bewildered, but happy. What could she have to say to him? A wonderful nameless hope set his heart beating quickly. If she should have found that, after all, she had spoken hastily—that she cared—if only a little. It was amazing how sweet the spring air suddenly felt, how pleasant the sunshine and the gay chatter of the moving crowds of people. The witchery and joy of life were in his veins once more.

He stole a glance at her, and was puzzled. There was a curious abstraction in her face. Her eyes were moving restlessly down the line of chairs, thick with people. She remained silent. At last he spoke to her.

"It is very pleasant to see you again once more," he said, in a low tone. "I came here this morning just to catch a last glimpse of you. It was all I dared hope for."

"You are really going, then," she murmured, without looking at him.

Her tone was indifferent, her manner scarcely one even of civil interest. A great chilling doubt stole in upon him. He crushed it masterfully.

"Don't you think that it is better?" he asked. "If there were the slightest hope for me I would stay gladly. If there were any chance that you might care, ever so little even at first, I would send in my papers to-morrow."

A change in her at last; yet she remained a riddle to him. Her eyes were suddenly bright, a faint, curious smile parted her lips. She slackened her pace. He almost fancied that he caught a rapid, sidelong glance over her shoulder—the shoulder remote from him, and nearest the chairs.

"You do not answer me," he went on, after a moment's pause. "Yet you have something to say; you told Sir Powers so. He may come back directly, and this seems to be my last chance of speaking to you alone before I sail. Eleanor, I am a clumsy sort of fellow, I know, and I didn't say half I meant to the other day. But I want you to believe that I love you, dear. I'm not much of a catch, I know—especially for you, who might marry anybody. But I'm awfully fond of you, and we like the same sort of things, and I'm sure I could make you happy. Give me a chance, Eleanor."

She turned towards him, he fancied unwillingly. There was a restlessness in her manner which he did not recognize.

"I thought that we had quite disposed of that subject the other day," she said coldly. "I did not imagine that you would allude to it again. It is quite impossible."

He caught his breath. He was scarcely prepared for anything so crushing.

"Then I must go back—next week?" he said.

"You know best," she answered. "It seems a pity to give up your leave."

He set his teeth hard, and turned upon her with a flash of something like anger in his eyes.

"Why did you call me to you just now?" he demanded. "What did you want?"

She glanced towards him coolly. "I wanted to get rid of Powers."

Her utter indifference was no longer to be doubted.

He was for the moment speechless, and before he could recover himself he saw a marvellous change in her. She had stopped before the first line of chairs, and a man had risen up, hat in hand, to return her almost eager greeting. Pale, colorless, and with his curious, negative smile, Trowse showed no signs of pleasure at the meeting, nor did he at first seem inclined to desert his chair. He exchanged cold greetings with Hood, and a few remarks with Eleanor.

"You are coming to lunch at Berkeley Square, are you not?" she said. "Shall we walk there? It is nearly one o'clock, and it is such a delightful morning."

"I shall be charmed," he answered quietly.

She turned to Hood.

"If this is really to be good-by, Captain Hood," she said, holding out her hand, "I hope that you will have ever such a nice passage, and a very good time up at Simla! Good-by!"

He bowed over her fingers, and she smiled with a perfect complacency which sickened him. Then he vanished amongst the crowd, inexpressibly relieved to be at last free from his torture. His mind rushed back over the events of the past few minutes. Such heartlessness was surely incomprehensible. It was something hideous—wholly amazing. It seemed to him that he could never think of her again without anger, that those foolishly sweet recollections which had given such color and passion to his life during the last few weeks must forever afterwards be wiped out by the nauseous memory of this last interview. He laughed bitterly, and lit a cigarette.

"After all," he muttered to himself, "the surgeon's is a kindly knife. I believe that I am cured."

Near the entrance he met Powers, who stopped him.

"Where is Miss Hardinge?" he asked abruptly.

"She has met a—friend," Hood answered, "and is walking to Berkeley Square with him."

"Who was it?"

"Spencer Trowse!"

Powers' face darkened, and his eyes flashed with anger.

"I left her in your charge!" he exclaimed.

Hood laughed hardly.

"I was — as you were — dispensed with," he answered.

Powers was furious, but speechless. He would have passed on, but Hood stood in the way.

"Sir Powers," he said, "I want a word with you."

"Well?"

"It is about Miss Hardinge!"

"Still Miss Hardinge!" Powers repeated satirically.

"Let us say the young lady who passes by the name of Miss Hardinge," Hood answered.

Powers started almost imperceptibly. He mastered his anger at once with the necessity for self-control. His pale face once more resolved itself into impenetrability.

"Still harping upon that old folly!" he murmured.

"I am not the only one," Hood answered, "who has had, and has still, grave doubts as to the truth of your story. Now I do not wish to fight you in the dark. I am going to give you a word of warning. There is at this moment on the way from India an authorized photograph and description of Miss Hardinge, also, I believe, some one capable of identifying her."

"Is this your doing?" Powers asked, with wonderful calmness.

"No."

"Is it that mad little shopwalker?"

"Yes."

"And how far are you concerned in this—plot?"

"To this extent," Hood answered. "I have promised to wait in England for the result. You, of course, can guess why. If your marvellous story should turn out to be false—then you will have to deal with me."

"I am wondering," Powers said, "what business it is of yours?"

"Miss Surtoes was engaged to marry me," Hood answered, passing on. "Any wrong done to her it is my right to investigate. And you may be very sure that I shall do so."

Powers laughed lightly.

"I am afraid," he said, "that it is not only the little shopwalker who is mad."

CHAPTER XXVIII

"THIS," Lady Fiske said severely, "must be the end of it. You can scarcely fail to agree with me, Powers. Frankly, I find Eleanor intolerable."

Powers stood with his hands behind him, looking out into vacancy.

"She is very young, mother," he said, "and she is very thoughtless," he admitted. "Still—"

Lady Fiske interrupted him—a breach of decorum of which she was very seldom guilty.

"Pardon me, Powers. It is not her youth or her thoughtlessness to which I take exception—it is her whole disposition. She treats this household and every one connected with it as though we existed solely for her convenience. I have watched her carefully, and I have never seen her betray a single scrap of real feeling. She has not an atom of consideration. You know that the Duke came simply because he wished to meet her. Before she went out I told her that we had people coming to lunch, and I asked her particularly to be in early. What happens? She strolls in just as we had finished, with Dr. Trowse, of all men in the world. She did nothing to make amends. There were half-a-dozen people besides the Duke to be entertained, and a nod is all she vouchsafes to any of them. She must insist, if you please, upon sitting next to Dr. Trowse, although the places were arranged quite differently, and she isn't even decently civil to anybody else—

not even to you, Powers, as I could not help notic-
ing. It is flagrant and inexcusable selfishness—and
I have had enough of it."

"What can we do?" Powers asked, in a low tone.
"We cannot send her adrift."

Lady Fiske raised her eyebrows.

"We cannot do that! It is not necessary. You
must find that uncle of hers at once. If you do not,
I shall write to Colonel Hardinge. Frankly, Powers,
I am not inclined to extend any further hospitality
to Miss Hardinge than is absolutely necessary. It
was at your request that I received her, and I have
done all that I promised, and more. The limit of
my inclination and my patience has been reached.
I wish you to understand that Miss Hardinge is no
longer a welcome inmate of this house. You will, I
trust, spare me the necessity of intimating as much
to her."

Powers walked moodily to the window, and his
mother watched him with curious eyes. He was
haggard and pale; his manner during the last few
weeks had changed completely. He had become
nervous and irritable. There were lines under his
eyes as though he had slept badly.

"For the moment, at any rate," he said, in a low
tone, "she is under our care, and I must admit that
her—conduct—gives cause for some anxiety. You
do not imagine that she is seriously attracted by
Trowse?"

Lady Fiske frowned impatiently.

"I do not think that she is ever likely to be seriously attracted by any one," she answered coldly.
"She is too utterly self-engrossed to be capable of
such a thing as spontaneous and disinterested affection. She is fond of admiration, and the very fact

that Dr. Trowse is reported to be proof against the
attractions of her sex, as a rule, would be sufficient
to excite her interest."

Powers was silent. Lady Fiske leaned forward in
her chair.

"Powers," she said, "I suppose it has never occurred to you as possible that Eleanor might be—
an adventuress?"

"What on earth do you mean, mother?" he asked
quietly.

"You are sure that you remember her—as the
daughter of Colonel Hardinge?"

"I am certain," he answered. "Why do you
ask?"

Lady Fiske sighed.

"For several reasons," she answered. "You see
the manner of her coming was so unusual, and the
Press never corrected their first report of her death.
Then this loss of her memory is, to say the least of
it, extraordinary. For her to have been born and
lived all her life in India, and yet know nothing of
the country, is a constant puzzle to people."

"Anything else?" he asked.

"Only that old General Gilbert quite expected to
recognize her, and I could see that he was completely
puzzled. He watched her all the evening, and kept
muttering to himself."

"He is in his dotage," Powers declared. "I remember her perfectly, mother. There is no possible
shadow of doubt as to her identity."

Lady Fiske looked resigned.

"If you are satisfied, Powers," she said, "of course
there is nothing else to be done. Only I can assure
you that I am quite in earnest. My chaperonage of
Eleanor was to be for a short time only. I have

found it too long already—and Marian also is of my mind."

"I will see what can be done," Powers promised wearily.

Lady Fiske raised her glasses and looked for a moment at her son.

"What is the matter with you, Powers?"

"I have a headache," he answered shortly.

"You look as though you were suffering from something more lasting than a headache," his mother said quietly. "I am beginning to feel nervous about you."

"It is nothing," he declared impatiently. "I am a little run down. I must get away for a day or two."

She surveyed him thoughtfully. He showed signs of a rare irritation.

"Is there anything troubling you, Powers? Anything upon your mind?"

"No."

"Better tell me! I might be able to help."

"There is nothing," he declared. "What should there be?"

She sighed, and looked away. He opened his lips as though about to speak, but the words never came. There was an interruption—tragical, unexpected. Ringing through the house, through closed doors and curtained hallways, came a sudden awful and thrilling sound—the cry of a woman in mortal fear.

Powers sprang to the door and threw it open. Outside all was silent. There was no repetition of the cry. Then a fainter sound reached him—a low convulsive moaning as of some creature in pain. He crossed the hall, ran wildly down a long passage, and flung open the door of the little sitting-room which had been given to Eleanor for her own. With his foot upon the threshold, he paused for a second. He heard stealthy movements in the hall, the front door softly opened and shut. On the floor before him, white and motionless, Eleanor was lying.

Marian, who had heard the cry in the drawing-room, was there almost at the same moment. To-gether they loosened her clothing, and Powers bent over her anxiously. Then he carried her to a sofa and sat down beside her. He beckoned Marian to him, and whispered in her ear:

"Did you see any one in the hall?"

She shook her head.

"I was just too late. Some one went out. I heard the door open and shut."

"Your guests had all left?"

"Yes. Some time ago."

He laid his hand upon her shoulders. His words sounded like a command, his tone was an entreaty.

"Go and see whether the servants let any one out —if any one saw who it was."

She was gone for several minutes. Powers sat with Eleanor's hand in his, watching for her return to consciousness. Her fingers lay in his, cold and passive, her hair was in wild disorder, and her face was still deadly pale. He bent over the closed eyes, and a fierce, passionate desire crept into his heart. If only she might wake up as he had known her first. If only these terrible months of her second existence might be blotted out forever. He was content to have failed in his great experiment. He had no longer any ambition to add to the sum of human knowledge. The memory of Halkar and his patients had become a nightmare to him. Forever he would have been content to remain ignorant of those things which lay now so short a distance beyond. It was an unexpected lesson which he had learned, a strange fever which had wrought so marvellous a transformation in him. The old ideals were dead and buried, life itself had become centred around the girl who lay by his side now, white and inanimate. Life seemed suddenly so much more simple, an unimagined sweetness mocked him.

Marian came back into the room.

"There was unfortunately no one in the hall," she whispered. "Groves heard the door, and came upstairs at once, but he was too late to see who it was."

Powers nodded, but his lips were set in a firm, grim line. Together they sat by her side until at last, with a little shiver, she opened her eyes.

"Is that you, Marian?" she said weakly. "Where am I? What has happened?"

"That is what we want to know from you, Eleanor?" Marian answered. "We heard you call out, and we found you on the floor in a faint."

Eleanor looked for a moment puzzled.

"Let me see," she said half to herself. "I came here to get a book, and—ah!"

She broke off suddenly. Her eyes filled with a wild, scared light. She stretched out her hands.

"Don't! Don't!" she cried. "I can't look. I daren't!"

She was trembling all over. She seized Powers' arm, and clung to it tightly. He set his teeth, and bent more closely over her.

"Tell us what frightened you, Eleanor."

"I can't—remember," she muttered. "I came here, and perhaps I fell asleep. I don't know! The room was full of white light, and some one was looking at

me—I heard them speak, and they were forcing me
to look, and it was like death. What was it I saw?"

"Try and remember," he whispered.

"Some one was holding my wrist, and their fingers
burned like fire," she murmured. "There was the
sound of the sea in my ears—or a great wind. And
everywhere the blinding white light, and beyond!
O God!"

She commenced to cry like a little child, and
Marian comforted her.

"Don't ask her any more questions, Powers," she
whispered. "She'll be ill again."

"I must," he answered. "Don't interfere! Eleanor,
listen."

She looked at him with streaming eyes.

"Some one spoke to you?"

"Yes."

"Whose voice was it?"

She shuddered violently.

"I don't remember. It frightened me. It said
two words only—'Look! Speak!' And I looked,
and on the other side of the light I saw—I saw—"
Her head drooped, her eyes closed. "I saw—"

Her voice died away. She had fallen asleep.

CHAPTER XXIX

TROWSE rose from his chair, and deliberately laid on one side the book which he had been reading. He affected to ignore the fact that his visitor took no notice of his greeting or of his outstretched hand.

"Is anything the matter, Powers?" he asked, with faint satire. "You look worried."

Powers looked behind him. The door was closed, and the servant who had ushered him in had departed. He advanced farther into the room, and the eyes of the two men met—challenging, subtly inimical. There remained between them no memory of their past friendship.

"I have come," Powers said fiercely, "to have an explanation with you."

Trowse raised his eyebrows.

"Your present attitude," he remarked, "seems to require something of the sort."

"You were in the Park this morning! You met Miss Hardinge?"

"Certainly!"

"What the devil were you doing there?"

Trowse stared at him.

"If you are going to behave like a fool," he said, "I shall decline to have anything to say to you."

Powers choked down a momentary fit of passion.

"You were in the Park—contrary, I suppose you will admit, to your usual custom, and you walked home with Miss Hardinge to Berkeley Square, arriving half an hour late for luncheon. You took leave of my mother and sister at three o'clock. Did you leave the house then?"

"No!"

"Why not?"

"At Miss Hardinge's request, I went into her sitting-room. I really forget what it was she wanted to show me—a picture or a book—some trifle! You can doubtless understand that the opportunity of being alone with her was not to be resisted."

Powers ground his teeth. "How long did you stay there?"

"An hour—perhaps more."

"You left her in a faint upon the floor?"

"Unfortunately, yes," Trowse admitted. "I was afraid all the time that we might be disturbed, and I attempted too much. It was a mistake which I regret exceedingly. I trust that she has recovered?"

Powers was white with rage. The coolness of the other man was almost past bearing.

"It is well that you are honest," he said, his voice unsteady with passion. "It simplifies matters. Now listen. Eleanor Hardinge is in my charge. I forbid you to speak to her. I forbid you my house. I have warned you once before. Understand me now. I will have none of your interference. Have I spoken plainly enough?"

Trowse shrugged his shoulders. His tone was deprecatory.

"Be reasonable, Powers," he said. "You cannot carry this thing through alone. It is big enough for both of us. You can take all the credit if you will, if ever we should place the result upon record. But I want you to understand this : I will not be altogether ousted. You brought me into this thing, and I decline to be turned out."

15

"You are not serious. You do not dare to tell me that?"

"I am perfectly serious," Trowse continued. "I should prefer that we worked this thing together like sensible men—it was your first intention, I believe. In that case, I do not wish to take any advantage of you. The result, I am sure, will be far more satisfactory."

"Damn the result—and you!" Powers cried. "What I have said is plain enough surely. I will not have you come near her. If you repeat this afternoon's attempt I will shoot you like a dog."

Trowse considered for a moment.

"You remind me," he said softly, "of a homely fable. I wonder whether you realize your position —the power which you have lost through this extraordinary fit of sentimentality."

"What do you mean?" Powers asked hoarsely.

"I think that you know," Trowse answered. "It is quite clear to me. You have lost all controlling power over Miss Hardinge. Your will against hers has become as the will of a child's. For you it is a most unfortunate occurrence."

Powers was as white as death.

"I am content," he said. "It is no concern of yours."

Trowse surveyed his visitor for a moment critically.

"I wish I knew exactly what was the matter with you, Powers," he said. "You appear to me to be on the eve of a nervous collapse. I am not sure whether I ought to take you seriously."

It was a deliberate attempt at provocation. Powers knew it, and held himself in.

"If you fail to do so, Trowse," Powers said, "you

will have only yourself to blame for the conse-
quences. For as you and I are living men, I shall
keep my word."

"We will waive the matter for a moment," Trowse
said. "Bearing in mind my knowledge of the slight
—irregularities which have already occurred as regards the introduction into your household of the
young lady in question, it may perhaps be worth
your while to deal with me reasonably. I should
like to understand the true cause of your change of
attitude towards me."

"Go on!"

Trowse swung his eye-glass backwards and for-
wards pensively.

"You want me out of it. Good! Now, is it from
a fear lest I might try in some way to steal a march
upon you, might acquire knowledge, say, which I
declined to share with you, or is it the fruits of this
extraordinary sentimentality which I have observed
in you during the last few months?"

"You can call it what you like," Powers answered
desperately. "If you want the truth, here it is! I
am ashamed and afraid of what I have already done.
Morally, I am nothing less than a murderer."

"I cannot follow you," Trowse said, shaking his
head. "A moral murderer. It is juggling with
words."

"It is you," Powers declared, "who are wilfully
blind. Can't you see that I have destroyed an intelligence? It is not only memory which has gone.
There is something else."

"This is folly!" Trowse murmured. "You have
seen the same results arrived at with others. You
found nothing to shock you in their state."

"They were natives and people of a lower order,"

Powers answered. "I cannot make you understand. It is not worth while. Only believe this or not, as you choose. I would give years of my life to undo what I have done."

"You have, I believe, contracted an affection for Miss Hardinge," Trowse said coolly.

"As between you and me," Powers answered, "that is of no consequence."

Trowse smiled quietly.

"We have called ourselves friends," he said. "I shall speak to you as though we remained such. I myself, as you know, am a person of few affections. I am not greatly concerned in your happiness or your misery. But it seems to be my duty to remind you that the young lady in question is in a most extraordinary position. She is, in short, mentally deformed."

"I will not listen!" Powers cried sharply.

"You must!" Trowse continued. "You have in Miss Hardinge a young woman of purely sensuous instincts. Her own pleasure is her law. She is wholly unconscious of any pain she may inflict upon others—she has, I should imagine, no moral judgment. With her memory has passed away something which neither you nor I can define. I am too thorough a materialist to try—you may have your own theories, which do not interest me. But the fact remains that Miss Hardinge, for all her physical attractions, is hopelessly deficient in all those qualities which go to make a desirable—companion."

"She is what I made her!" Powers cried hoarsely. "Trowse, you don't understand. I couldn't make you understand. It's outside any one's comprehension. But I love her! I can't help it! I love her!"

There was a deep silence. The clock ticked; a piece of coal fell into the fire; a small dachshund rose from the mat and yawned. But both men avoided speech. Even Trowse, though such things were outside his life, was conscious of the dramatic possibilities of that despairing confession. It was he who broke the silence at last.

"You have my sympathy, if that is any use to you, Powers," he declared. "It seems to me to be a very terrible retribution for an attempt in which I consider you had every justification. Now, I am bound to ask you this. We know that this girl, notwithstanding her present state, still represents to us huge possibilities. I have studied this question since last we talked, and I am convinced that so long as the memory of her past life remains lost, so long is there a chance that a faint echo of some former existence can be forced into her mind, and may be wrung from her lips. Your hand, Powers, is upon the curtain which hangs before the greatest mystery which the universe knows. Are you going to raise that curtain?"

"I am not," Powers answered firmly. "I have learned my life's lesson. I am going to devote all my time and skill to restoring what we have robbed her of."

Trowse made no immediate answer. His face was emotionless—like a white, still mask. But in his eyes there was for a moment a glitter like steel touched by fire.

"We have wasted our time then, Powers," he said. "We have talked to no purpose. At least, there shall not be any misunderstanding between us. I make no promise. I go my own way, and I accept your threat."

Powers turned to leave the room.

"Trowse," he said, looking back, with his hand upon the door, "as I am a living man, those were no idle words of mine. Be wise—and remember them."

CHAPTER XXX

PHYSICALLY, Eleanor became at that time a puzzle both to Powers and to the physician whom he called in to attend upon her. From an almost animal perfection of health, she passed after her recovery from that prolonged fainting fit into a state of nervous prostration, the more remarkable from its contrast to her former robustness. She lost her color, her light gracefulness of movement, her brilliant gayety of manner. She moved about listlessly, with pallid cheeks, and always with a strange gleam in her eyes —of expectancy, mingled with apprehension. They gave her the usual tonics, took her to a river picnic, to Ranelagh, and to several dances, at all of which her admirers gathered once more around her. None of these things roused her. She yawned in the faces of the men who laid themselves out to entertain her, she found punting and polo equally without charm. Lady Fiske took her openly to task.

"My dear," she said, "you were very rude to Lord Winandermere this afternoon."

"He wearies me so," Eleanor admitted. "He says always the same things; he makes my head ache."

"You seemed to find him amusing enough until quite lately," Lady Fiske answered. "I do not understand such a sudden change. There is Captain Hood, too. You are positively not civil to him."

"They should leave me alone, then," Eleanor declared irritably. "They are both very tiresome. I should be glad not to see either of them again so long as I live."

Lady Fiske raised her glasses and surveyed her charge in cold amazement.

"I presume you know what you are saying, Eleanor," she remarked. "In that case, it scarcely seems worth while your going to the Punchestons to-morrow afternoon."

"It isn't worth while going anywhere," Eleanor replied wearily.

Lady Fiske went at once in search of her son.

"Powers," she said, "have you heard anything yet from Eleanor's uncle?"

"Not yet," he answered.

"Or her father?"

"No!"

"She has been with us longer than the time Colonel Hardinge mentioned in his letter."

Powers shrugged his shoulders. "We can scarcely turn her away," he said.

"Perhaps not," Lady Fiske answered. "On the other hand, it is best for you to understand this. I am going to Homburg on the first of next month, and I shall take Marian with me. It will be necessary, therefore, for you to make some other arrangements for Eleanor between now and then."

"I will do so," Powers promised.

"In the meantime," Lady Fiske continued, "I think it will be better for her to keep quite quiet. She is evidently not in the humor for society."

"Just as you please," Powers answered. "Only you must remember that she is out of health. Don't be too hard upon her, mother. She is really in a very nervous condition."

"I do not wish to be hard upon her," Lady Fiske said. "I do not think that I am. But it is only natural that I should find her apparent ingratitude and ungraciousness a little trying."

"You do not know everything," Powers said, in a low tone.

Lady Fiske eyed him keenly.

"I am beginning to believe, Powers," she said, "that there are many things in connection with Eleanor and her visit here which I do not understand. Is it too late to ask you to give me your confidence?"

He shook his head. "I am afraid—it is too late!" he said sorrowfully.

Lady Fiske looked at him, and her face softened.

"I believe, Powers," she said, "that you would never do anything which was not honorable. If you have been deceived in any way, or acted foolishly, tell me about it. I may be able to help you—even now."

"It is not possible, mother!"

She hesitated for a moment, then continued :

"You can perhaps understand, Powers, that my position is not wholly a pleasant one just now. I hate gossip, but there is no doubt that there have been curious rumors about concerning Eleanor."

"What sort of rumors?" he asked sharply.

"Concerning her identity."

"Rubbish!"

Lady Fiske moved towards the door, but came back again.

"Nevertheless, Powers, there are people in London who knew the Hardinges in India, and who utterly fail to recognize Eleanor."

"She has changed!" he declared. "I did not recognize her myself."

"Yet you are convinced?"

"Absolutely!" he answered, with a faint smile. "I am as sure of her identity as I am of my own."

Lady Fiske did not pursue the subject.

"As regards the next few weeks—" she began.

"I am going to take her to Brindells," he said. "She needs a change, and I have wired Hassell to get the place ready."

Lady Fiske was surprised.

"Will she go there? It is the dullest spot in England. She will be buried alive! A girl like Eleanor will mope her heart out there."

"I think that she will go," he answered.

"And you?"

"I shall go, too, of course."

She looked at him fixedly. "What does it mean, Powers?"

"Can't you see?" he exclaimed. "How blind you are, mother! I love her!"

"Powers!"

Lady Fiske collapsed into the nearest chair. This, then, was the explanation of it all, the one possibility which had never even entered into her head. She was too surprised for words. She sat and looked at him.

"I thought women saw those things so quickly, mother! In any case, I don't know why you should be so amazed. A good many other men have admired her."

"That is true," Lady Fiske said, in a low tone. "All the same, I should never have believed this save from your own lips."

"Why not?"

"I should not have imagined," Lady Fiske answered, "that you would have been attracted by a girl of Eleanor's disposition."

"You do not understand her as I do! She is not really so frivolous as she has seemed lately. Already there is a change."

"But—have you spoken to her?" Lady Fiske asked.

"Not yet!"

She hesitated.

"Do you know, Powers, the more I think of this, the more I am bewildered. Just lately you and she seemed somehow always—at cross-purposes. I should have said that you almost disliked one another."

He was silent, and Lady Fiske's eyes slowly filled with tears. For a man's suffering is not a pleasant thing to watch, and the man was her son.

"It was fancy, of course," she continued hastily. "If Eleanor once knows how you feel towards her, she is scarcely likely to think twice of such men as Captain Hood and Winandermere. You must show her a little more attention, Powers."

He smiled wearily.

"Dear mother," he said, "it is a relief to me to know that you have no serious objection."

"You will have this question as to her identity finally settled first, of course, Powers?"

"It shall be absolutely settled, and before very long," he promised her. "As for the rest—very likely Eleanor won't have me. I am older than most of these men, of course, and—"

"It was only a few minutes ago," Lady Fiske interrupted eagerly, "that I spoke to her about Hood and Winandermere, and she quite annoyed me

by saying that she hoped she might never see either
of them again. Of course, I can understand it now."

Powers looked away.

"There is something, or rather some one else,
whom I fear a good deal more than those young
men, mother," he said. "But never mind about
that now. I want you to let Marian come down to
Brindells with us. Can you spare her?"

"I must," Lady Fiske decided. "You cannot go
down without her."

"I have sent for Nurse Endicott," he said. "She
attended Eleanor before, you know, and I think
that she needs some one with her."

Lady Fiske rose to her feet.

"If Marian is willing," she said, "I will spare her.
And Powers—forgive me, but this has come so sud-
denly! You are quite sure—that you understand—
Eleanor, and your feelings towards her?"

"I understand, mother," he answered. "For the
present you must take my word for it. There is
another Eleanor whom as yet you do not know.
She will be your very dutiful and your very loving
daughter some day—if I am fortunate enough to—"

He stopped short. Eleanor stood in the doorway.
She came slowly into the room.

"I wanted to see you," she said to Powers.

He smiled, and placed a chair for her.

"Is it a cheque?" he asked, "or some more young
men to be sent about their business?"

"I want to know how it is that nothing has
been heard from my uncle," she said, "or my
father?"

There was a dead silence. In her face were traces
of a strange new nervousness. Her interlocked fingers were moving restlessly.

"It is so absurd—so horrible—to look back—and to remember nothing," she continued, with a little break in her voice. "I want to see some one who really belongs to me—my father or my uncle, or some one. Perhaps that would help me—to remember."

"Your father is in China, dear," Lady Fiske said, "and I am sure that Powers is trying his utmost to find your uncle. It must be horrid, of course, to remember such a very little way back, but you have been so very brave about it. You musn't give way all at once."

She turned to Powers. "Have you heard anything from my uncle yet?"

"Not yet."

"Then, if you please," she said, "I should like to go back to my father."

Lady Fiske moved to her side and laid her hand caressingly upon her shoulder.

"My dear," she said, "I am afraid that you would never be able to find your father. He is in China on a secret mission for the Government. That is why he cannot write or receive letters. You must be content with us for a little longer. We may hear from your uncle any day."

Eleanor looked steadily into Lady Fiske's face. "You speak more kindly to me now," she said.

Lady Fiske laughed reassuringly.

"You must bear with an old woman," she said, "if sometimes she gets a little short-tempered. Powers has been talking about taking you to a little place we have in Lincolnshire close to the sea. I wonder whether you would not like that?"

"If I could get away—a long distance away!" Eleanor exclaimed, with a sudden tremulous emotion. "If only I could!"

Powers went quietly over to her, and took one of her restless hands in his.

"Eleanor," he said, "we are going to take you away to Brindells to-morrow. There will be no one there but Marian and me. You shall be alone as much as you choose. No one shall come near you whom you do not care to see."

She looked at him almost wistfully.

"To-morrow!" she repeated.

CHAPTER XXXI

"HARK !"

It was the first sign of her awakening interest in life. Towards the end of dinner on the evening of their arrival Powers had thrown open the French windows and let in the deep music of the sea. She started to her feet with a strange little cry.

"The tide is coming in," Powers said. "You see the beach is just below the gardens."

She attempted no excuse, but stepped at once through the window and crossed the lawn. From there a winding path led through a small spinney of stunted pine trees down to the beach. She never paused until she stood upon the shingle, with her pale, rapt face turned seawards. Powers followed noiselessly, close behind. Almost to their feet, the long waves came thundering in, weird and ghost-like, with their white, foam-flecked tops in the gray twilight. She stood like a statue, her lips parted, her bosom rising and falling quickly under the black lace of her dinner-gown.

"Listen," she murmured, "it is the old cry, unending, everlasting. Where have I heard it before? Oh, tell me! tell me!"

"I cannot," he answered. "Would to God I could !"

There was the scream of the pebbles ground together, drawn back by the long retreating waves, and around a rock a few yards ahead they saw the white spray leap up into the air as the waves broke over it. From the headland a bright light flashed out across the North Sea. She looked towards him and shivered.

"Why have we come here?" she asked. "You had a reason! Tell me!"

"None whatever," he answered promptly, "except that it is the purest air in England, and we thought that it would be good for you. We need not stay unless you like. It is for you to say, Eleanor."

She paid no more attention to him. She stood with her face turned seawards listening—always listening. And still the tide came rolling in, and its muffled thunder throbbed in their ears. He went back to the house and fetched wraps. She let him adjust them without thanks or remark. Soon the gathering darkness blotted out everything except the faint phosphorescent light which gleamed on the tops of the breaking waves.

"Come," he said at last, touching her arm gently, "it is late, and we have left Marian alone. You have only to open your window, and all night long you can listen to the sea."

She did not move, but soon Marian came out and called to them. Then she suffered him to lead her slowly towards the house, pausing every now and then to listen. A faint moon was shining through a misty sky, and he caught a glimpse of her face, which startled him. It was as though she were listening to voices which he could not hear. There was the breath of another world about her.

She bade them good-night, and went to her room. But Powers, smoking a late pipe in the garden, saw the outline of her still face at the window, and in the morning, though he himself was an early riser, he found her standing bareheaded upon a sandy knoll, her skirts blowing about her, her face once more turned eagerly seaward. He went up to her doubtfully.

"Still listening?" he called out. "After all, it is the same cry always."

She shook her head, but she did not look at him.

"No," she answered, "the sea has many voices. It has a different message for everybody. Only it is not everybody who can understand."

He held out his hand. "Come down," he said. "Breakfast is ready."

She came obediently. He walked by her side through the tangled garden.

"You are looking better already," he declared.

"There is nothing the matter with me," she answered.

"Are you afraid of being dull here?" he asked. "You see we have no neighbors, and the village is a mile away."

She smiled curiously.

"There is never any dulness," she said, "where that is!"

He was prepared for changes in her, but this sudden transition from a materialism almost gross was staggering. It was only a few weeks ago that she had flatly declined to move a yard to see the river flooded by yellow moonlight, and had yawned in the middle of a nightingale's song in the woods at Chertsey. He had watched in vain for a single sign of feeling in her face. Now she was pale almost to the lips with emotion.

"I did not know," he said, "that you were so fond of the sea. I never heard you speak of it."

"I think," she said slowly, "that the memory
16

of it lay a long way back—amongst the forgotten things."

He nodded.

"It is the beginning," he said. "Other things will come too. They will help one another."

"I pray," she murmured, "that it may be so! Powers, did I know you well enough to remember you before the illness?"

"Yes," he answered. "We were friends before then."

She nodded thoughtfully.

"From the first," she said, "I have always thought so. Your voice and your face both seem familiar."

"When your memory comes back," he said, smiling, "I hope that you will do me justice."

"I feel that I shall," she murmured. "I feel that you have always been good to me."

Powers for a moment was absurdly happy. Her next question, however, chilled him.

"When is Dr. Trowse coming, Powers?"

"Who?"

"Dr. Trowse!"

It was the first time she had mentioned his name. Powers watched her keenly. She seemed to have no anxiety concerning his answer.

"Dr. Trowse is not coming here at all," he declared firmly. "I should not allow him to come near you."

Her face showed neither relief nor disappointment. Only she was looking landwards now, and her eyes were a trifle dilated.

"Eleanor! You do not want him?" he asked anxiously. "Tell me that you do not."

She did not answer. She was moving on now towards the house.

"Eleanor," he begged, "do be frank with me! You do not wish to have him back, or to see him again? I am sure that you cannot! It was he who made you ill."

Still she kept her face partly averted, looking along the white dusty road which stretched far away back across the moorland. When she spoke her voice seemed to come to him from a distance.

"What does it matter," she murmured, "whether I want him or not? He will come. I believe that he is on his way now. He will come, and . . . . he will help me to understand. He will rest his fingers here," she touched her forehead lightly, "and the cloud will roll away."

"Do you remember the last time you saw him?" he asked.

She shuddered from head to foot.

"Don't ask me! I can't bear to think!"

"And yet you speak of his coming as though it were a matter of course! It is folly. He shall not see you. I will not allow it."

She laughed in soft derision.

"He will come," she said, "and neither you nor I will be able to stop him."

"Let him," Powers answered fiercely. "He shall not speak to you. Already I have warned him."

Marian called out to them from above. Breakfast was ready. They were to come at once. Eleanor ran lightly up the steep path with a sudden revival of her old grace. Powers followed with darkening face.

CHAPTER XXXII

She passed across the dew-wet lawn, and lifting softly the latch of the wooden gate, stepped into the road. Behind, the long, low house lay sleeping, all around was that deep mysterious silence of the hour before dawn. She laughed softly to herself and turned seaward.

Presently she passed through an iron gate. Beyond was half a mile of creeks and swamps full now of the soft rippling tide. The rough road to the beach had become a silvery river, with white posts to mark its course. She stooped and dipped her burning hands in the cool, soft water. Then she climbed the grass dyke which curved its way down to the sea. There came to her as she walked a flavor of salt on the slowly moving breeze, and she threw back her head and smiled as though with the delight of it. Around her the full tide had made a vast inland sea of the marsh land and sandhills. It came rippling almost to her feet as the tide grew lower, and again as she climbed away from it the sweet breeze cooled her hot forehead, and beyond she caught a glimpse of the sea itself, cold and gray, with white-topped breakers and spray falling about the rocks like driven snow. For the moonlight was waning, and the dawn had as yet barely streaked the heavy mass of clouds which seemed to rise from seawards.

And as she walked she began to sing softly and to herself. The place was a wilderness—no living thing seemed astir. So there was no one to wonder at that strange chanting tune, or at the time-forgotten words. And as she sang the color brightened her cheeks, and the wakening breezes blew the hair about her face.

As she came towards the end of the dyke there clambered up on to it from the shoreward side the strange figure of a man. He was short, and dressed in shabby black clothes plentifully besprinkled with sand. His hair was unkempt and his beard weak and straggling—of recent growth. He stood there watching her coming with straining eyes. So, as she never checked her pace, they came presently face to face upon the dyke at a spot where neither could pass. She broke off in her song and looked down upon him.

"Who are you?" she said. "Why do you not let me pass?"

"You have forgotten me—Miss Hardinge," he answered wistfully. "I am Henry Johnson."

Her face darkened.

"You are one of my persecutors," she said coldly. "What are you doing here?"

Tears stood in his eyes.

"Oh, don't call me that, Miss Hardinge!" he begged. "I would not do anything to annoy you for the world. I knew you once, though you have forgotten me—and I cannot forget you—I cannot forget you," he echoed, with a little sob.

A great sea-bird, disturbed by their voices, rose from the ditch below with a flapping of wings, and drifted away seawards. He started so violently that he would have slipped down the steep dyke side but that she caught him.

"It is only a bird," she said. "If you had seen as

many of them as I have you would not heed them.
I have seen them in droves when their wings darkened the sky, and I have heard them calling to one
another down the north wind. Afterwards there
comes the storm, the hurrying black clouds, the cold
breeze, the distant thunder. My little man, where
have you lived all your life that you know nothing
of these things?"

"I was sent to Bearmain's when I was so young,"
he exclaimed apologetically. "I have been to Mar-
gate twice, but it was in the summer."

She laughed softly.

"Come and sit with me on the sandhill there," she
said, "and I will tell you about the sea."

He followed her like a dumb animal. Almost to
their feet the long waves made harsh music upon the
shingle. He pointed inland to where the bare outline of the house was dimly visible in the twilight.

"For three nights," he muttered, "I have watched
your light at the window there. I knew that you
slept ill, for the light burned till dawn."

"Where the sea is I cannot sleep," she murmured.
"All the while I hear it crying out for me. What
does it say to you, I wonder?"

He was puzzled.

"I am not like that," he said doubtfully. "I do
not listen."

She looked at him as one who hears words which
are past all comprehension.

"Poor little man," she said softly. "Listen,
have you never heard this when the north wind
blows?"

And again she sang to him that wonderful song—
and his eyes grew big with wonder. When her voice
died away he shook his head.

"No, I have never heard that," he said. "It is very beautiful. I have never heard the music, and I do not know what language it is."

She smiled.

"It is the song of Ulric the Dane," she told him. "Many a time he has sung it to me as we stood on the prow of his ship, and the spray broke over our heads and leaped high into the sunshine. He sang it to me when the cold sleet stung our cheeks, and the wind came rushing about us, and we heard no longer the swirl of the oars. He sang it to me in the darkness whilst we stole into the harbor, and below his men sharpened their swords and fitted their spearheads."

"Who was Ulric?" he asked wonderingly. "Was it some one you knew before you came to Bearmain's?"

"Ulric was my lover," she answered, with her faraway eyes sweeping the gray sea-line. "Every night when the tide comes in he calls to me, but I do not know where he is. I do not think that I shall ever see him any more."

"Tell me about him," he begged.

Her eyes shone.

"He was tall and strong like a god," she answered, "with yellow hair and beard, and wonderful blue eyes. No man save he could wield his sword, and in battle men gave way before him as the corn falls before the scythe. And because he loved me he brought me here with him from over the seas. I sat in the ship whilst he and his men fought on the land. Oh, it was a grand sight, little man. How the poor Britons fled like sheep, for they could not face Ulric and his men, even to save their homes. And at night when the villages were burning, back came my lover with skins and ornaments, corn and wine, and we were all happy together."

He edged a little away from her. He watched her still with fascinated eyes.

"Do you mean that you remember these things?" he asked. "You have read about them in a book."

"A book!" she exclaimed scornfully. "What need have I of books to tell me of these things?—I, to whom their happening was but as yesterday. Only then my name was Hildegarde, and now they call me Eleanor."

"But this all happened very long ago," he protested. "You are only twenty-five, you know. It isn't possible for you to remember."

She eyed him with tolerant scorn.

"You foolish little man!" she exclaimed. "You do not understand. The things which have happened to me since I was Eleanor I do not remember at all, but the days when I was Hildegarde, and Ulric was my lover, are as clear to me as moonlight. I could tell you many things of those days if you cared to listen—how Ulric slew his brother because he lifted his eyes to me, and how once we were both taken prisoners by the King of East Mercia, and Ulric burst his bonds, the strongest they could forge, and slew the guards one by one. It was just such a dawn as this when we came running to the sea-shore, and when we smelled the salt wind how we laughed in one another's faces for the joy of our freedom. Behind the Britons were staggering with fatigue—for Ulric ran like a god, and when I was weary he caught me up by the waist, and I lay upon his shoulder, and never troubled him. Or I could tell you how he slew his chief captain because one night he whispered in my ear."

"Thank you, I'd rather not," Johnson answered, edging a little farther still away. "Can't you tell me about something a little less bloodthirsty?"

She laughed gayly, and her face seemed to catch a gleam of the coming sunlight.

"What a poor weak creature you are!" she exclaimed compassionately. "You would have made a poor woman in those days. What should we have done with you, I wonder? Ulric would have tied you down underneath and bound your arms to the oars. That was his way with the men who had no stomach for fighting."

His head dropped forward upon his hands. His thin frame was shaken with sobs. She looked at him in wonder.

"What is the matter with you?" she exclaimed.

"I can't help it," he moaned. "So long I have waited to see you. Ada was right after all. It is madness. And yet I can't get away from it. I've hung about here day by day, night by night, just for a word—even a glance. What have those devils been doing to you? Why do you talk—as though you were a madwoman? Is it part of their accursed work?"

She looked at him, suddenly sobered. She was very pale.

"You do not think that I am mad?" she asked, in a hoarse whisper. "It isn't madness, is it? No! It can't be that."

"No," he echoed, "not that. But you talk strangely, you know. You have forgotten things which have only just happened, and you have been talking about things which must have happened hundreds of years ago as though they had been only yesterday."

"You have frightened me," she said slowly. "I must go back now. See, it is morning."

A gleam of silver rested upon the ocean, a lark rose up from a grassy patch behind and circled over their heads, singing blithely. She shook out her skirts and turned to leave him.

"Tell me," he cried, "is there nothing I can do for you?"

She paused. Her eyes were fixed upon the dusty inland road. She looked from it to the strange little figure by her side.

"Are you braver than you seem, little man?" she asked doubtfully.

"I will do anything you ask me," he answered eagerly.

"Along that road," she said, "will come a man of whom I am afraid. It may be to-day or to-morrow, or the next day—but he will come. He is tall and thin, with no hair on his face, and eyes like cold fires. He stoops as he walks, and he limps with his left foot."

"I shall know him," he declared. "Well?"

"If Ulric were here with me," she murmured, "I should say kill, for the man is my enemy. He touches me, and I am helpless; he looks at me, and I am his slave. If Ulric were here he would kill him for me."

He stood on the knoll by her side.

"Kiss me," he said, "and I will do even as Ulric would have done."

She stooped and kissed him on the lips. Then she passed away without further speech, walking swiftly inland, with long, graceful steps. He watched her until she disappeared, a strange, wistful little figure, uncouth and dishevelled though he was. The touch of her lips had fired his blood. Slowly he made his way towards the long, dusty road.

CHAPTER XXXIII

At breakfast Eleanor appeared pale and heavy-eyed. The excitement of the early morning had passed away. She spoke but little, and she changed her place so that her back was to the window. Powers watched her anxiously.

"I am going to take you for a long walk by the sea, Eleanor," he said. "There are some places along the coast I want to show you."

She shook her head. "I am tired!" she said.

He pointed out of the window to a flight of birds passing over the marshes.

"Wild duck!" he remarked. "Would you like to come out in the punt with me down the creek, and try to get a shot at them?"

She shuddered.

"If I saw you kill one," she said, "I should hate you. I would rather stay indoors to-day. I have a headache."

He shook his head.

"I am your doctor," he declared, "and I can't allow it. You must be out of doors all the time. You can have a chair and a book on the lawn, if you like."

She remained impassive.

"I would rather stay indoors," she persisted.

"Couldn't think of allowing it," he said, smiling. "There has been a tremendous tide, and the sea is beautiful this morning. I will read to you, if you like, or we will sit and listen to the larks."

She was silent, but when he left the room to get some cigarettes from the study she followed him.

"Powers," she said, closing the door behind her, "I want to ask you a question."

"Well?"

"Is there any fear of my going mad?"

He started violently.

"Certainly not!" he answered. "Why do you ask me such a question?"

"I know that I am not like other girls," she said wistfully. "I cannot remember my father, or my life in India, or the voyage. When I try to think about these things my head plays me such strange tricks. I cannot remember where I was, or what I was doing a year ago—but—"

"Go on, Eleanor! I want you to tell me exactly how you feel," he said encouragingly. "It will help me to put you right."

"But behind all that," she continued hesitatingly, "I seem to remember many strange things—things which must have happened a long, long time ago. They are not things I have been told about, or read of! I can remember them. They must have happened to me. Powers, it makes me afraid."

He had been filling a pipe, but his fingers became nerveless. He looked at her with ill-concealed excitement.

"The very fact that you can ask me such a question in such a manner is a proof that you are in no danger of anything of the sort," he assured her. "You are quite as sane as I am. And, Eleanor, you must really remember what I have told you before. You lost your memory through an accident. There have been many such cases before, and it is a thing which is always likely to happen. But it is never more than a temporary thing. If you will only keep yourself in good health, and lead a natural life, it is bound to come back again. Remember that the very worst thing in the world for you is that constant striving to remember. If you find your thoughts leading you in an unnatural direction, try and stifle them. Read as much as you can, come for long walks and tire yourself physically. You must get rid of that desire for solitude. Nothing is worse for you."

"It is the sea," she murmured, "which seems always to be reminding me of things."

"Shut your window at night," he advised her. "You are too fanciful."

She came a little closer to him. His heart beat fiercely. Her eyes sought his—the appeal of the weak to the strong. He crushed down his joy—yet it shone in his face, trembled in his tone.

"Powers!"

"Yes, dear."

"Shall I ever be like other girls?"

He took her hands in his. She yielded them readily, but they were cold as ice.

"I am perfectly sure of it," he declared. "I have been to the hospitals, and I have talked it over with all the cleverest physicians. There has never been a case of loss of memory yet which was permanent. You must trust in me and be patient."

She held his hands tightly as though wrung with a sudden emotion—an emotion which he realized was one of fear alone.

"Powers," she begged, "will you lock my door at night? Lock all the doors in the house."

He looked into her strained, upturned face. There was the germ of a new thought in his brain.

"You have been walking in your sleep!" he said.
"Tell me about it. You must tell me everything,
Eleanor, if I am to succeed."

"Not in my sleep," she answered, in a low tone,
"but at night, when everything is quiet, the sea
calls and calls, and I cannot rest. I woke suddenly
this morning at three o'clock, and I went out. Powers, as I walked and listened, the wind and the sea
came to me like old friends. I remembered many
strange things. I remembered people whose graves
the sea has stolen from the land ages ago. I was
back in those days myself, Powers. I sang their
songs, my heart beat with their joys. Then I met
that strange little man who calls me Miss Surtoes,
and who thinks that I was once in a shop with him."

"What, that little lunatic here?" he exclaimed
incredulously.

"Yes! And I could not help it, Powers," she continued, "but I talked to him of the old life, for the
taste of it was between my teeth, and the sense of
that wild glorious freedom was in my blood like
warm wine. So I spoke to him, Powers, and he cried
like a woman. He thought that I was mad."

Powers was silent. The grim irony of this thing
which had happened held him speechless. It had
come, then, after all—the Great Awakening. He
looked at her with a curiosity almost reverent. His
voice trembled.

"Tell me, too, of those days," he begged.

She shook her head impatiently.

"They came back to me then," she said, "in the
twilight, when the whole world slept, and only the
sea kept calling to me. Now they are blotted out.
I am afraid to think of them. I want to forget!
Powers, help me to forget."

He hesitated. For a moment his love was in the balance against that unconquerable thirst for knowledge which had seemed to him once the whole aim of life. It was maddening to think that to a half-crazed little draper's assistant had been vouchsafed that marvellous moment of self-revelation. He, too, must look, if only for a second, into that land beyond.

"Eleanor," he said thickly, "think for a moment. Tell me, too, what you remembered of those days. Sing me that song. You need not be afraid. It is no sign of madness this! Think!"

She burst into tears.

"I cannot," she declared. "It is all gone now. Powers, why do you ask me? It frightens me—these strange thoughts and feelings. They make me feel that I am not myself. I want you to help me escape from them."

She lifted her streaming eyes to his, stretched out her hands—the impulsive gesture of a child, and the desire of his life became suddenly a faint thing beside his great love for her. He drew her tenderly to him.

"You are right, dear!" he murmured. "Those are not healthy memories. Sweep them away! I will help you, and you must help yourself."

"Tell me how?" she begged earnestly.

"Try and fill your life with some one great absorbing thing," he said. "Try and find something so important to you that all your thoughts are engrossed—that you can think of nothing else."

"But how can I?" she murmured. "That is all so vague. Where am I to look for it?"

He tightened his grasp about her.

"Dear," he whispered, "you yourself have done this thing for me. You have emptied my mind of all other thoughts. You have made life seem only a little place which holds you and me, and no one else. Eleanor, you know that I love you. Give yourself to me, to guard and to keep. Nothing evil shall ever come near you. You are the first woman who has ever come into my life. You will be the last. I will keep you from all harm. I will help you stifle those evil memories. You shall be my wife, and I will teach you that love is the greatest and the sweetest thing in the world."

He held her from him and looked anxiously into her face. There was scant comfort there for him. His heart ached at the sight of her.

"When you talk like that," she murmured, "I feel that I must be different from all other people. You expect something from me which I know nothing about. I do not feel towards you in the least like you say you feel towards me. Why is it?"

"It will come!" he declared confidently. "I am sure of it. In the future it must come."

"But it is the present which terrifies me," she cried. "He said that I was mad. He looked at me as though he thought so. There must be something strange about me, Powers, besides just this loss of memory. I can feel that there is."

"He is mad himself," Powers declared angrily. "The little fool has no right to be hanging about here at all. You must take no notice of what he said. I will see that he leaves the place."

She moved towards the light, and Powers watched her wistfully. She was thinner than he had ever

17

known her, and of that wonderful fresh beauty which had taken London by storm there remained but few traces. Yet to him there came at that moment a wonderful impulse of passionate love. The wistfulness which shone in her eyes, the wasted cheeks, the pallor of her once beautiful complexion, seemed in a sense to have spiritualized her. The child whose frank sensuousness had horrified him seemed to have passed away. Once more she was the girl whom he had met on the wet pavement of the city, brave and womanly, although in desperate straits—the woman who, however unexpectedly, had first found her way to his heart. Never, even in those days when her beauty had been unrivalled, and her train of admirers a constant source of embarrassment, had she seemed to him more to be desired than at that moment.

He moved a few steps toward her.

"Eleanor," he said, "do not think that I expect too much from you. I know that I am not exactly the sort of man you might have looked for—as a husband. But I love you very dearly, and to-day I ask from you only the right to give you my name, so that I may protect you from all evil, whensoever it may come. For the rest I am content to wait. I will take you right away from here. I will show you the beautiful places of the world. You will soon forget all that has frightened you, all of the evil that has come into your life."

She looked at him, still colorless, but with some eagerness in her wan face.

"You cannot know what you are risking," she said. "I do not know myself. You would be disappointed in me. You have been very kind, but—when you speak as you have done about caring for me, you speak of things which I do not understand."

He took her hands, and held them tightly.

"I will be your guardian, dear. You will grant me that?"

"If you are content!" she murmured.

CHAPTER XXXIV

POWERS went straight to his sister.

"I have some news for you, Marian," he said.

She looked up from her writing-table quickly. It seemed to her that she had never seen him so greatly disturbed. His eyes were bright, there was a flush of vivid color in his pale cheeks. His manner, too, was less reposeful. A significant nervousness possessed him.

"News!" she echoed. "Well?"

"After all, you will be able to have your month at Homburg. In a few weeks' time Eleanor will no longer require a chaperon; I am going to marry her."

Marian's pen slipped through her fingers. There was a moment's breathless silence.

"You are not serious, Powers?"

"I can assure you that I am."

"You are going to marry her—you!"

"Yes."

"And she has consented?"

"Naturally."

Marian's amazement was complete. A hint of this nature from Lady Fiske she had laughed to scorn.

"But have you considered her obvious unsuitability for you?" she asked.

"In what way?"

She frowned at a question which could be nothing but an evasion.

"Difference in tastes, disposition, character," she answered shortly. "Eleanor is more than usually

superficial, even for a girl of her age and good looks.
She reads nothing; she relies for her amusement
solely upon the chances of the moment. You must
know this, Powers. You must feel yourself that she
is shallow."

He shook his head.

"She is nothing of the sort, Marian," he declared.
"You have not had a fair opportunity of judging
her. She was a little frivolous in London, I know,
but you can see for yourself how changed she is
now. Her success was a little unsettling, perhaps,
and she is very young."

"She is quieter here, certainly," Marian admitted,
"but she is not happy. Powers, I think that there
is something beneath all this. Will you not give
me your entire confidence?"

"I am more fond of Eleanor than you would
readily believe," he answered slowly.

"Perhaps. But at least you will not mind my
saying that I have never seen her behave towards
you as a girl might towards her possible husband.
I cannot believe that she has ever seriously regarded
you in that light."

"Why not?" he answered coldly. "The difference
in our ages is of no great moment."

"You have actually asked her?"

"Certainly."

"And she is willing?"

"Yes."

"May I speak to her about it?"

"If you like. Don't say too much. Remember
that she is in a nervous, overstrung state."

Marian looked her brother in the face.

"I should like to know exactly what is the matter
with her, Powers?" she asked quietly.

He hesitated.

"I don't see why I should not tell you, Marian," he said. "The accident to her brain, which for the time has destroyed her memory, left certain effects upon her nervous system which render her peculiarly sensitive to mesmeric or hypnotic influence. Trowse knew this, and attempted to use her as a subject that Sunday afternoon in London when we found her in a faint. It was a most ill-advised and inexcusable attempt, and she is still suffering from the shock."

"And do you think, Powers, under those circumstances, knowing all that you do know about her, that she is likely to make a suitable wife for you?"

"You talk like a child's primer," he declared roughly. " 'Knowing all that I know—a suitable wife.' My dear Marian, these things are of no account at all. I am not a boy, am I, to wear my heart upon my sleeve and boast of my love-sickness. You have never heard me say that I cared for a woman before. Believe me now, then, when I say that I love Eleanor. If you understand what that means, you will realize at once what folly it is to talk about suitability and stuff like that."

Marian was silent, and there came a knock at the door. Powers stepped through the French windows as Eleanor entered.

"I am going to see about a punt for some duck-shooting," he called to them. "Take care of Eleanor, Marian."

He disappeared. Marian looked up with a smile, which she tried to make as friendly as possible, to the girl who stood hesitating upon the threshold.

"Powers tells me to take care of you, Eleanor," she said, "but it seems that he has arranged to do that for himself in future. Come in, dear, and tell me about it."

Eleanor came in and took the chair which Marian had wheeled round for her. There was scarcely a gleam of interest in her cold, still face.

"Powers wishes it," she said slowly. "I do not suppose that it matters much."

Marian looked at her in frank bewilderment. This was a little more even than she had been prepared for.

"My dear girl!" she exclaimed, "what an extraordinary way to talk about your marriage!"

Eleanor looked at her with lack-lustre eyes.

"If you were as I am," she declared bitterly, "you would find it just as hard, perhaps, to be enthusiastic about anything."

A sudden wave of sympathy prompted Marian—an unemotional person herself—to hold out her hand, and immediately it was clasped in the other's icy-cold fingers. Marian moved her chair a little closer to the other girl.

"Powers is very good, and very kind," Eleanor said, "but why he wants to marry me I cannot understand. I am quite sure that he will be very disappointed."

"You do not care for him—at all, then?" Marian asked.

"I do not care for anybody," Eleanor answered, with a little sob. "I have told him so. I cannot! I don't understand why. I don't understand why I should be so different from all other girls. It is very miserable."

Marian smiled encouragingly.

"My dear girl!" she said, "you are only a little out of sorts. You will soon be yourself again.

Think how different you were in London. You found life pleasant enough then."

"I shall never be like that again," Eleanor said sadly. "You cannot imagine what it is like, Marian, to be like me—to have no background to your life. When I first came to you I scarcely noticed it. It did not trouble me in the least. It was because I had no thoughts which turned backwards. The days were pleasant; I amused myself, and that seemed enough. Then—shall I tell you? Do you care to hear?"

"Of course I do," Marian declared warmly. "Go on, dear."

"Then there came some one whose voice, whose very presence seemed to have an extraordinary effect upon me. If he could not awaken my memory, he awoke at least the desire to remember. There were times, there are times even now, Marian, when it becomes a torture. Something seems beating about inside my head, and from the other side of the wall there are voices. I hear them, and I seem to recognize them, and yet—all the while—I know that they are phantoms. They belong to some other persons, some other world. I try to realize them, and they fade away."

"Dr. Trowse is that some one?"

"Yes. It was he who made me hear them first. He made me look, and he made me listen, and it seemed to me that I was passing into another world. Then—I suppose I was not strong enough. You remember it was that Sunday afternoon. He made me take him into my sitting-room, and he asked me strange questions, and somehow I found myself answering them as though with my own voice, but from the knowledge of some other person. Before this, I wondered what it was that attracted me to him. When he came near all my will went. I believe that he could restore my memory. But I am afraid —hideously afraid."

Marian was looking very grave.

"Eleanor," she said, "you must not think me unkind, but do you think that you ought to marry my brother when there is another man who has such an influence over you?"

"I do not want to marry Powers," Eleanor said slowly. "It is his wish, not mine. I cannot think that it would make him happy, and it would make no difference to me."

"Have you told him how you feel about Dr. Trowse?"

"He knows," Eleanor said simply.

"Yet he wants to marry you at once," Marian said. "I wish I could understand what it all means."

Eleanor smiled vaguely.

"You must not blame me," she said. "I would rather that he did not want to marry me at all. He is so much in earnest about it, though, and with me there is always a sort of feeling that nothing matters. I have no will to set against his. Then, too, he promised to take me a long distance away. The thought of that is restful."

"This is the strangest engagement I ever heard of," Marian exclaimed. "Do you feel that some time in the future you could care for Powers?"

Eleanor shook her head.

"I cannot tell," she answered. "I do not think that I have the power of loving anybody."

"You did not care for Captain Hood or Winandermere?"

"Not in the least. Cannot you see that I am not like other girls?" Eleanor said bitterly. "It isn't my fault. I want to be. There is something which you all have—and I have not. I do not know what it is, but I feel the want of it. It is as though I were living always upon the surface."

"Can you tell me this?" Marian asked. "Supposing you were left entirely to yourself—how and where would you like best to live? Would you rather go back to London?"

Eleanor shook her head. Her deep-set eyes had turned towards the window. Her head was bent a little forward, and a far-away look had stolen into her face—she seemed to be listening to voices whose message was for her ears alone. Marian had a curious feeling that she was in touch for a moment with that mysterious part of the girl's being, always elusive—that part which sent shadows from the unknown land.

"I think that I should like to stay here," she said slowly. "Do you hear that?"

She drew nearer to the window. The faint music of the sea, with its muffled undertones, stole into the room.

"You hear it," she murmured. "To you it is just the sea, to me, ah, it is something far more wonderful. There are voices there which you cannot hear—calling—always calling. I listen, and some day I believe that the black wall will crumble away. It seems to me that I was born with that music in my ears. It comes back to me, Marian. It comes back to me."

There was a moment's silence. A dark shadow passed across the window, and Powers stepped in.

"Well," he said cheerfully, "who is coming out?
You girls have finished your talk."

Eleanor glided away. Marian looked up at him
gravely.

"Yes," she said. "We have been here ever since
you left."

"Well?"

"Powers," she said, "if I were you I would give it
up."

The slight color which the rapid walking had
brought into his cheeks faded away. He regarded
her coldly.

"What do you mean, Marian?"

"I mean that if you marry her I do not think
that you will either of you be happy," she said. "I
do not think that Eleanor is in a fit state to decide
for herself upon anything of the sort. You know her
condition quite well. You know that what I say is
true."

"I know nothing of the sort," he answered, almost
roughly. "She is alone and unprotected. She needs
some one to look after her, if ever anybody in this
world did—and she needs some one who understands
her peculiar condition."

"But she does not love you, Powers."

"It will come," he answered.

Marian shook her head.

"There are many things about Eleanor and her condition, Powers," she said, "which I cannot pretend
to understand. But I cannot think that it is right
or wise of you to marry her when there is another
man whose influence over her is over-mastering."

Powers seemed to answer quietly enough, but the
words came through his set teeth, and his eyes were
lit with silent anger.

"It is from Trowse that I would protect her. He cannot leave England. I shall take her for a long sea voyage."

She shook her head slowly.

"I think that you are very foolish, Powers," she said firmly. "It seems strange to be reminding you of such things, but there is, after all, something due to your forebears. Our family is one of the oldest in the kingdom, and your baronetcy could be exchanged for a peerage at any time you chose. I tell you frankly that I think you are doing a very foolish thing. The girl does not love you. She is not in a condition to make you a suitable wife."

His anger was no longer silent, his eyes blazed, his voice shook with passion.

"You do not understand!" he cried. "How should you? If I were a fairy prince, and she were the most wretched beggar who ever tramped the earth, I might yet marry her and make insufficient amends. For what she is I made her. Her sufferings are a heritage of misery to me."

"Powers, you are mad!"

"Mad, am I? Ask Trowse. He knows. She is the miserable victim of our smatterings of science."

"It was no accident, then?" Marian cried, a sudden light breaking in upon her.

"Accident! No! It was my cursed bungling."

"Then who is she? Those people were right. She is not Eleanor Hardinge."

Powers hesitated. He had gone farther than he had meant, too far for any further concealment.

"Yes, they were right. She is Eleanor Surtoes. What does it matter who she is?"

"You have deceived us—both of you."

"I have—and Trowse. No one else. She believes

still that she is Eleanor Hardinge. Don't undeceive her, Marian. It might do harm. Listen!"

There were footsteps in the hall—a knock at the door. The trim maid-servant announced visitors.

"Captain Hood, Mr. John Hardinge, and Mr. Johnson."

They entered the room together.

CHAPTER XXXV

HOOD entered belligerent. He bowed coldly to Marian, who, in obedience to a gesture from Powers, left the room. But when he faced Powers he stood with his hands behind his back, and his fair, honest face was grim with anger.

"Sir Powers Fiske," he said, "I have a few words to say to you. This is Mr. John Hardinge, brother of Colonel Hardinge, of Calcutta."

The two men exchanged frigid bows.

"You have under your roof a young lady who is living here under a false name."

"It is possible," Powers answered coolly. "I should like to know whose business it is—save hers and mine. If she is not Eleanor Hardinge, daughter of Colonel Hardinge, late of the Bengal Lancers, well and good. To borrow an identity—supposing she has done so—is not a punishable offence. You can call her what you like. I have no objection."

"She is Eleanor Surtoes, and my betrothed wife," Captain Hood said doggedly.

"What of it?" Powers demanded. "She herself denies it—and she should know. She is under no restraint here. My sister is her chaperon. She is of age, and her own mistress."

Hood interposed.

"Look here," he said. "Here is the point. The young lady's name is Eleanor Surtoes. She came to your flat one night from Bearmain's shop, and was apparently taken ill there. On her recovery she is

introduced into your household and to society as
Miss Hardinge. I can prove that she is Eleanor
Surtoes. What we want is an explanation."

"I have no explanation whatever to give you,"
Powers answered firmly. "I do not recognize your
right to come here, and I beg you to leave at once.
You can take whatever steps you like."

"So far as I am concerned," Mr. Hardinge said
gravely, "my interest in this matter is purely acci-
dental. The young lady whom I have just seen
outside is not my niece, nor is she in the least like
her. I could have wished, sir," he added severely,
"that you could have invented some other identity
for your—young friend; but beyond taking steps, as
I shall do for my brother's satisfaction, to prove
that Eleanor Hardinge was drowned in the *Colombo*,
and that this young person has no connection with
my family, I have no further concern in this most
unpleasant affair."

Powers turned towards his other visitor.

"Mr. Hardinge," he said, "has adopted a sensible
view of the matter. Later on I may be able to offer
him some explanation of the origin of this unfortunate—mistake. I am perfectly willing for him to
adopt the course he suggests. Now, is there anything else you wish to say?"

"Not to you," Hood answered. "I must speak to
Miss Surtoes before I leave the house."

"You have spoken to her about this phantasm of
yours so often," Powers said impatiently. "Surely
her manner has conveyed to you by this time that
she does not desire to be worried any more."

The slight irritation in Powers' tone determined
Hood.

"I shall not drop this matter, or leave this neighborhood," he said firmly, "until I have had another interview with Miss Surtoes."

Powers shrugged his shoulders.

"Supposing that she is willing to see you," he said, "will you promise to accept her decision as final?"

"I am leaving for India in a fortnight," Hood answered. "I shall not trouble you again in any case."

Powers rang the bell and sent a message to Eleanor. In a few moments she appeared.

"There is an old friend of yours here, Eleanor," Powers said, "who declines to go away without see-ing you."

She shook hands with Hood, and looked at him inquiringly.

"I thought that you had gone back to India, Captain Hood," she remarked listlessly.

"I am going in a few days," he answered. "Eleanor, we know everything. I cannot leave without a definite explanation with you."

"What do you mean?" she asked coldly. "You have no right to talk to me like that."

"I have the right which belongs to the man whom you promised to marry," he answered. "You de-ceived me very cleverly and very wonderfully once. I know you now, Eleanor Surtoes. I am as sure of you as of my own identity."

She looked at Powers with a puzzled frown.

"Can you tell me what it all means?" she asked.

"I believe that Captain Hood is mistaking you for another young lady," he said coolly. "I have promised that you shall listen to him."

She sighed, and leaned back in her chair.

"Very well, then. Go on," she said.

He bent over her.

"Eleanor," he said, "I am determined that you should know this. I never received the letter which you wrote to me from your home in Yorkshire until a month before I left India."

She sat up again and looked at him with wide-open eyes.

"You must be mad," she declared. "I have never written you a letter in my life, nor have I ever been in Yorkshire."

He bit his lip and flinched before her steady, inquiring gaze.

"I can well understand, Eleanor," he continued, "that my silence must have seemed very cruel to you. The fault was not mine. I wrote to you by every mail after hearing of your father's losses, and your own misfortunes. I applied at once for leave, and I have come home to ask you to redeem your promise, and return with me as my wife."

"It is absurd!" she answered scornfully. "I never promised to marry you. I never had the least intention of doing so. You were an amusing companion for a short time in London, although you bored me now and then with your strange talk about some wonderful likeness. You asked me to marry you, and I declined. I am quite sure that I never encouraged you in the slightest. I never regarded you as a possible husband."

A light flashed in his eyes strange to both of them.

"You adhere to that statement?" he asked. "Of your own free will you tell me that we were not engaged in Yorkshire; that we met for the first time at Lady Fiske's house in Berkeley Square?"

"Certainly I do!"

18

He opened his locket and held it out to her.

"That, I suppose, is not your picture?"

She looked at it at first carelessly—afterwards with a vague trouble in her eyes.

"Where did you get that?" she asked.

"There is the photographer's name," he answered. "Brown & Sons, of York. You gave it to me yourself on the night I left England."

She looked suddenly at Powers. His face was inscrutable. She sat for a moment as though thinking.

"It is like me," she said quietly. "I can say no more."

Her tone grew softer. The sense of trouble lingered in her eyes. He leaned over her, and his face was stern no longer.

"Eleanor, let us make an end of this," he begged. "If there is anything to be explained between us, let us have it out. Don't keep up this deception any longer. You owe me at least the truth, and I will have it. Remember that I am not pleading my own cause any longer. I will accept my dismissal. Everything is over between us. Only do not ask me to go back to India without having this mystery explained to me. I want to be certain that your actions are uncontrolled, that no one is exercising any evil influence over you."

She half closed her eyes. Powers alone realized that her composure was severely taxed. A great fear was keeping him silent.

"Once and for all," she said slowly, "you are mistaken. You must be mistaken. I am not Eleanor Surtoes. I am Eleanor Hardinge. I came from India on the *Colombo*, and was saved from the wreck by some fishermen. That is true, is it not,

Powers?" she asked suddenly, turning toward him.

"It is true," he answered calmly.

"It is false!" Hood cried fiercely. "Here is John Hardinge, brother of Colonel Hardinge, and he declares that you are neither his niece nor in the least like her. Here is the photograph of Eleanor Surtoes"—he dashed it upon the table before him. "Eleanor, what has come to you? Why do you lie to me like this? You are Eleanor Surtoes. I would stake my life upon it. With my last breath I would swear to it."

Johnson, unseen before, sprang up from his corner, his shrill voice tremulous with excitement.

"I, too! I, too, will swear it; in Heaven or Hell I will swear it. You are Eleanor Surtoes, and I checked your bills day by day at Bearmain's, and took you and Ada to the theatre only a few nights before you ran away. It's that devil over there who's put it into your mind to try and deceive us all," he cried passionately. "Curse him!"

Eleanor half rose, and tottered back. She was white to the lips.

"Powers," she said, "send them away. I must talk to you alone. Go away, all of you."

Then Powers knew that a crisis had come, and if a wish could have killed Hood he would have been a dead man. He opened the door and pointed to a room opposite.

"Go in there," he ordered, in a fierce whisper. "You shall have your explanation presently."

He closed and locked the door after them; then he returned to Eleanor. Her face was buried in her hands. She was sobbing convulsively.

CHAPTER XXXVI

IT seemed to him as she sat there, with tear-stained face and quivering lips, that it was indeed the weary shop-girl of the Edgware Road who was with him once more. There was a light in her eyes as of some new understanding.

"Listen," she said slowly. "You must tell me the truth now. Who am I?"

"You are Eleanor Surtoes," he answered. "You lived in Yorkshire, and I have no doubt you were engaged to Captain Hood. You came to me from Bearmain's, the drapers, in the Edgware Road."

She drew a little breath through her teeth.

"This time," she said, "the truth! The truth, mind!"

He assented gravely.

"I first met you," he said, "by accident when you were employed at Bearmain's. You had no relatives or any friends. You had been brought up in luxury and amongst gentlepeople. Your father lost all his money, died, and you were penniless. Bearmain's was your last resource. When I met you you were utterly miserable. . . . You went out with me once or twice. To some extent I was your confidant. Once you said this to me: that for one year of full, untrammelled life—life at its best—you would give all the rest of your days—you would gladly risk death. It was to me you said that, Eleanor, and it set me thinking."

"This is truth?"

"God's truth, Eleanor."

"It is the black wall," she moaned. "It is always there."

"I was just back from India," he continued, "fresh from the strange teachings of an old Indian professor. He had shown me how in certain cases of great mental shock or acute unhappiness it was possible to restore health by the destruction of memory."

She cried out, holding her hands before her. Her face was white with horror.

"It was your work!"

"It was my work," he echoed, with faltering voice. "I proposed it to you. I told you of the risks; I offered you the life you desired if all went well. You deliberately accepted. But I took no account of temperament. The cases which I had been shown were all successful. I knew nothing of complications. I did not dream that it would change you so."

"It was your work!"

"Eleanor," he cried, "be fair to me. I showed you all the risks; you yourself were in the depths of despair—you hinted even at suicide. And am I not punished? I am like the man who slew the thing he loved. If only I had realized before. Dear, you must trust in me still. I will give my life to undo this evil thing. At least, I swear this. If I cannot break down that black wall I will fill your present and your future with happiness. We will travel, and you will get stronger. I can give you health, Eleanor, if only you will trust in me."

She roused herself as though from an apathy.

"Why was I called by a name which was not my own?" she asked.

"I will explain. My bargain with you was that

you should be found a place in life where the best
of all things should be open to you. I could only
keep my word by having you socially recognized.
It happened that on the day you came to me I
received a letter from Colonel Hardinge, committing
his daughter to my care, and almost immediately
afterwards I heard of the shipwreck, and that she
was drowned. I knew that he had no friends in
England, and that he would never return here. My
mother was, of course, prepared to receive Eleanor
Hardinge, so I decided to risk it. I never dreamed
of your becoming such a figure in society, or I
should never have ventured it. You see, it was
my only chance of really keeping my word to
you."

"Did Dr. Trowse—know of this?" she asked slowly.

"Yes."

"You have quarrelled with him?"

"I have."

"Why?"

"Perhaps it is better, Eleanor, that you should
know. In your weak state of health, and on account
of certain brain disturbances, you are an excellent
subject for—further experiments."

"Oh, how can you!" she cried.

He caught her hands tightly.

"Dear, never believe it of me for a moment," he
said passionately. "It is Trowse who is anxious to
make them. I have told him if he dares even to
come near you with such an intention I will shoot
him without mercy. Have no fear, Eleanor. I go
about armed, and Trowse knows that I am in
earnest. He is not the man to risk his life."

"I am afraid of him—oh, I am afraid!" she whispered brokenly. "He will come here, Powers; he

will find me alone. He will call to me, and I shall have to go."

"I will not leave your side," he declared, "until you are my wife; and after then you will be as safe as though he were dead. Eleanor, I have told you all the truth. Remember how I have suffered. Dear, as my love for you has grown day by day, and I have watched—and realized what I have done, it has been like a knife in my heart. You will forgive me, Eleanor?"

"Yes," she said slowly. "I must forgive you. It was a bargain, and you have kept your part. But, Powers, I have no pleasure in living. All day long my head aches; there are strange sounds in my ears. I seem scarcely able to recognize myself from hour to hour. Let me die, Powers. You could do it without risk."

He threw himself on his knees before her. The words had left her lips so coldly—she spoke as one whom suffering or dejection has robbed of all fear.

"Eleanor," he cried, "do you want to send me mad? Don't you know that I love you? I couldn't live without you, Eleanor! My love!"

He covered her face with kisses, but his passion wore itself out before the marble-like coldness which neither rejected nor encouraged him. He rose slowly to his feet. He was chilled and miserable.

"You will try not to think of this any more, Eleanor?" he pleaded.

"I will try," she promised.

He made an effort at cheerfulness.

"Come," he said, "we must remember those people in the other room."

Eleanor rose to her feet.

"You have been very cruel," she said, a dull note

of irritation in her tone. "All this time I have been trying to build up for myself a past. Now you have destroyed it. . . . What are you going to say to them?"

"You are sure that you do not want to marry Captain Hood?" he asked, looking at her with an anxious smile.

"I am quite sure that I do not," she answered.

"I will get rid of them quietly," he said, "if you will promise not to interfere or contradict me."

She assented. He opened the door and called to them.

"Captain Hood," he said, "and you, Mr. Johnson, you have both of you exercised yourselves considerably as to the identity and welfare of this young lady—my ward! Whether her name be Surtoes or Hardinge is no longer a matter of any moment. In a very short time she will have changed it, for she has promised to become my wife."

She was suddenly the cynosure of all eyes. Her face remained unmoved, colorless, weary. Powers, who was watching her closely, found something chilling in her composure. To Hood it was unnatural. He turned at once towards her.

"Is it true?" he asked.

"Yes, it is true!"

Hood hesitated. The situation was now beset with complications.

"This—engagement is of your own free will?" he asked. "You have not been forced or coerced into it?"

"It is of my own free will," she answered. "I have not been forced into it."

Hood's face hardened. He stood before her doggedly.

"I have come from India," he said, "with but one object—to find you, and to take you back with me. I am to understand that you wish to forget or deny —our past. You intend to marry Sir Powers Fiske."

"I intend to marry Sir Powers Fiske—certainly," she repeated. "I do not understand half of what you say, and I wish you would go away."

Hood glanced towards his companions.

"There is nothing left for us to do but go," he said. "Eleanor, at least let me tell you this. If ever I had a single moment's doubt as to your identity, it is now. The Eleanor whom I knew and loved was something better than a heartless jilt. You are she, sure enough, but none the less you are a changed woman."

The shadow of a smile flickered upon her lips.

"That is quite true," she said. "I am a changed woman."

Hood turned to Powers.

"Sir Powers," he said, "I shall remain in England until your marriage is announced. You have deceived me from the first. I don't know why, and I am no longer curious. I shall interfere in this matter no longer, provided that your marriage to Miss Surtoes takes place. Come, Johnson."

But Johnson had for the first time approached Eleanor. He stood looking at her, the dumb fidelity of a dog in his common little face.

"If only you would say just once that you remembered me, Miss Surtoes—Henry Johnson, you know. You always brought me your bills to check before any of the others."

She looked at him fixedly.

"I do remember you," she said slowly. "You are the little man who is going to—"

She paused, and for a moment he was puzzled. Then a smile broke across his face.

"Quite right, Miss Surtoes, quite right!" he exclaimed, shaking his head vigorously. "I shall attend to it. Never fear. I shall see to it. That's all right."

Hood took him by the arm. The visitation was over. Powers drew a long sigh of relief.

"What did that little man mean, Eleanor?" he asked.

She laughed.

"Can you tell me what any of them mean?" she answered. "They are all mad."

CHAPTER XXXVII

"Powers!"

He sprang up. He had scarcely expected to see anything more of Eleanor that day; yet there she stood in the open window dressed for walking—her deep brown hair pinned down beneath a tam-o'-shanter, her morning gown changed for a tailor skirt and coat. Even in his first rapid glance he saw a wonderful change in her appearance. Her cheeks were flushed, and her eyes bright. Once more she carried herself with the old lightsome grace. She called to him gayly,

"Come for a walk, Powers! I am going to take you somewhere."

He caught up his stick and hat, and followed her down the garden path. Then he saw that the color in her cheeks was not wholly natural. She was nervous and excited. At the gate he paused.

"Why not inland, Eleanor?" he suggested. "Let us go to Turton Woods."

She seemed scarcely to have heard him. Already she was well on her way shorewards. He caught her up in a few strides. The tide had gone down, and they walked dry-footed along the road. To their right was the marsh-land, with its long creeks, sinuous belts of silver, and its pools ebbing slowly away. Above their heads the larks were singing, and in their faces the freshening sea wind blew.

"You were right, Eleanor," he exclaimed. "There is no other walk but this. It is magnificent."

She ignored his speech. Her head was thrown back, her lips were parted. She drank in the breeze as though it were wine.

"This is the wind which Ulric and his men always loved," she murmured. "A wind from the north to the shore. Can't you feel the sting of the Iceland Snows?"

"Not I!" he answered, laughing. "To me it is soft and warm enough. But then, you know, I have no imagination."

They had reached the shore, but she turned sharp to the left along a low range of sandhills, faintly green with sprouting grass.

"Does this lead to any place in particular?" he asked. "If not, let us sit down. I am lazy."

"It leads to Rayston Church," she answered. "We are going there."

He looked at her in quick surprise.

"How did you know that?" he asked. "I have heard of a place called Rayston, but there is no church there."

She laughed softly.

"I will show you where it stood, then," she answered. "I will show you, too, what sort of man Ulric was. It was the last of our raids. We had twelve ships, and nearly five hundred men, and everywhere the people fled without fighting, for no one could stand against Ulric and his men. For once I, too, was allowed to land, for we knew that our coming was unexpected, and there was no fear of defeat. Village by village they plundered, and sacked, and burned. Never had the spoil been greater. Night by night we made great fires, by which the ships followed us along the coast, and I sang to them till the embers burned low."

He clasped her fingers in his. They were hot and feverish.

"Shall we turn now, dear?" he said. "We have walked far enough in this sun. You shall tell me more of Ulric another day. I want to ask you about our cruise. You know that I am in treaty for a yacht."

She stopped short with a little cry, and pointed inland. To their left was a ploughed field, and in the top corner were three grass and ivy-covered stone walls of immense thickness.

"See," she cried, "there stood Rayston Church! When we came here an old man met us waving a green bough. He told Ulric that all the folk had fled, and that their dwellings might be spared they had collected all their treasures and belongings and stored them in the church. Ulric believed him, and they hastened to the church, all shouting and singing together for joy of such an easy victory. But when they were within a dozen yards of the building there came suddenly upon them from the slit apertures and the tower a cloud of poisoned arrows, and Ulric lost more men in those few minutes than ever in his life before. I was far away behind, but I saw all. I saw Ulric raise his great two-edged sword and cut down to the ground the old man who had led them there. I saw them drag the trunk of a tree to the church door and batter it in, and not one Briton escaped. Ask that old man, Powers, what they have found in the fields here."

Powers called to a laborer digging on a potato patch close at hand.

"What is the name of that ruin?" he asked.

The man surveyed it doubtfully.

"There ain't any one as rightly knows, sir," he

admitted. "Our vicar has looked at the walls, and reckoned it must have been a church."

Powers nodded.

"Have any Danish trophies ever been found about here?" he asked.

The old man smiled.

"You see this field, sir?" he answered. "I've heard my grandfather say that when he used to plough that one day it must have been sown with human bones. There's an old horn mug been found here, too, that they say, from the shape of it, must have belonged to some foreigners. It's in the British Museum in London."

Powers threw him a shilling and turned away with Eleanor.

"You have been here before," he said, in a low tone.

"Never since I came with Ulric," she answered dreamily, "and that must have been a very, very long time ago. There were no houses in those days, nor any fields. Yet the land is the same, the land and the sea. They do not change."

They sat down on a sandy knoll. Powers took her hand in his.

"Dear," he said softly, "it is not well for you to dwell upon these fancies. Try and think instead of the future—our future. Tell me what countries you would like to visit."

"Fancies, do you call them," she repeated scornfully. "They are not fancies. They are memories."

"Call them what you will, dear," he said, "but let them lie. They belong to a dead past. It is the future which concerns us."

She drew a little closer to him. For the first time he felt his pressure upon her fingers returned.

"Powers," she said, in a low tone, "have you seen him? He is somewhere about."

"Whom do you mean?" he asked quickly.

"Trowse!"

Powers set his teeth.

"I have not seen him," he answered. "He will not come here now. I have warned him."

She shook her head.

"He is here now," she said. "I know that he is not far away. Look along the sea path, Powers."

He turned round. Save for a flight of seagulls, he could see no living object.

"There is not a soul in sight, dear," he said reassuringly. "Believe me, you need have no fear."

"Look again," she murmured, without turning her head.

He stood up and gazed along the sea-shore with his hand shading his eyes. And this time, in the far distance, he saw the figure of a man coming towards them. Something in the walk, even though as yet he was a long way off, seemed familiar. A sense of sudden excitement thrilled him. This was to be a day of crises.

"What do you see?" she asked.

"There is a man coming towards us," he answered slowly. "It is too far off to say who he may be. A fisherman perhaps, or a tourist."

She laughed hardly. "It is Trowse," she said.

Powers felt in his pocket, and as he withdrew his hand something flashed like steel in the sunlight.

"If it be he, what matter?" he said. "He knows my mind. I am a man, Eleanor, and I am able to protect you. I will not suffer him even to come near."

"You cannot stop him."

"We shall see," he answered grimly.

They sat together in silence. The color had faded from Eleanor's cheeks. Her eyes were dilated, the fingers which Powers still held were as cold as ice. Once or twice she shuddered as though seized with a sudden spasm of fear. And as he watched her, Powers was filled with silent rage.

Nearer and nearer the man came. Soon there was no longer room for any doubt. It was Trowse. He wore a gray homespun suit and a soft hat. In the fierce sunlight he looked thinner and paler than ever. When he saw them he raised his hat with a little flourish; but they neither of them returned his greeting, and Powers rose to his feet.

"Stay where you are, Trowse!" he called out.

Trowse came to a standstill. He was about twenty paces off. He addressed Powers, but his eyes travelled beyond him to where the girl sat, pale and terrified.

"This is strange hospitality, my friend," he said. "I have come down to see you—and to have a talk with Miss Hardinge."

She rose quietly to her feet. "I am here!" she answered.

Powers' grip upon her wrist was like iron. He replaced his revolver in his pocket. After all, here in the open, man to man, he was more than a match for Trowse.

"You have had fair warning, Trowse," he said. "I will not suffer you to come near Miss Hardinge, nor am I prepared to receive you at my house."

Already she was struggling to leave him, but Powers held her as though in a vise.

"Let me go!" she cried, in a low, wailing tone. "Let me go!"

"Not I!" he answered firmly. "Trowse, you have your answer. Miss Hardinge in a few weeks will be my wife. I have, therefore, every right to protect her. And I shall do it."

Trowse laughed softly.

"It is an excellent method of appropriation, my friend," he said. "Am I to conclude from your—somewhat belligerent manner that you propose to exclude me from the benefit—and the pleasure—of Miss Hardinge's society?"

"That is my intention," Powers answered. "Be wise, Trowse. You cannot understand my attitude. No matter! We are cast in different moulds. My scientific curiosity is dead. Eleanor is to be my wife, and I will suffer no more of these hellish experiments."

"You appear to forget," Trowse said slowly, "that I am the sharer of your knowledge as to this young lady's antecedents."

"There is no longer any secret to be kept," Powers answered. "Eleanor's identity has been admitted. She herself knows everything."

Trowse looked at her keenly. "Is this true?" he asked.

"It is true!" she answered.

"I want you to come to me," he said.

"I want to come. He will not let me."

She struggled with Powers, but he would not let her go. Trowse shrugged his shoulders.

"Perhaps not to-day," he said coolly, "or to-morrow, but my power is for always. You have only to turn your back, and she will come to me. It is true, is it not, Eleanor?"

"It is true," she murmured.

"You will marry her—knowing that?" Trowse asked.

19

"You waste your breath, Trowse," Powers declared. "I shall marry her, and your infernal power will wane and die away as she grows into a more natural state of health. And remember, Trowse, that I am in deadly earnest over this. Don't think I'm talking heroics. I shall kill you, whatever may happen to me, if you defy me."

Trowse laughed scornfully.

"It may be," he said, "that you will have to drag the young lady to the altar. Hold her tightly, Powers. Mind, or she will scream."

She cried out, obeying the suggestion almost before the words were out of his lips. Then Powers, in a sudden passion, caught her up, and turning towards the house, strode away with Eleanor, still unwilling, a dead weight in his arms. Trowse climbed to the top of the little sandhill and watched them till they were out of sight.

CHAPTER XXXVIII

At dinner-time Eleanor was in turn brilliant and sullen. At times she talked with all her old spirit, even spoke of their cruise, and delighted Powers by a certain wistfulness in her tone, and in her deep, clear eyes, at every reference to it. Then there were intervals when every vestige of color faded from her face, when her eyes became fixed and expressionless, and when, with head turned toward the window, she seemed to be listening intently. At such times she became deaf to all questions and remarks. She ignored both Powers and Marian. She looked through the French window across the marshes seawards, and was peculiarly susceptible to all sounds from outside. She started from her seat at the call of the sea-birds, the heavy tramping of feet as a group of fishermen passed along the road upwards towards the village filled her with alarm. Afterwards Powers took her by the arm and led her out into the garden.

"Eleanor," he said, looking at her steadfastly, "I want you to listen to me for a moment."

"Well?"

"You are alarming yourself unnecessarily. Trowse is a man of ordinary common sense. He will not trouble you again, I am sure. He will go away."

She shook her head.

"You are wrong," she said. "To-night he will come—and I must go to him."

"I forbid it," Powers said firmly. "You understand, Eleanor. You have promised to be my wife. I have the right to a certain amount of control over you, of consideration from you. I will suffer no interference between us. I will permit no intercourse between you and Trowse."

She laughed strangely.

"You cannot stop it. I cannot prevent it," she said, "if it is his will. When he calls I must go."

"If he comes," Powers said, "he risks his life. I do not think that he will come."

She leaned over towards him. Her fingers burned his wrist, her eyes were lit with fire.

"Why don't you kill him, Powers? You could do it. You are strong—much stronger than he is. And whilst he lives there will never be any rest for me."

Marian came sweeping out to them through the open window. In the twilight she saw nothing of the horror on her brother's face.

"I forgot to tell you people," she remarked, "that I had a visitor this afternoon."

There was a moment's intense silence.

"I suppose you met him—Dr. Trowse. I sent him along the sands. He is staying close here."

"Yes, we met him," her brother answered.

"I quite expected that you would have brought him back to dine," Marian remarked, settling herself down in her easy-chair. "I offered him some tea, but he would not stop. What is it, Morton?"

A servant had approached noiselessly across the smooth-shaven lawn.

"A fisherman from the village desires to see the master, miss," the man answered. "He said that his name was Gregg, and that he had come about a punt."

Powers rose up at once.

"It is quite right," he said. "I must go in and
see him for a moment. Perhaps we can arrange for
our duck-shooting to-morrow."

He crossed the lawn and entered the house. The
two girls were alone. Marian leaned over through
the twilight.

"Eleanor," she said, "I have been thinking a good
deal about the events of the last twenty-four hours
here. Powers has told me everything. I want to
wish you every happiness, dear."

"You are very kind," Eleanor whispered faintly.
Once more her head was raised as one who listens—
her thoughts seemed to have taken flight.

"I am afraid you must think me a little unsym-
pathetic," Marian went on. "You see, your whole
story sounded so strangely at first. But I have been
thinking it over, and I am very glad that you are
going to marry Powers. I hope that you will both
be very happy."

There came no answer, and Marian, looking more
closely towards Eleanor, surprised at her silence, was
amazed at the sudden change in her appearance.
Every vestige of color had left her cheeks—even to
the lips she was ashen pale. Her eyes, dilated and
lit with fear, were turned fixedly seawards. She was
trembling, and she gave no sign of having heard a
word of Marian's speech. She rose hastily to her
feet and stood for a moment breathing convulsively,
swaying a little as though not certain of her balance.
Marian was startled.

"What is it, Eleanor?" she asked. "Are you
ill?"

But Eleanor raised her hands for a moment in a
gesture of despair almost tragical. They dropped
heavily to her side. With surprising swiftness she

turned speechless away towards the bank which alone divided their gardens from the marsh-land. Even while Marian watched she vanished amongst the shadows.

Powers came out and found his sister standing upon the bank, straining her eyes through the gathering darkness. A sudden fear struck terror to his heart.

"Where is Eleanor?" he cried.

Marian turned round.

"She is a foolish girl," she answered severely. "She glided away like a ghost a few minutes ago. I—Powers, are you mad?"

For Powers, running up the steep sloping turf like a man possessed, had leaped from the top of the bank on to the marsh-land below. The black mud oozed up over his ankles. He took no heed of it, but turned at once seaward.

"Marian," he called out, "send one of the men after me with a lantern! At once, please."

He waded through a small creek, stumbled through a ditch, and reached the bank which led to the shore. Below the road was under water. The tide swept past him with a soft, deep swirl. Away to the right was a great tidal lake, with here and there islands of uncovered marsh-land wreathed in gray mist. He could see only a yard or two in front of him—and the top of the bank was narrow. He stood quite still for a moment listening intently. Everywhere was silence, save for the soft murmuring of the dark waters below, and the far-away changeless undernote of the sea itself, breaking upon the rocky shore. Nowhere a sign of any human being. Yet she could not be far away. Once more he listened. Away ahead he almost fancied that he could

"'Brave little man!' she cried, approvingly."

[*Page* 295

catch the sound of a stifled cry. He moved on a few paces, then stopped short. For the night was suddenly made hideous by an awful sound. The blood in his veins ran cold, he reeled and nearly fell down the steep bank. It was worse than any cry of pain or terror, worse than any frantic shriek for help from one hard beset. It was the mad laughter of a woman. Too well Powers knew the sound. Surely this was the knell of his hopes."

He sprang forward, fired with a sudden fierce passion. At least he would keep his word. He would not be flouted with impunity. The blood rushed to his head, his thoughts were murderous. Then there loomed suddenly before him the gray figure of the girl whom he sought, dimly visible against the empty background of sea and sky. She was leaning forward, peering eagerly into the water below. He called to her softly :

"Eleanor, is that you?"

She turned sharply round. The darkness enveloped him closely.

"It is I—Powers!" he cried hoarsely. "What are you doing here, Eleanor? What is it that you are watching?"

She caught at his coat-sleeve and dragged him down. The first note of her voice terrified him.

"Can't you see? Can't you see, Powers? Look there !"

He went down on his knees and peered forward. A dark object bobbed up and down in the water. It was like a log of wood or a bundle of old clothes.

"What is it, Eleanor?" he asked. "I can see nothing."

Again she laughed, and again he shuddered.

"Brave little man !" she cried approvingly. "He

kept his word. They are both there, Powers—locked together. Trowse was taken by surprise. The little man stole up behind him, and when Trowse would have called out he stuffed something in his mouth. Then they struggled, and Trowse lost his footing, and they rolled down the bank. The little man was like a limpet, Powers. He wound himself round Trowse like a weed, and I think that they are both drowned."

Powers woke from his lethargy, shouted to the servant, who, with a lantern like a great will-o'-the-wisp, was already in sight, and scrambled down the side of the bank into the dark, cool water. It was up to his waist, and for a moment or two he stretched about aimlessly. Then his hand struck something soft, and a low cry of horror broke from his lips. The light from the servant's lantern came travelling up over the surface of the water. It stopped upon a hideous sight. Trowse and Johnson were locked in each other's arms. Their clothes were already sodden and stained with seaweed—the faces of both were still distorted by that last desperate struggle. Powers, scarcely able to keep his feet owing to the strong, silent tide, was suddenly sick and dizzy. For a moment he closed his eyes. Eleanor called softly out to him:

"He is dead, Powers. I am sure that he is dead. I am free!"

He looked up at her. She suddenly threw her hands up to the skies.

"Free!" she cried. "He is dead! The little man has killed him."

Again she laughed, a long and evil laugh, and Powers caught his breath and watched that ghastly burden borne slowly seawards. Mason, with his lantern, had stopped short in the dyke path. The sound of her laugh was terrifying. He was afraid.

"You must come down here, Mason. Scramble down the bank. Keep the lantern well over your head."

Mason obeyed, and Eleanor watched the two men groping about.

"You will never find him!" she cried. "He has gone out to the sea, and the little man's arm is tight around his neck. He has gone where Ulric and the others lie. Let him sleep there, Powers. Better there than the churchyard."

CHAPTER XXXIX

THE great German doctor looked at Powers benevolently through his thick, double glasses. He closed the door behind him carefully.

"My young friend," he said, "the work is finished. My last visit to this most interesting of patients has been paid. I await now only the confirmation of our theories."

Powers, though outwardly cool, was trembling with excitement.

"I can go to her?" he asked. "You recommend it? The moment has arrived?"

"It has arrived," Herr Rauchen affirmed. "She is strong enough to bear your presence—to talk in moderation. Myself I will await here the result. It is an experiment the most interesting of any I have ever known."

Powers moved towards the door, but the Professor called him back.

"My young friend," he said, "one moment. There is no hurry. I would ask you a question."

"Well?"

"You say the room is the same, the nurse is the same. Good! Have you the clothes she arrived in?"

"They are there in full view," Powers answered. "I have spent many hours thinking out the details. She has come back to consciousness amongst precisely the same surroundings as when she first came to me eight months ago."

"Very good indeed," the Professor declared. "Now you shall go to her, and I will smoke. Do not hurry. Assure yourself completely. Meanwhile, I wait for you here."

Once more Powers hesitated, with his foot upon the threshold of her room. It seemed so short a time ago since he stood there before on his way to his first interview with her since his great experiment. But his interest was no longer scientific. He knew very well that the next few minutes must make or mar his life. The Professor had given him hope; their theories had been based upon at any rate a sound basis. But the issue was the greatest he had ever put to the test. With it was bound up the whole welfare of the woman he loved. His heart was filled with a great longing. He entered the room without his usual confidence. Yet the moment he saw her his heart beat with passionate hope.

She was lying upon a sofa, her hair loosely coiled upon the top of her head, clad in a becoming morning wrap, white, with streaming ribbons. At the sound of the opening door she turned her head, and she greeted him with a faint smile. As their eyes met he felt once more that passionate thrill of hope. For the change in her face was manifest. This was neither the brilliantly beautiful but soulless child who had taken London by storm, nor the mystic, moody girl, hovering ever on the brink of insanity, who had sung to him upon the sea-shore, and laughed with unholy joy at those later and more tragical happenings. It was the girl who had been his companion at the theatre, the Eleanor of his earlier knowledge, who greeted him now half shyly, yet with a certain mischievous look in her clear, soft eyes.

"So, after all," she murmured, looking up at him, "I am a disappointment. The great experiment is a failure. I really haven't forgotten a single thing."

He sat down beside her, and returned her smile.

"Hang the experiment!" he declared cheerfully. "I lost all interest in that long ago. All that I have been anxious for has been your recovery."

She smiled again with pleasure.

"I am so glad," she said. "I was afraid you would be terribly disappointed. It really isn't my fault, is it?"

"Not in the least," he assured her heartily. "You were an excellent subject. I suppose," he added, struggling to keep the anxiety out of his tone, "there is no doubt about the failure of it?"

"Not the slightest. My memory feels particularly clear. You can cross-examine me, if you like."

He nodded.

"Well, I will ask you a few questions," he said. "Tell me your last recollection before you came to yourself."

She answered him readily.

"I came to you, here," she said, "and told you that I was dismissed from Bearmain's. I heard your proposals and agreed to them. You sent for a nurse, and you gave me chloroform here. The very last thing in my mind is that you walked to the window, and looked at your watch just before I went off."

He drew a quick breath—it sounded almost a gasp. "It is wonderful!" he exclaimed.

"Everything before that day—my miserable life at Bearmain's, your kindness to me, and our little jaunts together," she said, "I can remember quite clearly. I am sorry to wound your vanity, but your experiment has been shockingly unsuccessful."

He smiled.

"It was a very foolish one," he declared. "I have been terribly worried about you."

Their eyes met for a moment, and a spot of color burned in her cheeks.

"You need not have worried," she said softly. "You made it all quite clear to me before I consented. I knew the risk I ran."

He braced himself up for the final test.

"You have been unconscious for a very long time," he said. "Often I used to listen to you talking to yourself. You don't mind, do you? You see it was part of the experiment."

"Of course not," she answered. "Was I very foolish?"

"You spoke of a lot of things which, of course, I did not understand," he said. "For instance, there was Ulric. Who was he?"

"Ulric?" She repeated the name wonderingly. There was no comprehension in her face.

"Are you sure of the name?" she asked. "I never heard it in my life before."

He smothered his agitation with a strange laugh.

"Perhaps," he suggested, "Ulric was one of your companions when you were a child."

"Perhaps," she assented. "Yet the name is so uncommon that I think I should have remembered it."

"Well," he continued, "there was a person of the name of Trowse—an enemy, I should think, or some one you disliked. What of him?"

Again the blankness of non-comprehension. She shook her head at him and smiled.

"Do you know," she said, "I shall believe soon that it is you who have been raving. Trowse!

Ulric! I never heard such names in my life. Tell me, was there any one else?"

"You spoke of my mother and sister as though you knew them," he said.

She shook her head.

"I saw them with you in a box at the theatre one night, you know," she reminded him. "Never before or since, to my knowledge."

"Then," he continued, keeping his eyes fixed upon her, "there was a person whom you called sometimes Hood, and sometimes Angus. Ah!"

She dropped her eyes.

"Yes," she admitted, "I had once a friend of that name. What did I say about him?"

"You seemed to expect to hear from him—to have him come to you."

"Yes," she admitted, "that is very likely true."

There was a moment's silence. She raised her eyes to his.

"I was once engaged to be married to Captain Hood!" she said.

"So I understood."

He was watching her closely, and permitted himself a little sigh of relief. The mention of Hood's name had not in the least discomposed her. Already she seemed to be thinking of some one else. She was looking out of the window at the faint November sunshine which was doing its best to brighten the dull afternoon.

"There is one thing which I do not understand," she said. "The people in the street all seem to go about muffled up as though it were winter. Now I came here on the 17th of April. There is another proof of failure for you, you see," she added, with a smile. "It certainly does not look like April now, or May, and the trees are all bare. How long have I been here? What is the date now?"

He hesitated.

"I will tell you, Eleanor," he said, "but you must prepare to be surprised."

"You have already surprised me," she said, laughing at him. "Are you taking advantage of my weakness that you use my Christian name without permission?"

"Forgive me," he answered gravely. "But, after all, we are older friends than you imagine. Your illness has lasted a very long time."

She looked at him in amazement.

"You cannot mean," she exclaimed, "that the summer has gone?"

"It is true," he answered. "This is the 10th of November. You have been ill nearly seven months."

"It is wonderful!" she exclaimed.

"It was not natural," he hastened to say, "but you must remember that your illness was not exactly a natural one. It was the result of the operation and the drugs you took."

"Seven months of my life gone," she murmured, "in a sleep."

"No one can repent it more bitterly than I do," he said. "I have robbed you of more than half a year of your life. I wonder whether I shall ever succeed in gaining your forgiveness."

She looked at him with eyes suddenly dimmed.

"That is so foolish of you," she whispered. "You ought to understand, for you know just how valuable my life was when I came to you. Why, it is a joy to me, not a sorrow. When I think of Bearmain's, and the misery I endured there, I am almost tempted to ask you to experiment upon me again, only to let me remain as I have been seven years instead of seven months."

"God forbid!" he cried, with sudden passion. "No more of such ignorant dabblings so long as I live."

She smiled.

"You are changed," she murmured. "You were so cold—so self-confident."

"A good deal has happened to change me."

"You are looking older! You have had troubles?"

"I have been terribly anxious," he said.

She looked at him with wide-open eyes.

"About me?"

He nodded. "Yes," he answered. "About you."

The feeling in his tone was unmistakable. A delicate flush of color stole into her cheeks.

"I think that is rather nice," she said quietly, "to find oneself—once more—of any account. But perhaps," she added half shyly, "you were afraid that if anything happened to me your experiment might have been talked about."

He shook his head.

"No one could ever have discovered that," he said. "My anxiety was—on your account only. As soon as there was danger—I think that I began to realize how pleasant our friendship had been."

She closed her eyes with a little smile. In the strong light he noticed more clearly the fragility of her appearance. He rose hastily.

"I have stayed longer than I meant to," he said. "Here comes nurse with beef-tea. Remember that you have nothing whatever to do but to get well, Eleanor. I shall come in and see you, if I may, every day."

Her eyes filled with tears.

"You are very good to me," she said, "and I am afraid that I am a shocking disappointment to you. It wasn't my fault—was it?"

He laughed at her cheerfully.

"Oh," he cried, "if only I could make you under-stand how thankful I am that it failed!"

.   .   .   .

He burst in upon the Professor and slapped him on the back.

"Professor!" he exclaimed, "it's marvellous. I tell you that it is marvellous."

The Professor groped for his cigar, which had fallen upon the carpet, and set his glasses to rights.

"Well, well!" he exclaimed. "Such muscle you have, my young friend, and of so much vehemence. Well, well!"

"I tell you, Professor, that our theory is proved," Powers cried. "She thinks that she is recovering from a long illness. She remembers everything which happened before her first coming here, and nothing between then and now. I have tested her with names. She is herself again."

The Professor relit his cigar and nodded.

"Well, well!" he said. "I knew it! It is a most interesting case."

20

CHAPTER XL

"Do you mean to tell me, Powers, that this is really Eleanor—the same Eleanor?" Lady Fiske asked impressively.

"Undoubtedly, mother," Powers answered, smiling. "Further, this is the real Eleanor. The girl whom you knew was very different."

"It is most extraordinary—the most bewildering thing!" Lady Fiske declared. "Why, she is charming."

"So I think," Powers remarked.

Lady Fiske smiled an understanding smile.

"But, my dear Powers," she declared, "the complications are endless. There are all the people who knew her as Miss Hardinge; then there is the scandal about those people who discovered that she was not Miss Hardinge. Oh, how foolish you were!"

"I know it," he answered dolefully. "But, mother, if all turns out as I hope, it will be very easy to ignore all that. Besides, I shall take her abroad for some time. You know that I have chartered Errington's yacht provisionally, and you and Marian are to join us at Pisa."

Marian laughed lightly.

"Hear this impetuous lover!" she exclaimed. "Mother, do you recognize your staid son?"

"Indeed I don't," Lady Fiske answered. "But, at least, it is delightful to see you looking yourself again, Powers."

"And, Powers," Marian said, drawing on her

gloves, "I withdraw all that I said against Eleanor
number one. Eleanor number two is delightful. We
shall be so fond of her, and we wish you luck—don't
we, mother?"

"Indeed we do," Lady Fiske assented. "Come,
Marian, let us go now. If you should have any
news for us, Powers, come and dine. We shall be
alone."

. . . .

Powers saw them to the carriage, and then made
his way to Eleanor's room. It was easy to see that
her recovery was now an assured thing. She was
standing by the window when he entered, and he
fancied for the first time that she greeted him a
little nervously.

"Your mother and sister have been to see me,
Sir Powers," she said. "Wasn't it delightful of
them?"

"Well, I don't know," he answered. "It seems
to me a very natural thing for them to do. I hope
you liked my mother, Eleanor."

"How could any one help it," she said simply.
"Your sister was very kind too. They spoke as
though—I was to go and stay with them—but—"

"Of course you are going to stay with them some
day," he said. "That is all arranged."

"Some day—perhaps," she said. "Sir Powers, I
am glad you came in now. I have been waiting to
have a talk with you."

"I am in the same position," he said, drawing a
chair up to hers. "I want to have a talk with
you."

"I claim priority," she declared.

"On what grounds?" he asked.

"Well, my sex."

He smiled. "You have proved your point. Go on."

She was a little nervous, but she began at once.

"It is about that ridiculous bargain of ours. I don't know how you have regarded it, but I have been ashamed of my part of it ever since. The things I asked for were absurd. I have no wish at all to occupy an unsuitable position. So, if you please, I want to alter it."

"Well, go on," he said. "You have kept your part of it loyally, and I am prepared to carry out mine to the very best of my ability."

"You have all been so kind to me," she said, "that my convalescence, at any rate, has been like a long holiday. But now as to the future. If you still feel that you owe me anything at all, will you pay me in the way which I myself shall select?"

"Most certainly," he answered. "I am prepared to give you exactly what you asked for; but if you have changed your mind, you can still command me up to the limits of possibility."

"If you could—if you help me to find some more pleasant way of keeping my independence—and incidentally," she added, laughing, "earning my living. That would be real downright kindness. I am afraid that I wasn't a success at Bearmain's, and I hated it. But there are plenty of things which I could do."

"As for instance?" he asked gravely.

"I could typewrite if some one would start me with a little work. Or I think I could take a situation as secretary. I can write quickly and legibly, and I know French and German pretty well. Or perhaps there is something which you could suggest. I wouldn't mind what it was—except a big shop like Bearmain's."

"Well, I don't know," he said thoughtfully. "There is something, Eleanor, which I ought to tell you—and which might affect your views."

She looked at him questioningly. "What is it?"

"You have spoken to me of Captain Hood. Well, he has been back in England—looking for you."

"How do you know?" she asked.

"I have heard of him through friends. There was some question of a letter which he never received. He is, or was, very anxious to find you and marry you."

"Was?"

"Yes; his leave was up. He has gone back to India."

She was unmistakably relieved. Powers felt his heart grow lighter every moment.   ·

"Will you do me a favor?" she asked eagerly.

"Well?"

"Do not let him know my address. I do not want him to come back again. I will write to him."

He raised his eyebrows. "But—you are still engaged to him."

"I am nothing of the sort," she declared. "It would have all been broken off long ago but for my troubles. We were drifting apart—I was very young when we were engaged, and so was he. I am glad that he was willing to keep his word. But I should never have consented. Let us leave Captain Hood out of the question."

"I will do so," he assented, "with great pleasure. Exit Captain Hood."

"Now tell me," she said, "what do you think about a secretaryship?"

"I think," he said slowly, "that I know a position which would suit you much better."

"What is it? Please tell me. I want your advice."

"My wife."

The hot color burned in her cheeks. She looked at him confused—reproachful.

"Sir Powers!"

"I mean it, Eleanor," he said very earnestly. "You cannot think that I was jesting. I am very much in earnest."

She drew a little away from him.

"You are asking me," she said, "because you remember my foolish words, and it is the only way in which you can keep your share of the compact. It is quite unnecessary, Sir Powers—although I thank you very much, and I appreciate your generosity. Do forget that foolishness once and for all. If you consider yourself in my debt, help me my own way. I mean it."

He drew very near to her.

"Eleanor," he said, "I ask you for no such high-minded reason. I ask you because I love you, because you are the first woman I have ever seen whom I have wished to marry. Dear, you must believe me.

She looked him in the eyes. He was speaking the truth. It was amazing to her, but it was the truth. Nevertheless, she hesitated.

"But you never seemed as though you cared at all!" she faltered. "I don't understand."

He caught her to him. His eyes were bright, his face was hungry with the love of her.

"Dear!" he cried, "look at me. What does it matter when first I cared for you? Look at me now—listen. I love you, Eleanor! You believe me! You must!"

She laughed softly as she leaned towards him.

"It is so easy," she murmured, "to believe when one wants to—very much."